THE GIRLS IN QUEENS

A Novel

CHRISTINE KANDIC TORRES

HARPERVIA

An Imprint of HarperCollins*Publishers*

To all my Day Ones: this is for us.

This is a work of fiction. Names, characters, places, and incidents are products of the author's imagination or are used fictitiously and are not to be construed as real. Any resemblance to actual events, locales, organizations, or persons, living or dead, is entirely coincidental.

THE GIRLS IN QUEENS. Copyright © 2022 by Christine Kandic Torres LLC. All rights reserved. Printed in the United States of America. No part of this book may be used or reproduced in any manner whatsoever without written permission except in the case of brief quotations embodied in critical articles and reviews. For information, address HarperCollins Publishers, 195 Broadway, New York, NY 10007.

HarperCollins books may be purchased for educational, business, or sales promotional use. For information, please email the Special Markets Department at SPsales@harpercollins.com.

FIRST EDITION

Designed by Terry McGrath

Library of Congress Cataloging-in-Publication Data is available upon request.

ISBN 978-0-06-321678-5

23 24 25 26 27 LBC 5 4 3 2 1

2006

*T*hese girls are the truth."

Brian had remained stoic when he introduced us that way to his lawyer near the courthouse in Kew Gardens. He looked at Kelly and then me, faint roses blooming beneath the dark stubble of his cheeks.

"They got my back like family." He'd smiled then, a single finger resting on the back of my hand where I gripped my purse, the skin at the corners of his eyes folding like sunshine filtered through blinds. *"Better than family."*

Brian's words from that day echoed in my ears as I walked up to the suburban front door, sweat curling the hair at my temples into tight, angry spirals that mirrored the manicured cypresses lining either side of the yard. It was confusing, how proud I'd felt when he described us that way, me and Kelly, his girls, who'd been there from jump, since childhood. How proud I was to witness his success as a high school, and then college, baseball player. How lucky, I'd thought, to have been his first girlfriend, to hold that status entirely on my own, separate from Kelly, who so often was the one of us booed up at any given time.

Behind the red-painted door in front of me, framed by clear glass panels that invited strangers to look inside, was a border beyond which I could not return: Janet. Stepping into the world in which this suburban girl lived, a world where people felt entitled to the safety of unarmored windows, meant, I suspected, accepting a truth about Brian that I'd never been able to grasp entirely, like the tail of a mouse in the dark of the night as it scurries around a corner, always just a disorienting inch out of reach.

Pressing my thumb against the smooth black button of the doorbell, worn, I imagined, from scores of dinner-party guests and prom dates calling with corsage in tow, scenes from a safe suburban life I'd only ever seen in movies, I knew one thing for sure: Kelly was going to kill me for this.

I toed the wooden slats of the porch with my boot and in my pocket fingered the sharp grooves of my apartment keys, metal against flesh to ground me in the moment, keep me from running away. This is what I wanted, I reminded myself.

The seconds passed, heavy with anticipation, but I heard nothing but birdsong in the cool autumn air. A twig snapped in the distance, but when I turned to look, I saw only a branch's burnt-orange leaves shaking on a large elm in the front yard. How could I ever think I'd have anything in common with a girl who lived here? How could I trust her?

I took one last breath and turned to leave, when the slice and sweep of the front door opening startled me.

"You're early," Janet said, popping one white earbud out and narrowing her hazel eyes at me. She wore ratty old gym shorts and an oversize JUMP ROPE FOR HEART T-shirt that reminded me of field days in elementary school with Kelly, who always sat out the games because her mother never gave her any cash to participate.

"Sorry," I stammered, thinking her appearance didn't match

what I expected of this pristine-looking home. "I overestimated the distance from the train station. I can leave if you're not—"

"No." Janet reached out an arm. "I was just working out. It helps when . . ." She trailed off. "Well, whenever I don't want to be in my head anymore."

"Hmm," I said, nodding, my brain filling in all the scenes Brian had painted for me with her face, her body, in them. What she looked like when Brian first saw her after his game, what she looked like at the party, in her dorm room . . .

"Let me change," Janet said.

She pulled the door open wider and stepped aside to let me in. "Then I'll be ready to talk."

1996

Kelly crouched over, a single finger against my lips, her breath humid and sickly sweet from the Sour Patch Kids we'd stolen from the Indian deli down the street. She pressed me down onto the ground of the abandoned overgrown lot next to her family's home and whispered in my ear.

"You can still smell her cigarette."

She was right. Above the fresh scent of overturned soil and empty Doritos bags, it lingered heavy around the two of us. If I waited, if I searched for it, I could still smell the smoke from her mother's Virginia Slim wafting toward us on a breeze that barely tickled the heads of the tall weeds surrounding us. I blinked at her in recognition of the danger we were in, and she flopped her skinny bones next to mine with a distracted huff.

My bare shoulders still flattening the patchy grass of the sloping earth behind me, I turned my head to hers and saw that her eyes were clear and focused on something straight ahead, in the sky. I inched my pinkie finger inside her clenched, clammy fist, and she squeezed it. Digging my jelly sandals into the gravel to lift my hips, I shifted over quietly so that no one could detect us hiding there. To our left, trucks barreled down the road and onto Queens Boulevard, rolling metal doors clanging against iron bumpers. In the distance, we could hear plastic skateboard wheels growing closer as the new kid, Brian, sped down the hill.

"How long you think we'll have to wait?" I asked. But before Kelly could answer, I heard Brian scrape his skateboard against the sidewalk in an abrupt stop. Through the weeds, we could see him crouch down and squint toward us.

"¿Quién está allí?" he asked. "Who's there?"

Brian and his mother had been introduced as newcomers during mass one Sunday, having recently arrived in New York from La Paz.

"Shh," I whispered over Kelly's body, emphatically shooing him away with my hand. "Go away!"

I could make out the shape of his shoulders shrugging before his skateboard clattered once again against the sidewalk as he sped away. Kelly didn't move.

I nudged my head closer to hers on the ground and searched the sky to find what Kelly had been watching. It was a plane. Two planes, in fact, crisscrossing the clouds, and from our vantage point, seemed to only narrowly avoid crashing into each other. It was hypnotizing to zero in on the space between the flashing red lights underneath the aircraft, each beat taking longer than the last.

I blinked and refocused my eyes on Kelly's dry, cracked bottom lip.

"Coming or going?" I asked.

"Coming," she said. She'd been looking at the other plane, descending into LaGuardia.

"From Cancún," she said, nodding.

Her older brother had gone there on spring break a few months ago. He was the first person in either of our families who had ever flown somewhere on an actual vacation, besides our fathers. Kelly's left often to return to family she had never met in Colombia, and mine never looked back when he left for Puerto Rico via Miami when I was three. As far as kids, Patrick was the only one who'd ever had the pleasure of seeing his name printed on a boarding pass except for Timothy, the high school senior who lived in the spare bedroom of Kelly's house, and from whom we were now hiding.

"How do you know?" I whispered.

I felt her bony shoulder shrug beside me in response.

I turned my attention back toward the plane that had by then nearly disappeared in the distance, and I imagined all the waves in the Atlantic Ocean it would have to cross over to get to Italy, or to France, or to Greece. All countries I'd only run my stubby fingers over on the topographical globe in our elementary school library.

From the shallow grave we dug ourselves to hide inside of in this abandoned Woodside lot, it was hard to imagine tiny little people inside those tin birds, always leaving, always coming. In this neighborhood, people seemed to always be arriving anew or moving away. But never us. No, we had been planted there right from the start on Clement Moore Avenue.

⟡

Her house always smelled of ferrets and melted butter. It was one of the few old, yellow clapboard homes on the street that predated the expansion of Queens Boulevard. When the city widened the road, they dumped the rubble at her grandmother's doorstep, forcing the family, newly arrived from Cork, to build a steep set of concrete stairs to the new hill paved along Clement Moore, which became home to more and more three-story, red brick apartment buildings.

The steps had become chipped and worn by the generations of Irish, and then Irish Colombian, schoolchildren running up, away, and always back down again. Inside, their sponge of a sea-green carpet hid stains created by animals and kids alike; in addition to the two kids, her mother, Frances, took in every stray, human and nonhuman, she could find. The rolling French pocket doors that separated Kelly's bedroom from the living room had long ago bounced off their tracks, allowing gray feathers to float from Frances's living room birdcage and land on the colorful ruana—the sole gift her father had brought her from Colombia—that lay across the foot of Kelly's bed.

"Some women are like that," Mami had said once after suffering through a coffee with Frances, straining to hear her over squawking birds. Mami kept her purse clamped shut in her lap the whole time.

"Like what?" I'd asked as we walked back to our one-bedroom apartment down the street.

"Scared to be alone."

The latest stray to arrive at Casa Morales (Frances kept the name after the divorce) was Timothy. Timothy was a senior on winter break at Monsignor McClancy when his parents kicked him out for getting a blow job from a sophomore girl in their basement. Patrick, who spent a year with Timothy on varsity before enrolling at Baruch, convinced Frances to offer him a room in their house so he could finish out the year and graduate high school.

"He told her it was the Christian thing to do. As if." Kelly had rolled her eyes when she first explained the new housemate sleeping in their converted old utility closet.

Frances took to Timothy right away, I could tell. She saved him the biggest baked potato, served him iced tea first. He was attractive, but as an eleven-year-old only child to a single mother, the presence of any man, really, was reason enough for excitement.

Timothy had a thick neck that had tanned peach by June, and

wore scuffed Timberland boots as if he already knew he was destined to work construction. He had curly brown hair that he kept cropped close in a fade and offset with a sparkling blue stud earring. It was his birthstone, he had told us.

"Virgo," he'd said. "Like a virgin. Do you know what that means?"

Kelly and I broke into a rendition of Madonna's song immediately, swinging our neon, Lycra-clad hips and running our hands through our frizzy hair.

He smiled and his healthy pink lips curled at the sides. I would spend hours in the mirror that summer staring at my own pale mauve lips, Herbalife commercials and lead paint contamination PSAs blaring between Ricki Lake segments in the background, wondering if I might be sick or deficient in some kind of vitamin, because mine weren't the same color.

Sometimes he would sit with us on the shaded back stoop of the house that overlooked a steep, littered valley of freight train tracks that rumbled to life every twelve hours like clockwork, at 2:00 p.m. and 2:00 a.m. The tracks were separated by a fence along the cracked asphalt of the Moraleses' driveway, at the end of which sat the sole tree on their property. Timothy had built a swing in woodshop and installed it on one of the tree's branches to thank Frances for letting him stay at her house. Kelly and I took turns pushing each other on it as high as we could, reaching for the tracks all spring.

Timothy had a harmonica that we thought was stupid.

"Who do you think you are, Blues Traveler?" I asked him once while he played.

He flourished the end of his song with what looked like big, fat, turkey-tail hands flapping against the instrument and strained to widen his green eyes.

Kelly, her bony, narrow thighs and hips too tiny for her hand-me-down shorts, slid in close to sit next to Timothy and rested her hand on his knee.

"Can I try?"

He looked at her and, for a second, I could see that he was nervous. He raised a scarred eyebrow at me briefly, but then quickly flashed that strawberry-pink gum smile at us both.

"Nah, I don't think so, Kels." He tugged on her right earlobe and brushed her cheek, freckled by the sun, with the back of his hand.

"It'd be like we were *swapping spit*," he had said. "Like we were boyfriend and girlfriend. Kissing or something."

Kelly took her hand off his jeans.

"You don't want to kiss me, do you?"

We both erupted in nervous laughter and Kelly screamed, "Gross!" as she leapt up from the pebbled steps, but not before discreetly swiping the harmonica sticking out of his jeans pocket. She shot out across the concrete yard and swung the broken chain-link gate open, and it bounced back on its hinges with a loud whine, as she ran into the empty lot next door. I followed closely behind, not wanting to be left alone with Timothy, and found her in the plot of soil we'd excavated to be our hideout. The dugout, we'd called it, long before we knew all that much about baseball.

She lifted the large, flat rock under which we hid a hand-me-down Spider-Man lunch box full of chica chica cards, matchboxes and loose cigarettes, and a cubic zirconia ring we found on the schoolyard. She popped the lid and tossed Timothy's harmonica inside with a loud clatter.

"Shh," I giggled. "He'll hear it!"

Kelly slid the cover back on and smiled without teeth. Her eyes were just a little too far apart, and sometimes when she had this calm, satisfied look on her face, she looked like a frog that had swallowed a fly.

"Let him."

⁀

On the third straight day of a New York City heat wave that July, Kelly and I retreated to the cool, damp air of her basement to read the latest installment in my fan fiction saga based on *The X-Files*.

Kelly flipped the last page closed, revealing dollar signs and zeros; the manuscript was printed on the backs of old medical bills from Mami's job at St. Vincent's. The maintenance men always knew to save a box for her to take home before trashing them.

"So," Kelly said, blowing silky strands of black hair from her face, "the chick is Mulder? Or—"

I snatched it out of her hands.

"Never mind," I said, rolling it up and shoving it into my back pocket.

"No, no," Kelly said. "I liked it!"

I tugged at the hem of my shorts, which were already too tight from the beginning of the summer, and sat down. I'd grown several inches taller—and fuller—than Kelly in the last few months.

"Forget it."

Kelly humored my fan fiction, especially when I wrote her into it, but couldn't be bothered to watch much television beyond what was on at my house when she came over.

"I'm a liver," she'd said, "not a watcher."

"You're an internal organ?" I asked, eliciting a groan.

"How you such a *nerd* sometimes, yo?"

Our forearms on the cold concrete floor in the one furnished room of the basement, where her older brother used to make out with girls, we listened to Boyz II Men cassette tapes on his boombox for a while before we decided to explore the dark corners of the cellar. Kelly and I regularly searched for love letters, or mix tapes, or condom wrappers, anything to piece together the intimate lives we knew the adults around us must have lived. Toward the back of the house, where cellar doors swung out onto the concrete backyard, a washer and dryer sat underneath lines of rope hung from the exposed wooden beams of the ceiling to dry delicates. That day, we found the silk and cotton boxers that had come out of Timothy's wash hanging on the lines.

"*Oh là là!*" Kelly said, as she tugged a black pair with red kisses on it down from the clothespin on the line. She held it up in front of her face and made it dance between pinched fingers.

I laughed.

"How the hell he got these kinds of boxers?" I asked. "You think your mom bought them for him?"

Kelly let the pair drop from her fingers and sucked her teeth.

"My mom don't buy him shit," she said, looking up at the line for another one.

"Do you think he's cute?"

Kelly rolled her eyes as she ripped another silk pair down and threw it on my face.

I tore it off and tossed it back at her. "Yo, that's disgusting!"

"What," she said, cocking her brow. "I heard you say you thought he was cute."

"Did not!" I leaned on the clothesline with my right arm and caught myself in the mirror above the sink. I sucked in my stomach and adjusted the tank top over my chest; Mami had graduated me from sports bras to the polyester sheen of Conway's back wall a few weeks ago for my eleventh birthday, and the underwire dug uncomfortably into my rib cage. "I asked if *you* thought he was."

Kelly pretended to ignore me and ran her hands along the line of boxers as if she were a rich woman admiring her art collection.

"Besides"—I shrugged—"even if I did think he was cute, I don't want to rub my face in his underwear."

Kelly sighed, tired of me, I could tell. I got the sense oftentimes that I was too dumb for her, or too prudish. Too naive, for sure.

"What's the big deal, you baby," she said, gesturing toward the washing machine. "It's not like they're dirty."

She ripped down a cotton pair with a silkscreen print of Porky Pig on the butt and threw it at me, but that time I caught it.

She smiled and opened her arms wide, grabbing onto the lines overhead, and ran her face across each pair of shorts, one long motorboat through a sea of his unmentionables.

I laughed at her audacity, her brazen disregard for other people's personal property. I wished I could be more like Kelly.

"What are you doing?"

His voice was deep and reverberated against the low ceiling of the cellar, stopping my laughter cold. Timothy stood behind us with an empty laundry basket at his hip. His face was hard; I couldn't quite read if he was mad at us, but there was heat in his eyes, an excited self-awareness of the scene he'd just walked into.

I looked at Kelly, but she didn't look scared. She looked amused. Defiant. As if she'd been expecting this.

"Laundry." She shrugged, a blue-and-orange pair of Mets boxers hanging off her fingertip.

He snatched it from her and threw it in the plastic basket at his hip. Just as quickly, he grabbed her wrist in his thick fist and twisted it behind her. Kelly was so short she only came up to his chest. He pulled her close to him.

"You wanna do my laundry?" he asked, his voice frighteningly intimate. It wasn't the same voice he used when he played his harmonica for us on the stoop.

Kelly didn't look at me, or him, but at the line of clothes above her. She didn't seem shocked or afraid at all—only embarrassed. She tucked her chin to her shoulder to turn toward him.

"You're hurting me again," she said low, as if reminding a scene partner of their lines. "Not so hard."

Timothy turned to raise his eyebrows at me.

"You want to feel my boxers?"

He dropped the laundry basket onto the concrete floor and the sound echoed throughout the basement. Underneath it, I could hear the metal of his belt buckle coming undone.

I gasped and took a step back, my bare heel banging into the empty washing machine behind me. It was like a gong, the sound of its quivering hollow walls echoing through the house and snapping Kelly out of her dim fog. She elbowed Timothy away from her hard. He staggered back, but trained his hungry eyes on me instead.

"I saw you," he said, his right arm reaching for me, the alarm of leather and metal sounding off at his waist. "You wanted this, too."

His fingers barely grazed my neck before I ducked out past him and ran for the far back door. I made it up the warped wooden steps and out into the yard, where Frances sat with a freshly lit Virginia Slim. I ran past her and past the broken fence, losing one of my chunky jelly sandals in the process.

When I got to the dugout, I hugged my knees at the far edge of the dirt lot where the tall weeds grew strong and thick from the ground. It wasn't until Kelly followed shortly thereafter, trailed by

Frances's coughing wails for us to come back and apologize for being rude to Timothy, that I realized I was still clutching a laundered pair of his underwear.

Kelly lay panting, back flat on the ground next to me.

"Has he done that before?"

She cut her eyes at me. There I was again: so silly, so naive.

She propped herself up on one elbow, her eyes still on mine, sizing me up.

"We practice," she said.

"Practice what?" I asked.

"Shh!" She clamped her perpetually wet palm over my mouth.

"Kissing," she said. "We practice kissing. It's like a game."

I stared at her, not comprehending what she was saying even though, on some level, I had suspected it for some time.

"But he's almost eighteen," I said.

Kelly lowered herself back onto the ground, and I could feel the wall go back up between us.

If we listened, we could just make out Frances apologizing to Timothy and offering to buy him new clothes. Occasionally she would shout out in our general direction, "Come get your shoe!" or "You lost your shoe, dingbat." And she'd laugh, and we'd hear Timothy laugh, too. I dug into the cool soil with the bare toes of my non-sandaled foot and imagined myself as a worm crawling into the earth.

Suddenly, Kelly scrambled to her knees, snatched the boxers that I'd been gripping in my fist, and pawed at the ground like a dog with a bone.

"What are you doing?" I flicked dirt off my thighs and peeked back through the weeds, my body still humming with adrenaline. "Why don't you just stuff it inside the lunch box with everything else?"

"I can't leave this out," Kelly grunted. "It's too dangerous. I have to hide it." Her hands were claws, the star-shaped plastic ring on her finger collecting more and more soil like a miniature trowel.

"Dangerous for who?" I asked, but Kelly only lifted a wrist to wipe sweat from her brow. Beneath the cars whizzing by and the cicadas above, I could hear Frances's lighter catch in the distance.

I pulled myself to my knees alongside Kelly and grabbed clumps of earth to pile on top of the garish fabric. I wanted to bury this moment and forget it as soon as possible. But Kelly, it appeared, was burying treasure. She hadn't put the boxers in the lunch box with our other naughty items; this was something else, something precious, and something that was hers alone. I got to run away, I understood, but she was stuck in that house. So I helped her, and I clawed so deep that I was cleaning soil out from under my nails for a week afterward.

We lay back down over the fresh earth, panting. I tried to synchronize my breathing with hers so that our lungs functioned as one, one beast hiding in the bush. I squeezed her wrist so hard I felt ligaments press against the bone beneath her skin, but I tried to still my nerves and match her pulse with mine. If we could share a soul, I'd felt, a body, if I could give her mine, we'd survive. We'd make it through.

She turned to look at me and shook her head.

"You can still smell it," she said, motioning back toward the house with a puckered mouth. "Her cigarette."

⁊

The St. Agnes fair was held each Labor Day weekend to raise money for the parish. New York City public schools traditionally started the Thursday after Labor Day so, for us, the carnival marked the unofficial end of summer. The spinning Big Eli grew larger as we made our way toward the church parking lot, hundreds of multicolored bulbs flashing in preset sequences from every available surface on the wheel. We jumped at balloons bursting atop open-mouthed clown busts getting shot full with water from a line of gun-wielding children aiming across a table. We heard the screams and laughter from the nearly vertical Tilt-A-Wheel, and beneath that, faintly, the beat of music playing from KTU through strategically located speakers. The air smelled of beef fired on a charcoal grill and oily paper bags of deep-fried zeppole coated in clouds of confectioner's sugar.

Kelly nudged her hip against mine as we walked down the hill toward Queens Boulevard.

"Chica chica!" she said, pointing toward wild dandelions growing out from under a wooden fence that walled off a tiny concrete yard and an aging rottweiler.

I bent down and peeled the black-and-white chica chica card off the sidewalk. A curly blonde with lace gloves held a finger to her pouting mouth, the angles of her elbows covering her nipples. A number was printed in hot pink at the bottom promising DELIVERY on one side and ENTREGA on the other.

"Nah." I flicked it back into the grass. "We've already got her."

Inside the old, tin lunch box we hid in the dugout, we maintained a stack of those cards that we'd occasionally find strewn across major avenues on our walks to and from school. We collected them like baseball cards and imagined names and backstories for them: Lexi, Paulina, Amber.

"Who you think is gonna be at the fair tonight?" I asked, pulling my ponytail tight inside its scrunchie.

The church was close enough to our houses that if we stood on our tiptoes, we could spot the top of the Big Eli once it had been erected. Kelly and I had been baptized as infants at St. Agnes's and attended religious instruction classes there since first grade. But we were on the wrong side of the Long Island Rail Road tracks, in the northern half of Woodside, with better transit options but darker skin tones. To the south of the LIRR, past the mechanic shops and auto yards, homes grew taller and statelier, sprouting side lawns of fresh grass and backyards with vegetable gardens. Woodside grew into Maspeth there, an Irish-, Italian-, and German-American enclave of Queens where SUVs were parked in double-wide driveways and kids played Manhunt after dark without fear of much more than their shadow.

"I heard Nicky Gargiullo got back from Sicily last weekend," Kelly said, tugging on her Bugs Bunny embroidered denim shorts that hung loose around her swaybacked waist.

Kelly and I had crushes on many of the boys from those families, and Nicky Gargiullo was king. There was virtually no girl who'd met Nicky Gargiullo and didn't immediately go weak in the knees and start scribbling his name in hearts in the back of her notebook. He had perfectly gelled hair, a sparkling diamond stud in his left ear, and a St. Anthony medallion dangling on a thin silver chain around his neck, where soft blond hairs sprouted down his spine like a fawn. He always smelled like fabric softener exhaust from the laundromat down the block, like blue bottles of Downy and Saturday nights when Mami would blow-dry my hair straight with dollops of Dippity-Do.

"Who told you that?" I asked. "Who told you he's back?"

Kelly shrugged and reached in her pocket to pull out and count the crumpled dollar bills she was bringing to the fair.

"That kid Brian," she said.

Brian's family had moved into the basement apartment of the

small building around the corner from where we lived. When Mami came to Kelly's one evening to drag me home for dinner, I heard her whispering to Frances about the Vargases having arrived from *Bolivia*, as if the word itself were a threat, as if Mami hadn't come here from Puerto Rico or Kelly's dad from Colombia.

"I didn't know you talk to him," I said, a twinge of jealousy in my chest.

"I don't *talk* to him," she said. "I just spoke to him. Once or twice."

Brian went to our school but was in an ESL class. He had apparently been born in New York but returned to Bolivia when he was just a baby. He had joined the baseball team at St. Agnes, too, though we usually never saw him at mass on Sundays.

"He speaks English?" I asked.

Kelly rolled her eyes.

"I guess so?" she said, throwing her hands up. "I sure wasn't speaking Spanish."

I felt the unresolved questions I still had about Timothy catch inside my throat, so I chose instead to listen to the cars barreling down Clement Moore Avenue, rubber tires rolling over metal plates NYNEX had installed in the road.

Mami and I had watched through the venetian blinds in our living room as Timothy packed his stuff into a white Ford Explorer one morning. Mami explained, her chin knocking against my shoulder as she shook her head in pity, that he got his GED and secured a job in Mount Vernon as a nursing-home attendant. Kids came from all over the city to attend Monsignor McClancy, and rumor had it, Timothy had already been offered a full ride to play basketball for Seton Hall. That was supposed to be Timothy's future. For him to end up working in a nursing home, despite everything I knew he'd done to Kelly during his six months in the Morales house, still didn't make any sense to me. Mami sucked her teeth and agreed it was "no place for a young man with his whole life ahead of him."

After the incident with his boxers that July, Kelly told me that Frances had thrown my abandoned jelly sandal at her head and sent her to bed without dinner. Later that night, Kelly confessed to Frances everything that had been going on: the kissing, the touching, the games, the "practice." Frances listened to Kelly, not breaking eye contact as she slid a fresh cigarette out of her pack and lit it with a rose-engraved Zippo that she flicked on by snapping it against the side seam of her black jeans. (She wore black jeans every day, she said, "in case Aunt Flo reared her ugly head.") Frances had inhaled when Kelly was done and asked her with one of her penciled eyebrows cocked, "So?"

She exhaled the smoke with a deep, phlegmy laughter that grew in intensity.

"You think," she'd coughed out, "you think you are special?"

Kelly said she heard her laughing through their broken French doors while she tried to fall asleep that night. It was the last time Kelly mentioned Timothy's name to me—she didn't even mention it when he moved out.

We stopped at the corner to wait for the WALK sign and start the trek across the twelve-lane Queens Boulevard, when a Toyota Corolla slowed down in front of us, blasting a Cover Girls song. Dance music had just returned to the local KTU radio station, and freestyle was once again everywhere. A man with tight, baby-oiled curls and hairy arms leaned over and puckered his lips at us.

"Mamita, I like those legs, honey."

He didn't even have to shout. He was driving closely and slowly enough for us to hear every word clearly over "Show Me You Really Love Me." I didn't know if he was talking to one or to both of us, but I shrank underneath hunched shoulders in my holographic-printed baby tee and curled my toes inside my white shell-top sandals, looking east down the boulevard at oncoming traffic.

Kelly, on the other hand, bent down to pick up a pebble resting in the tacky rubber cracks of the cement sidewalk and launched it at his sideview mirror. It didn't crack the glass, but I heard it bounce off his exterior.

"Get out of here, you pervert!" Kelly screamed, her voice breaking, veins swollen in her neck. So much anger coming from such a tiny body.

"Little bitch," we heard him mutter before accelerating his NOS-powered engine down the road and onto the Brooklyn-Queens Expressway ramp, drowning out the freestyle beats from his stereo.

We'd been getting catcalled since we were eight, when I started developing the tiniest shadow of what would become my fifth grade B-cup breasts. We'd already learned to raise our voices when anyone got too close to us on the sidewalk, or to tuck into a neighbor's yard so that no one would be able to track us home and return to stalk us later on.

I turned to Kelly, who was once again tugging up her Bugs Bunny shorts. She had already turned her attention back to the crosswalk, dusting off dirt from her hands on her back pockets.

"Good aim," I said.

She chuckled.

"Too bad. I loved that song," she said.

"Do you realize?" I asked as we stepped onto Queens Boulevard. "We're gonna be sixth graders this year. We're gonna *rule the school*!"

Grease had become our favorite movie that summer, and fully aware that we would never be Sandy, we desperately wanted to be Rizzo. The two of us weren't exactly popular, part of a divorced kids support group that met every Tuesday (or Wednesday or Thursday) afternoon—whenever one of us needed to talk. In reality, we used it as an opportunity to get out of class, and play cards, and dance to songs by Selena and Mariah.

"Yeah." Kelly beamed. "I know."

She swung around the streetlight pole on one of the median islands and slapped it once for emphasis.

"And this is the year I'm going to make Nicky Gargiullo my boyfriend."

⇛

Kelly ripped the cash out of my hands and slapped it down on the ticket counter along with her wad of crumpled bills.

"Let's start slow," she said, eyelids low, urging me to act cool.

I nodded.

"Work our way up," I said, motioning behind her to the brown potato sacks flying down the enormous yellow slide in the middle of the parking lot—by far, the worst attraction that year. Our strategy was to build to the Flying Baron, a seesaw of sorts that not only swung twin cabins around in circles, but also spun each cabin on its own axis. Watching it twirl as I climbed the steps to the slide made my stomach churn.

From the line at the top of the yellow slide, we could see the entire layout of the fair. In the thick of a crowd of Italian boys, Kelly managed to spot Nicky Gargiullo waiting to board the Flying Baron, silver chains glinting in the twilight. My stomach lurched again, nervous at the sight of his ripe-peach cheeks, fresh off of two months of sun and travel through a world beyond our expressway-bound borough.

"Killing Me Softly" was playing over the speakers, and Kelly grabbed my hand.

"Follow me," she said, plopping her legs out in front of her on the plastic slide.

"One," she said, as I hurriedly slid the rough burlap over my legs, trying to ignore the pain in my gut. "Two . . ."

Kelly pushed off, tugging me along once Lauryn Hill hit the bridge and we sang the note together. It felt like a brief freedom to fly down like that, in unison. It felt like we were cruising in from the clouds, like we were making our debut to an adoring crowd below.

As I was heavier and taller than her, the gravity of my sack catapulted Kelly farther out than me onto the ground ahead of us at the bottom of the slide. We laughed about it and checked, out of the corners of our eyes, to see if anyone—Nicky—had caught our duet down the slide.

I stumbled getting up off the wobbling plastic and felt my stomach gurgling again. When I lifted the sack to return it to the pimple-faced line attendant, I noticed a slick black stain on it. With a dread that reverberated from my tailbone to my temples, I reached around and touched the seat of my shorts. Wet.

Immediately, I snatched the burlap sack back and pinched it around my waist. I elbowed Kelly in the ribs, where she stood flirting with the gawky, fifteen-year-old attendant. More practice, I caught myself thinking.

"Kelly," I shout-whispered through clenched teeth, "I shit my pants!"

I cleared my throat and shuffled a step closer.

"I think I shit my pants!"

Kelly's eyes bulged, and she opened her mouth wide to laugh.

"Again?" she asked.

I had soiled myself once in kindergarten, on the day I transferred out of my ESL class. I was terrified to find myself there, and so was Mami; she purposely hadn't taught me Spanish at home to avoid the fate she'd experienced as a new student in Sunset Park back when Abuelita brought her here from Isabel Segunda. After bumbling through the few Spanish phrases I did know, the school figured it out and placed me in Kelly's class, but not before I'd been so nervous to speak up that I held off going to the bathroom until I just couldn't hold it anymore. Kelly, recognizing me from the block, offered me her sweater to tie around my waist, and we had been friends ever since.

"No." I swatted her wrist, in no mood for a trip down memory lane. "Shut up, let's go!"

She followed, but laughed so hard while trying to jog up to me that when I turned to enter the church basement bathroom, I saw she had doubled over at the corner of the rectory, squeezing her knees together to keep from peeing and trying to catch her breath in front of where a Mary-on-the-half-shell was planted.

I hobbled down the dark marble steps to the girls' bathroom, where I safely locked myself inside a stall and pulled my pants down.

"Oh my god." I looked down, expecting to find something much different than what appeared to be grape jelly and the contents of an old ketchup packet. My mind raced with contrasting commercial images of elegant, blue liquid pouring onto white cotton and the mimeographed worksheets from sex ed class that diagrammed the angry goat of the female reproductive system. Everything felt like a lie, a letdown. At least Frances had called Aunt Flo ugly.

Kelly, still giggling, pinballed into the bathroom and broke out into a full cackle again when she heard me mumbling, "Oh my god." She locked herself in the stall beside me.

"I think I made it," she said, banging an open palm on the metal wall separating us. "Wait, maybe not."

"Kelly," I called.

"Nope, these are soaked," she continued. I listened as the lid to the metal trash receptacle whined open and her wet underwear landed with a crinkle and thud inside its brown wax paper lining.

"Kelly," I repeated. "I think I got my period."

I heard her wrap a mitten of toilet paper around her fist as she reined in her laughter.

"No, you didn't," she said, her voice dismissive.

We both started laughing again then, an infectious high taking over our shared embarrassment of the absurdity of our bodies' betrayals, when I heard her flush.

"I'm eleven!" I said, wiping at the crotch of my underwear with one-ply.

"You can have babies now," Kelly said, as she flushed.

"Yeah." I unspooled fresh toilet paper and folded the long sheet into a tidy stack to sit inside my underwear. "That's not exactly my top priority at the moment."

We decided our best bet was to make a run for it through the double-door exit we'd entered through, down the street to the twenty-four-hour laundromat, where we could swipe some new bottoms or at least something large enough to wrap around our waists and conceal each of our messes.

But just as we passed the exit, we nearly collided with Joey Di-Prima, the beefiest of Nicky's boys and the widely accepted bodyguard and protector of his popular holiness. I could see he'd grown a faint shadow of a blond mustache above his top lip since class ended in the spring.

"Whoa, whoa, whoa," he said with a smile, looking at us with his palms outstretched. "Where you goin', Speedy Gonzalez?"

Again, I wasn't sure which one of us he was insulting, but this time, Kelly chose to ignore it instead of throwing the nearest projectile.

"I'm not feeling well," I announced, immediately regretting it. We clearly had just left the bathroom, and those boys would be all too willing to fill in the blanks.

"I think the clams are bad," I continued, as if that would help.

Kelly looked at me. Why couldn't I shut up?

Joey laughed, along with his cronies, Nicky Gargiullo, and the Bolivian boy, Brian. I wondered what he'd had to do to be accepted by the rest of these Catholic Youth Organization boys. I wondered if he'd caught the Speedy Gonzalez comment and how the white boys felt they could get away with those kinds of insults even with a South American in their crew. Joey patted Brian's chest as if to say "watch this" and turned suddenly to snap the potato sack off my waist.

"Did you forget something?" Joey asked. "Or is this"—he gestured to my waist—"a new fashion statement?"

The boys snickered behind him, and I prayed that nothing had seeped out the front of my pants in the rush up the stairs from the bathroom. No one pointed or laughed any harder, so I figured I was in the clear.

"What do you care?" I asked, doing my best to keep my lips pursed and muscles tight. "Get a life."

Proud that I set off a chorus of *boo*s and *ooh*s from the boys in the crowd, I took a step to start backing away slowly, when Kelly lunged forward to steal the Coke can out of Joey's hand and the strawberry Slurpee out of Nicky's.

Before I could raise my arms to shield myself, Kelly dumped both drinks over my head, to an even louder chorus of jeers.

"Ohh snap," Nicky said, clapping his hands together before covering his snickering mouth.

The liquid was cold and sticky as it congealed, creating a vacuum seal of fabric against my skin. I glared at Kelly, enraged that she would use me for an opportunity to impress those herbs. I felt my fists tensing when I realized amidst the whistle-pitched laughter of the boys that she was tilting her head at an odd angle and widening her eyes at me. She wanted me to retaliate.

"Don't you talk that way to him!" she shouted too loudly, performing for our audience.

"You," I started, the Coke trickling down my back, "you two-faced bitch!" I didn't have to pretend much.

I stepped wide and grabbed Brian's Mountain Dew from his hand and pulled her slack waistband away from her belly. I squeezed the paper cup, and the soda and ice exploded down the front of her shorts and onto her bare legs, leaving electric-green streaks of corn syrup on her skin. Her eyes were wild again, the same wildness as when she dug into the earth of the abandoned lot to bury Timothy's boxers in our dugout. She threw her head back and charged at me, emitting a squealing, antagonistic laugh as she shoved me and ran, as if tagging me to follow her down the steps, past the crowd of pre-adolescent boys doused in their own weather system of Cool Water and perspiration, and I did, praying all the while that her plan had worked and that no one would notice the original stains on either of our outfits.

In the laundromat across the boulevard, I grabbed my knees, trying to breathe through a stitch in my side. I pulled out a soggy string of green tickets from my front pocket.

"You owe me ten bucks," I told Kelly.

She grabbed them from me and threw them in an active dryer.

"There," she said. "I think we're even."

&

We kept a low profile for the rest of the fair, hanging out between the zeppole cart and the dunk tank toward the back. By Sunday though, Kelly had gained back most of her resolve. Mami invited her over that morning to help clear out the fridge, since the electric company cut our power Friday evening, and it wouldn't get turned back on until Tuesday at the earliest. We fried salami and eggs, and toasted onion bagels on the stove, pressing the bread down on the griddle with the weight of our coffee pot.

"So," Kelly said between greasy bites, eyeing me up and down, "you, like, wear a diaper now?"

I flicked a potato chip at her. I snuck the bag of Lay's to the table while Mami was rifling through a box in the bedroom, looking for her latest notice from Con Edison.

"You're the one who may actually need diapers here, in case you forgot."

I couldn't shake the feeling that Kelly was jealous of me for starting my period. For the first time since the basement incident, she volunteered information about Timothy. He had sent her a postcard.

"What does a postcard from Mount Vernon look like?" I asked. "A picture of the Metro North? A factory?"

"Don't be stupid," Kelly said. "The card is from Virginia."

She emphasized the word "Virginia" like it was exotic.

Timothy had driven down to Virginia to pick up a pair of ventilators for the nursing home. Kelly produced the postcard from the back pocket of her overalls and framed it for me between pinched fingers. It was glossy and unbent, and on the back was printed VIRGINIA IS FOR LOVERS.

"I wiped oil from my mouth with a paper towel, grateful to be able to hide my dropped jaw behind a Bounty.

"Didn't your mom see it?"

"No, you know she never checks the mail. I'm the one who brings it in."

"What does it say?" I asked.

"Eh." She shrugged. "Nothing special. He misses me, you know. Misses"—she cocked an eye up at me—"my lips."

"Gross!" I pushed my plate away, knocking over burnt-to-the-base votive candles on the dining room table. "He did not write that!"

"¿Muchachas?" Mami called out, poking her head from the kitchen. She was on the phone with the gas company.

Kelly ripped up the postcard and stuffed it in between the two bitten halves of her bagel. I watched his blocky handwriting blur in the grease, the fibers of the postcard turning gray as it soaked up the margarine Kelly had slathered on both halves.

"Don't believe me," she said, crossing her arms. "I don't care. I told you I didn't care about him anyway."

She leaned in toward me.

"Besides, his postcard gave me the best idea. For Nicky Gargiullo."

I swallowed a gulp of my orange juice.

"You gonna kidnap him and take him to Virginia?"

"No," she said with an eye roll. She reached into her other back pocket and waved a crumpled white envelope with Nicky's name on it written in orange Magic Marker.

"I'm going to write him a love letter."

ॐ

It was a sleepy Sunday afternoon at St. Agnes's, and the festivities were winding down. Kids had grown bored of gorging themselves on fried, fatty foods, and the novelty of being catapulted through the air had worn off with headaches and sugar highs. I could sense the carnival workers itching to pack up their trailers, fold up their rides, and travel to the next Catholic church on the calendar.

"Are you sure this is a good idea?" I asked Kelly, sitting on the stoop of the gymnasium where St. Agnes's CYO basketball games were held. "He doesn't really seem like the romantic type. Maybe I can help you write something . . . I don't know, different."

Across from us, Brian was attempting to recreate some WWF move by jumping off the railing of the wheelchair ramp and striking his elbow square into Joey's chest. It was still odd to me, how seamlessly he fit in with the Maspeth boys. *What is the trick*, I wondered, *for getting them to see past the color of our skin? Are only boys allowed to be brown?* Beyond the acrobatics, Nicky watched and laughed as he waited to place an order at the sausage and peppers truck parked on the street.

"Please," Kelly said, ripping me from my thoughts. "Don't start acting like you know Nicky now. You don't know everything."

"What does that mean?" I asked.

"Don't act like now that you're on your period, you're *enlightened* or something. It's just blood." She leapt off the step she'd been sitting on and tugged on the leg of her shorts. "You may know something about tampons." She smiled. "But I know about boys. Trust me."

I let out a guffaw, but froze when Kelly shot her eyes at me as if to say don't you dare. I wanted to shrink further inside my bootleg oversize Knicks T-shirt, to clam up and close off, to keep any other new biological development in my life from her. I felt my blood run hot beneath my skin like it did that day in the basement with Timothy, and I crossed my arms through my gaping sleeves to hug my ribs.

Behind the WWF moves off the accessible ramp, I noticed Pablo, another kid from our school, leave the rectory with his dad and older brother, all of them dressed head to toe in black. I recalled hearing their mother's name butchered at lecterns over the past several months during the prayers for the sick, until Adela Cabanban disappeared from the mass, and the Cabanban family joined the list of names of the bereaved, for whom we were asked to bow our heads and pray.

Father Manuel, who led both Tagalog- and Spanish-language masses, was the only Filipino priest at St. Agnes. He thumbed the sign of the cross on Pablo's forehead before rubbing his arm in compassion. Pablo looked tired, his cheeks puffy. I lifted a timid hand to Pablo in recognition, but he never looked my way. Instead, Brian alone paused his wrestling moves to walk over and give Pablo a pound and a solemn hug. I felt embarrassed, considering I'd never even talked to Pablo in school, and turned back to Kelly.

"So," I sighed, "what are you gonna say to Nicky in this letter?"

She slid the envelope out of her pocket again and tossed it to me so that she could bend down and adjust the buckle on her iridescent platform sandals. I jumped a little when it landed in my lap.

"I'm just gonna tell him that I wanna be his girlfriend." She patted both her thighs as she stood up straight.

I turned the wrinkled envelope over in my hand. There were coffee and grease stains on it from breakfast, and on the back, where the flap was glued shut, she'd written "S.W.A.K." in marker, anchored on both sides by kiss-marks in a dark red shade of lipstick she must have swiped from her mother's purse.

"What does 'S.W.A.K.' mean?" I asked.

"Ugh," Kelly said, as she stomped her foot on the step behind me before plopping herself down two stairs above. She yanked the envelope out of my hand and admired it in her own.

"Sealed with a kiss," she explained. She made a smooching noise and bopped me on the head with the envelope.

"But," I started, the blood in my veins coursing quicker, "you don't even know if he likes you."

"Why are you being so mean?" she asked, her eyes turned to slits.

"I'm just being realistic."

"Well," she said, "screw your reality." She emphasized "reality" as if it were a made-up word, but for a brief moment, we shared a look—I could see in her eyes that she recognized she'd spun a witty turn of phrase against me, and my eyes, I felt, were beaming with pride for her ability to do so. But just as quickly as we shared this flash of recognition, Kelly blinked and turned away from me.

"Besides," she said, looking at Nicky, the late-summer breeze blowing back the black bangs she was growing out, "once I become his girlfriend, then maybe you can go out with one of the other boys. Like Joey?"

I screwed up my face at her in response.

"I don't like Joey!" I swatted her shoulder with the back of my hand. "He called me a wetback, remember?"

Last summer before religion class ended, our teacher took us for our final session to St. John's Hospital, where we helped repaint its parking garage facade. Under the midday sun I was drenched with sweat, and Joey, somehow managing to escape actually doing any work, exclaimed to Nicky and all his buddies, "Look! I told you Brisma was a wetback!"

"Okay." Kelly stood up. "What about the Bolivian kid then?"

I shook my head emphatically.

"Why are you roping me into this?"

"Fine." Kelly pulled a white scrunchie from her hair. "Sue me for thinking of you."

She tossed the scrunchie onto my lap as she skipped down the stairs two at a time.

"Never mind," she called back, exasperated, long arms flopping at her sides, nodding toward the old Victorian convent to the right of us. "Be a nun!"

Kelly marched up to where Nicky Gargiullo was waiting on line for sausage and peppers. He was assisting his dad all day at the milk-bottle toss and was ordering two heros when Kelly walked up, both hands in her back pockets, the tiny mounds on her chest thrust forward. I followed at a safe enough distance so that neither of them would be able to detect me. Hiding beside the red, white, and blue ticket booth, I could just make out what she was saying over the bells and whistles of the carnival games and the crescendo of screams from the Tilt-a-Whirl.

"Hi Nicky," Kelly said, toeing the asphalt with her right foot.

"Hey!" he replied, his crystal-blue eyes lighting up when he saw her.

Maybe he does like her, I thought.

He pointed at her with a fist that clutched the dollar bills for his food.

"What you did to your friend the other day was cold." He smiled, nodding his head in approval. I let out the breath I realized I'd been holding and looked around, suddenly self-conscious again.

"Yeah." Kelly tucked her hair behind her ear. "Well . . . she shouldn't have talked to your friends like that," she said, gently brushing his shoulder.

I pursed my lips and bit the inside of my cheek to keep from shouting at her.

"You're cool, you know that?" Nicky accepted his change from the hairy arm that offered it to him through the steamy window of the sausage truck. "How come we don't talk more?"

"We don't go to the same school," Kelly said.

"We don't?"

I frowned. He didn't even know?

"Look," she said, and I could tell by the way she inhaled that she was committed to her mission. "We don't go to the same school, but . . . I did write you something."

She handed him the envelope.

"Here," she said. "Read it when you're alone."

She turned on her rubber Conway heels and walked back toward our spot near the dilapidated convent. I saw Nicky flip the envelope around in his hands a few times before shaking his head and shoving it inside his back pocket. I could hear the metal of his wallet chain jingle as I skipped past him, rushing to catch up with Kelly.

"How'd it go?" I asked.

Kelly was excited, the baby hairs on her forehead wet with perspiration, her chest flushed.

"He said I was cool!"

We both squealed and jumped over to the bush near the nuns' kitchen window, where the scent of ammonia would occasionally slice through the cloud of confectioner's sugar and grease that emanated from the zeppole stand.

"Hey," I asked, "why did you have to throw me under the bus?"

Kelly glanced at me with what looked like disappointment, before bending down to adjust the strap on her sandal again.

"It don't mean anything," she said, her voice muffled against her knee.

She pulled her scrunchie back off my wrist and stood up straight to sweep her heavy black hair into a ponytail. Her oval eyes, what Kelly's mom called Aztec eyes, despite the freckles that surrounded them, despite Kelly's Colombian heritage and Tairona ancestors, remained trained on the asphalt just ahead of her.

"I had to keep up the front," she said, finally looking at me and dropping her arms heavily at her sides. "Who cares what he thinks if we both know the truth?"

I dug my hands into my own back pockets, mimicking how she'd stood with Nicky, contemplating what she said. Was this what people on daytime talk shows meant when they said all is fair in love and war?

"I know," I said. "I know."

Inside my denim, I felt the ridged edges of sharp card stock against the pads of my fingertips and realized we still had some tickets left.

"Wanna watch Nicky Gargiullo open the letter from the Ferris wheel?"

∽

We'd extended our ride twice already, handing the very last of our tickets to the Big Eli conductor from our swaying seats, when we finally spotted some action at the bottle toss. We reached the top of the wheel with a jerk as it stopped to let new people on, while in the distance, Nicky's dad lumbered down from the trailer steps and hobbled over toward the bathroom.

"This is it!" Kelly said, squeezing my knee.

We leaned over the safety bar as far as we could, twisting our necks to catch a glimpse of Nicky under his milk-bottle awning. His back was to us, but we kept our eyes trained on him as best we could. As the wheel screeched forward for another revolution, we rose up and then back down again.

To our horror, we watched Joey and Brian and their goons from the first night sidle up to his booth. Without paying to play, they started tossing blue-and-brown beanbags at the milk cartons stacked in a pyramid on a cake stand. Brian was the strongest of the bunch, and he threw his beanbag so hard that it pinged the metal tin back of the trailer like a gong. The sound snapped Nicky to life; he lifted both arms up to high-five Brian, laughing along with his buddies, who appeared to be just as surprised by Brian's strength as we were.

Then, just as our car came to a creeping halt at the top of the wheel again, Nicky stood up and leaned over to hand his boys something . . . something that looked an awfully lot like a white piece of paper with red lipstick all over it.

"No!" I grabbed Kelly's shoulder.

"Oh my god," she said, staring into the ether.

"What did you write in it?" I asked. "Tell me *exactly* what you wrote!"

Crestfallen, Kelly shrugged. She kept her shoulders pulled back as she stared ahead, sitting up as straight and tall as the starched-stiff straps of her overalls.

"I wrote that I wanted to be his girlfriend." She turned to me with hopeless eyes. "And kiss him like they do on *90210*."

"Oh no," I said.

"With tongue," she added.

"Oh my god!" I covered my face with my hands. "You wrote that?"

The wheel jerked into motion again, causing us both to yelp.

"What are we gonna do?" Kelly asked.

"We?" I asked, crossing my legs so they faced away from her. "I dunno about *we*, but it looks to me like you've got no choice but to leave the country."

"Brisma!" She shoved me against the side of the cart. "Be serious."

As our cart scraped past the landing, whizzing by the motor as it lifted us up again over the wheel, we could see that the crowd of boys had already begun laughing, some doubled over. Joey looked up, his face red and eyebrows raised in disbelief, and by some cruel magic, locked his sights on us immediately. He pointed up at us, and we saw the other fruit-punch faces turn to look, too. Brian kept his nose inside the letter, reading it intently, as if it were scripture. The others ran over to the gate around the wheel to point and laugh at us with each revolution.

I shrank against the padded vinyl back of the seat and balled a fist against Kelly's hip.

"We are like animals at the zoo."

Kelly shook the security bar across our laps.

"Nowhere to hide," she said.

I hated them all at that moment, the immature, sadistic lot of them. *Why do we even bother with these white boys?* I wondered. No one at our school would care enough to bother—it felt like back on our side of the boulevard, we were all too busy dealing with our parents' unpaid electric bills, or translating their mail, or restocking their cigarette cartons.

"I want to die," Kelly said, shielding her eyes and tugging the bottom of my shirt.

The conductor let us out with a grunt, and we took our first dizzy steps off the swinging carriage and onto the metal platform. The chorus of boys at the gate started making smooching sounds, following Joey's lead. We rolled our eyes angrily and slipped past them. I noticed Nicky was in the crowd, having left his post at the milk bottles when his father returned from the bathroom.

We made it a few steps away from them when Joey balled up Kelly's letter and threw it at the back of her head. I heard it fall to the ground with a soft, hollow scrape.

"Slut!" someone bellowed.

This got an uproar from the boys and some dirty looks from mothers passing by with babies. I looked at Kelly, who kept her eyes trained on the ground, grinding her teeth.

"What a whore!"

I recognized that voice as Nicky's. They were high on themselves, whooping and hollering.

I squeezed Kelly's hand and stopped us just before we exited the yard. I couldn't do much about Timothy, but I could do something about this.

"What are you doing?" she whispered, tugging my fist along. "Let's jet!"

I turned around, walked back up to them, and stood with my hands on my hips, all five foot five of me towering over most of them. I widened my stance and felt the adhesive of my maxi-pad pull on the delicate skin of my inner thigh. I winced, but surprised myself by maintaining my inner Rizzo.

"You guys are so immature," I said. "You think a kiss makes you a slut? What do you think you're gonna do with your girlfriends? Play Parcheesi?"

Some of the boys giggled; some looked embarrassed that I was speaking to them at all, seemed unsure of what to do with their tongues and arms now that they weren't hurling insults.

"It's not that big a deal," I said and reached for Brian, the boy with the least social collateral, the only boy in my caste I could touch. I hooked my finger inside the stretched-out neck of his St. Agnes CYO baseball T-shirt and pulled him into me, hard teeth against soft tissue, kissing him forcefully on the lips.

The boys gasped around us. Their chanting turned to teeth sucking and random mutterings of "gross," and "ugly," and "yikes." I left Brian stunned, his lips pink from the pressure of mine, and walked away, making sure to hold my head high, back to Kelly standing at the exit, and slipped my arm around her elbow to leave.

"I can't believe you just did that," she said, our steps falling in unison.

"Just keep walking," I said, my head light from all the blood draining from it. The truth was, I couldn't believe it either.

"You kissed that weird-ass Bolivian boy in front of everyone!" she stage-whispered.

"Who cares?" I asked at the corner, but I could already feel the adrenaline wane with each shaky step I took toward home.

When we hit Queens Boulevard, the cars rushed past us at top speed, kicking up dust and flattened trash, the disco-dance beats of KTU trailing behind them. In the distance, the sun was setting behind the Twin Towers in the Manhattan skyline. I could detect in the air the slightest hint of the coming fall, of sweaters and backpacks, and the heady lead of pencil shavings. I looked Kelly in the eyes, and after a pause, we collapsed into a fit of giggles, all the tension from the evening erupting from our prepubescent throats.

Wiping tears from her eyes, Kelly turned to me.

"Still think we're gonna 'rule the school'?"

SEPTEMBER 2006

We climbed the steep rows of the upper reserved section, cast-metal seats chipping red paint after forty-two New York winters, and looked for our spots in the second-to-last row of Shea Stadium: Row VV. They were the cheapest tickets in the house for a Thursday night game against the Dodgers in early September, at six dollars a pop.

Kelly balanced her Victoria's Secret beach tote on her shoulder to let a greasy beer vendor make his way past her, ice sloshing against aluminum inside his waist-high tray. She winked back at me where I stood on the concrete step below her and pressed herself up against the vendor's hairy arm as he passed.

"Sorry about that, honey," she purred, nodding toward the bag on her shoulder. "A little top-heavy over here."

We had just turned twenty, and although we had fake IDs that suggested we were Jewish girls from Long Island (Kelly argued my tight curls could pass for Sephardic), they only worked half the time. The other half, we needed to resort to alternative measures to ensure a buzz by the third inning.

Settling into our seats with the beer Kelly scored, we were relieved to find that there weren't many other fans around us. We could stretch out with our oversize bags, and oversize plastic cups, and oversize fleece blankets, if the evening turned cool enough after the sun went down. We could shout all we wanted, in whatever language we wanted, without worrying about getting into a race riot with a drunk Nassau County white boy. Earlier that spring, Kelly held me back from punching a season ticket holder who told me to go back to my country.

"We're American, hijueputa!" I had yelled in defense of Puerto Rican first baseman Carlos Delgado, who infamously refused to stand for "God Bless America" in protest against the war in Iraq.

"Yeah, okay," the frat douche in an upturned collar said. "Why don't you come over and clean my apartment sometime, Maria?"

I had lunged up at the row behind us, my flip-flop catching on the seat with a smart *thwack*, allowing Kelly to grab my ankle and then my waist.

"We're American!" I shouted, swinging at air.

It was the age of Los Mets, after all, with their Black and Latino star players José Reyes, Carlos Beltrán, Carlos Delgado, and Pedro Martinez. Omar Minaya, another Black Latino, was the general manager and, more importantly, a former student at our local neighborhood high school, which sat just three stops away from Shea Stadium on the 7 Line. LosMets.com had launched, created for Spanish-speaking fans, and advertisements along and inside of the 7 Train and throughout our neighborhood were usually printed in Spanish.

They played bachata, and reggaetón, and hip-hop in the stadium during games. José Reyes taught a Spanish word of the day in the seventh inning of each home game. For Black and brown kids growing up in the shadow of Shea Stadium, it felt, slowly but surely, like America's favorite pastime was finally acknowledging that we were Americans, too.

"Where's the salami?" Kelly asked.

"What?" I said, as I adjusted my sunglasses on my nose.

"You packed the sandwiches," she said. "I've got the Funyuns and the potato chips." Then she coughed and said, "Oh!" as she slid a hand inside her orange ribbed tank top behind the rhinestone-studded New York Mets logo printed on her chest and produced a sleeve of roasted peanuts.

"My favorite!" I exclaimed, plucking the peanuts from her hand.

"I got you, girl." Kelly smiled, her palm still open, waiting for her sandwich.

I dug through my purse, the top layer filled with stray tampons and the green plastic of ultralong maxi-pads. We'd learned years ago to distract stadium security guards from looking too closely at the bodega contraband we were smuggling in, by hiding it beneath a sea of feminine products they were too uncomfortable to sift through.

"All we're missing is the Cracker Jacks," I said, handing over her sandwich.

"Nobody really eats that stuff," she laughed, wrinkling her nose.

"Little old grandpas do."

"Whose grandpa?" Kelly asked. "Your abuelo been chomping on some Cracker Jacks over on la finca?"

"No," I laughed. "You know, people on TV. My point is, it's always folks with dentures who love that crap."

"That's true." She nodded, rapping her knuckle against her front teeth. "Living on the edge."

Overhead, the announcer began to list the starting lineup for the Los Angeles Dodgers and Kelly booed.

"Brisma," she said before chomping into the sandwich, "LA is a cesspool of fake tits and fake tans."

I bit the paper sleeve tip off a straw, and blew the fleck of white away in a huff.

"Kelly, the farthest you've been out of Queens was driving thirteen hours down to Georgia to bail your mom out of—"

"Too soon," she warned with wide eyes, wiping mayo from the corner of her mouth with the back of her hand. "Besides, I heard Patrick say it once after a business trip to Santa Monica."

The Morales children had the most Irish names their mother Frances could dream up: Kelly and Patrick. I assumed it was a passive-aggressive dig at Andrés, their Colombian father, who'd returned to Barranquilla each time Frances turned up pregnant. They might have both carried his last name and arrowhead nose, with or without his active presence in their lives, but to Frances, at least, they'd always be children of Eire.

"I don't know," I said, dreaming of palm trees and perpetual summer. "LA seems kind of nice. All that sunshine. No sea of winter coats packed into a subway car."

I used to be jealous of Kelly's more American, more white-sounding name. I was named Brisma by my mother after a childhood friend of hers from Vieques she lost touch with over the years. She'd caress my cheek with the back of her hand and tell me we shared the same trigueño skin.

"I will never move out of New York," Kelly said, as she opened the bag of Funyuns with a pop. The stale, synthetic smell of onions overwhelmed me.

"And now," she said, "neither will you, right?"

Mami had been let go that summer from her job as an RN at St. Vincent's in the first wave of massive layoffs at the hospital where she had worked since I was a toddler, when my father cut out on us for Puerto Rico. She took the layoff as an opportunity to get her real-estate license and had dreams of buying and flipping old brownstones in Ridgewood, including one that she and I could live in and renovate together, living off the rental income from the other two floors.

"Absolutely," I told Kelly, as I watched the gray shadows of planes taking off from LaGuardia grow small in the distance until they disappeared in the setting sun.

"I mean, unless this fellowship comes through."

"Right." Kelly cleared her throat, and as I lifted my beer to take a sip, I thought I could detect in my peripheral vision a slight rolling of Kelly's eyes in response. "But that's just for a few months, isn't it?"

A week into the fall semester, I submitted a fellowship application to write for ABC Studios. Last spring, I'd completed a spec script for a drama about a New York sports psychologist helping baseball players navigate their personal and professional traumas. My mentor and screen-writing teacher, Professor Acevedo, liked it so much she suggested I start applying for network fellowships: ABC, NBC, FOX, even HBO. If I was going to be graduating from college early, she'd cautioned, then it was time to start planning for my future—in LA.

"Yeah, I'd be gone like three months, tops."

I pulled a Funyun from the bag in Kelly's lap, as a cool breeze blew off Flushing Bay and across our bare arms.

"If I get it," I added.

The announcer raised his voice to welcome the New York Metropolitans to the field, and the fans rose to their feet.

Kelly and I jumped, cupping our hands around our mouths to holler for the team as they jogged out of the home dugout.

I felt Kelly elbow me gently in the ribs and turned to look at her under the roar of the crowd. She nearly matched my height now, but remained slender, still fitting into clothes from the juniors' section, while I needed a belt to secure my size 14 jeans over my ever-widening hips.

"You'll get it," she said, her eyes trained on the field, where players in black-and-blue burst onto the diamond.

"Oh," I said, thinking about all the nights she'd spent at my house since her mom was sent to Albion Correctional Facility six months ago for running a fake Hurricane Katrina charity. I didn't want her to think I was abandoning her, too.

Kelly snuck a glance at me.

"You just better come back home afterward."

Cold fingers, just then, patted softly against the back of my neck, ripping me from my thoughts. I smacked the area hard, a reflex from a summer spent thwarting mosquitoes, and trapped the offending fingers under mine.

I turned around, ready to pounce and attack the man (surely it was a man) who was brazen enough to touch me, when I saw who it was.

"Hey, boo," Brian cooed, his thick lips spreading smoothly into a smug smile. "Long time no see."

It was disorienting seeing him there. His face was at once familiar and yet older, more masculine, his jawline defined beneath a suggestive shadow, brown neck thick with muscle and veins. The last time I had seen him was a few years ago at high school graduation. We had dated sophomore and junior year, but our once-hot relationship smoldered for too long in a spiral of shame and self-doubt until I finally found the strength to throw water on it and move on. We didn't keep in touch after that beyond cold glances across student-filled auditoriums.

"How you been?" he asked, when I still hadn't responded.

I hated that looking up at him in the row behind me, I felt my chest tighten and my lungs fill with elation at the sight of him there, talking to me, in a very steep, very cheap, section of Shea Stadium.

"Good." I coughed to clear my throat. "Um, I've been fine."

Feeling dizzy looking up at him like that, I sat down in my seat. Brian followed, sitting in the identical seat in the row behind us, but I watched his eyes wash over Kelly as he did.

"Hey, babe," he said to her loudly, performative, his long, dark eyelashes flitting between us.

Kelly. Because of an unspoken agreement to never bring up that dark period in our lives, it was easy for me to forget that Kelly and Brian had nearly hooked up once early in my relationship with him.

"Hey, douchebag," Kelly said. She smiled and crunched loudly into a Funyun, her hoop earrings bouncing against her full cheeks as she chewed.

"Always the charmer," Brian said, and retrained his dark, liquid eyes on me.

"What are you even doing here?" I asked, taking off my canvas Mets cap to smooth my frizzy flyaways back up into my ponytail.

He raised his eyebrows and pointed toward the field. I saw that he had a new scar on his left eyebrow, or maybe he had directed his barber to shave one in after his last tape-up. I wasn't sure. But it made him look hard, tougher than I knew him to be.

I glanced back toward the field at Tom Glavine warming up on the mound for the Mets. I felt my cheeks flush and closed my eyes.

"No, I know. The game. You're here for the game," I said, turning back to Brian. "But what are you doing *here*?" I asked, drawing my arms wide to encircle our two rows. "Your seats just happen to be right here? With us?"

Brian stretched back in his seat, allowing me to see the full spread of his grown body. The soft belly I knew to be stuffed with Oreos from coffee hour at St. Agnes had flattened out, and the muscles in his arms were solid and toned; veins now bulged where chicken pox had scarred the inside of his biceps in fifth grade. His skin was a deep russet color from a season spent on the baseball diamond. He was a catcher for St. John's University baseball team, and they were actually good, a great difference from the games I watched him play on our barely ranked high school team.

Brian folded his arms behind his head.

"I guess it's just meant to be," he said with a wink, his dancing eyes always too quick to catch for long. He jumped up to signal his boy over, and I saw that it was Pablo, the Filipino kid we used to hang out with who I'd stopped speaking to after Brian and I broke up. Last we knew, he'd joined the army after graduation, served a tour in Iraq, and came back to Elmhurst calling people *boss* and *chief*, instead of *son* and *player*.

"Jesus, Mary, and Joseph," Kelly said, rubbing salt off her fingers when she saw Pablo ascend the stairs. "What is this?" she said, as she wiped her hand on her jeans. "A high school reunion?"

Brian hitched his basketball shorts up and sat back down, placing a hand on my bare shoulder.

"So what's good with you?" he asked. "It's been a minute since I seen you last."

He licked his lips as he lifted a sweating plastic cup of Bud Light from Pablo's outstretched hand. Just before tipping it back, I caught him giving me a quick once-over.

"You look great," he said.

Out of the corner of my eye, I saw Kelly reach over to greet Pablo with a hug.

"Private Cabanban," she said, as she saluted him.

Brian leaned in closer to me, his brow creased, and mouthed the word "beautiful," and I realized I'd stopped breathing at some point.

I rose to greet Pablo myself, clearing my throat.

"So," I said, pursing my lips, remembering that things had ended sour between us at the same time my relationship with Brian ended. I squeezed his hand. "What you been up to, G.I. Joe?"

He shook my hand and said nothing, not once breaking eye contact. I frowned and looked at Kelly and then at Brian. Pablo's grip was strong, but I was most unnerved by his silence. Looking back at him, at his eyes still trained on mine, searching, I felt the skin on my arms prickle as my imagination filled in the space between us with sandstorms, IEDs, and impossible violence.

"Been a while, Brisma," he muttered, bending his neck to wipe his brow. He turned to Brian.

"Are you really trying to sit up here?" Pablo asked. "My brother is waiting for us in Row B. You know, with the tickets he paid for?"

Brian giggled in a way that folded me in, as if Pablo's question had touched on some kind of inside joke we shared—only we didn't. It was a self-important giggle meant to make Pablo feel dumb and self-conscious. I remembered it well from when we dated.

"So you're telling me," I said, "you spotted us from all the way down there? This is Row VV!" The skin around his eyes wrinkling from laughter, Brian leaned forward on his elbows again.

"What can I say, Brisma?" He reached out and gently rubbed my earlobe between his thumb and forefinger. "You've always stood out in a crowd."

At this, both Kelly and I rolled our eyes.

"Give me a break," I croaked and turned around in my seat.

"Do you know how corny you are?" Kelly asked, punching a broken fragment of one of her last Funyuns toward him. I giggled. It pleased me that Kelly was giving him a hard time; she never talked much about him after we reconnected back in high school, and I think we both preferred it that way.

Pablo tossed Brian's ticket down on the empty seat beside him.

"I'mma be down there with my brother," he told Brian. "I don't want to miss the game."

He straightened his shoulders back and nodded at Kelly and me. "Ladies," Pablo said, and started back down the steps toward their actual seats.

Kelly and I looked at each other, our chins tucked into our necks.

"Ladies," we repeated with a giggle.

I watched Pablo find his brother, Ariel, in Row B and tiptoe between other people's feet to sit down in the empty seat beside him.

"Don't mind him," Brian said. "He's just salty that I didn't invite him to this party last night up in Connecticut."

I elbowed my arm around the back of my seat to look at Brian better, as Glavine recorded his second out of the first inning.

"Oh yeah?" I raised my eyebrows. "Pablo went off to war"—I looked back down toward him to make sure he was out of earshot—"and he's brokenhearted that you didn't invite him to some Waspy-ass frat party?"

Brian widened his eyes and grabbed my forearm.

"How'd you know?" He shook his head. "It was such a messy night, Brisma, 5–0 and all."

I smirked, but there was something sobering about the way he said this that made me think for a second that there was really something he wanted to tell me, something serious maybe, but I shrugged it off. This was the first time we were having anything close to a conversation in nearly five years.

He lowered his voice, and I leaned toward him.

"Can't say it was my first time sneaking out of a girl's dorm room," he said, his jaw tight, brows raised.

My breath caught in my throat as I studied him. Behind me, I heard the crack of the bat in the batter's box. I turned to see who'd just hit a double and peeked at Kelly as I did; she seemed intent on watching the game, not eavesdropping on us.

"Sounds like you're really living it up," I sighed.

"Nah," Brian said, drawing his knees together. "You know I'm just playing."

I glanced back at him, side-eyed, and saw that he was looking down the V-neck cut of my top, when the next batter hit a pop-up that looked for a second like it was going to count for a hit. Kelly dug her fingernails into my bare thigh as we watched the ball sail through the air until it curved at the last minute, a foul ball. Kelly released her grip on my flesh and grunted in relief beside me.

"But for real," Brian said, inching forward in his seat. "We should hang out again sometime. I'd like to catch up. You been following the Mets?"

I whistled in the direction of the scoreboard.

"You already know," I said, clapping as the batter finally grounded out, the team retreated to the dugout, and the Dodgers took to the field. I turned back to face Brian. "This is the year. Can't you feel it? Twenty years?"

The last time the Mets had won a World Series title was 1986. There were all sorts of commemorative specials airing on the

Mets-owned SNY network, and the stadium had been hosting special events with players from the last championship team all season.

I saw something change in Brian's face; an old softness returned that I recognized from childhood, from before we even dated. For a moment, he wasn't the smooth-talking lothario he usually portrayed himself to be. He was just a kid from the block, rattling off stats and studying the pitching arms of Ron Darling and Doc Gooden. His body visibly relaxed, and his eyes were excited and light.

"Maybe we should watch a game together, then."

"Am I the only one watching *this* game?" Kelly interjected, annoyed.

"Sure," I answered Brian, ignoring Kelly. "Just give me a call. Same number. Or email me?" I regretted rambling, making myself so available to him.

"I will," he said, and before I could turn away, he squeezed my shoulder.

"I mean it, though," he said. "I'd like to see you again."

"Okay, cool," I said with a shrug.

I checked Kelly beside me to see if she had noticed the exchange, but she was ripping open a new bag of Sour Cream and Onion Ruffles. I considered whether she was using every odious-smelling weapon in her arsenal to physically repel Brian from our area in an effort to look out for me or to keep me to herself. Either way, I enjoyed it.

"Good," he said.

I watched him bounce down the steps and back to his seat. I tried to concentrate on José Reyes at the plate, but his at-bat music transported me back to sticky summers filled with salsa, and bachata, and dancing with Brian on the newly built piers off of Long

Island City, the slight breeze off the East River the only thing to come between our sweating skin grinding against each other underneath the streetlamps.

Kelly elbowed me hard as she slammed her arm across my lap to reach the chair on the other side of me.

"Hey!" I cried out in pain.

She stretched to grab the baseball cap I'd left on the seat next to me and tugged it on hard over my head.

"Your ID, numbnut."

I adjusted my cap and looked up at Kelly's beer vendor from before, towering over us with an impatient look on his face, back and apparently willing to serve Alyssa Rosen and Rebecca Stern their sixteen ounces of alcohol in exchange for a little more cleavage as we bent forward to fish around in our back pockets for our licenses.

"It's like you're in a trance," Kelly muttered.

And she was right. It felt a little like I was.

1996

Maybe we already are witches."

Kelly and I had walked home from Elmwood Movie Theatre in the middle of a late June downpour, the air heavy like in the rain forests our fathers came from, down the length of Queens Boulevard without a single Q60 passing us by. School had just let out and we lied to Mami about going to Queens Center Mall so we could watch *The Craft* again instead.

"What makes you say that?" I asked, tonguing a popcorn kernel off my molar as we waited for the sun to burn through the lingering clouds. I had made the mistake of telling Mami I wanted to become a witch after seeing the movie the first time. She slapped me and muttered that the devil always collects his debts. When I asked what that meant, she sent me to my room. The following Monday when I came home from school, a rosary had appeared, hanging from a nail over my bed.

"Well," Kelly said, leaning back on her ankles, her legs bent into the shape of a W beneath her.

"Our addresses," she said, nodding to the stickered numbers on the door at the end of the dark communal hallway of the three-family house I lived in with Mami. "You're 66-06? I'm 66-61. You think that's a coincidence?"

She bounced a handball in my direction, which I caught with one hand.

"Only one digit away from 666."

"Yeah." I shrugged. "Maybe."

Maybe that was part of what worried Mami all along. Maybe I did possess some kind of powers on account of having been born here. Maybe the devil already knew my name.

I bounced the ball against the concrete walls painted a delicate gray and white to mimic marble.

"But isn't that number for evil people?" I asked. "I don't think witches are necessarily evil."

Kelly placed both palms on the floor to push herself up to her feet.

I tossed the ball again. "Do you?"

She caught the ball before it could bounce back to me.

"Oh, I am definitely one of the damned," she said. "Let's give it a try!"

"Give what a try?" I leaned back.

"A spell."

Kelly pushed open the front door, beckoning me to follow. She skipped the two pebbled concrete steps to the bottom of the stoop and spun around, her left foot slipping out of its cracked leather sandal, the ones handed down to her from one of her Jersey cousins. The air was sweet with the smell of fresh rain and loamy soil emanating from skinny, neglected rows of vegetation along the sidewalk.

"What do we do?" I asked.

Kelly shrugged.

"Wriggle your nose."

Kelly used to come over and watch Nick at Nite with me and

Mami on nights when Frances hadn't come home from her boy-friend Zayid's apartment during one of her separations from An-drés. *Bewitched* and *I Dream of Jeannie* were her favorite old shows to watch. She liked the furniture, she said, and how neat, and clean, and colorful everything was. My favorite was *Laverne & Shirley*.

I tried wriggling my nose, but all that conjured was a sneeze.

"You're such a nerd," Kelly said.

"I think I need an intention."

"An intention?"

"Yeah," I said. "I need to want something. I need to concen-trate on making something specific happen, don't I? Like breaking a glass or lifting a rock?"

At that moment, we heard the whine of a chain-link fence gate swing open in the distance, and we groaned in unison, knowing who it was even before we turned to see. Julio was an out-of-work actor who lived across the street and who, as far as we knew, had never held a real job for which he was compensated, ever; he claimed to have a tricky back, which allowed him to collect disability. Our mothers told us he lived rent free in his abuela's musty old house that sat on the other side of the railroad tracks across from Kelly's. We could hear their rusty wind chimes rattle each time a freight train passed. We had been inside exactly once, at the invitation of La Señora (his grandmother must have had a name, but that's the only one we were ever given), and I remembered wondering how long it must have taken for dust to accumulate fingernail-deep in-side the closed doors of their china cabinet.

Julio had bleached his skin so many times that he always looked a little dusty, too. He wore very strong glasses that magnified his prawn-like irises and maintained a daily uniform of white tees and black or blue Dickies, no matter the weather or season. When we were little, he used to attend block parties and barbecues along with the other neighbors and always found excuses to play with us. He'd load up our bubble wands but then put them so close to our faces that our lips would get covered in solution, and he'd wipe our mouths with his thumb a second too long. He brought out Hula-Hoops to watch us swivel our hips, and his favorite game after church or on special occasions was to playfully lift up our skirts with the cane he sometimes used. It was all done in plain view of other adults, but no one ever seemed to see or acknowledge it. He was just playing around. Everyone was having a good time. But lately, he had been secluding himself from all types of social situations.

"This is perfect," Kelly said, snapping her fingers and peering into the square plot of dirt we called a "yard," looking for something. She pulled out a dark, oblong rock behind a spot of wild scallions and turned it over in her hand.

"Good weight," she said. "Good shape."

Over the winter, Julio was spotted spying in the windows of several people's homes on the block, but most often, my own. Frances had caught him standing in the alley next to my house, wearing no shirt or shoes, despite the February frost on the ground, staring into our bathroom window. Another time, he rang our doorbell, similarly shirtless and shoeless, and when I answered, he insisted I fetch my mother. When she came to the door, fresh from the shower with her hair in a silk bonnet, he snatched at her towel and asked if she wanted to come over to his place, "y que le pases bien." Mami sent him home, but never got angry enough. "Drogas," she said with a shrug, and lit a candle on the Virgin Mary altar in our living room.

"Maybe she liked it," Kelly had said after a thoughtful pause, when I told her at school the next morning.

"No way." I frowned. Mami hadn't dated anyone after my father left seven years ago.

"Maybe she's lonely and doesn't mind letting him watch you shower, if it gets him to keep coming over," she said, fingering the collar of my T-shirt as I shoved her arm away.

"Are you out of your mind?" I asked, my heart rate quickening. "You don't know what you're talking about."

Kelly and I referred to him solely as El Cochino after that night, and I mastered showering in under five minutes, always afraid he was lurking outside the frosted window, watching my naked silhouette. We went out of our way to throw empty platanitos bags and used Kleenex over his tall fence and onto his property. We ignored him anytime he tried to call out to us. He had finally crossed a line coming to my door, training his dilated pupils on my mother, snatching for her. I wanted to make it clear he was not welcome—that I had him figured out, Kelly and I did. We knew danger, even if our mothers didn't.

"What are you doing?" I asked Kelly.

"You wanted an intention, right?" Kelly responded, kneeling down in the paved front yard the size of a freight elevator to draw a circle big enough for the two of us, with the sharp edge of the rock. She nodded back at Julio, who was already making his way toward us.

"Let's banish him."

I stepped inside the circle, and she pulled me down to sit with her, ankles crossed beneath our knees. Facing each other, we repeated the lines from the movie we'd just watched.

"With perfect love," Kelly began.

"And perfect trust," I answered.

Julio crossed the street towards us, whistling to get our attention, but we didn't break our gaze from each other. We chanted louder. When we sensed him step onto the curb of our sidewalk, Kelly frowned and leaned in close to me.

"Repeat after me," she muttered.

I nodded.

"Protect us, Goddess, from the perversions of the pathetic."

I stifled a laugh, both because I felt embarrassed for Julio, but also because I didn't know how Kelly had strung that sentence together, sounding archaic like a black-veiled viejita.

"Protect us," I repeated, "Goddess, from the perversions of the pathetic."

Kelly joined me for a few repetitions before we devolved into simply chanting "pathetic" and "perversions."

"Qué lo que, nenas?" Julio asked, gum popping between his teeth. He leaned his full weight on the fence that separated him from us. The measly clasp on the gate an empty gesture of safety when it could be swung open at any time.

"Pathetic," we said, turning to face him.

"Perversions."

"What's that?" he asked, squinting, the curve of his belly pressing into the diamonds of the chain-link.

"Pathetic," we screamed. "Perversions."

"Pathetic!"

"Pervert!"

A woman pushing a stroller moved to the far side of the sidewalk to speed past us.

"Pathetic!"

"Pervert!"

I could see in Julio's face the moment when he finally registered what we were saying. His already beady eyes narrowed, and he reached for the latch on the gate, the tinny scrape of metal against the gatepost. He was coming in. The anger I had felt peering at him that frosty night from the cracked spine of the front door as he tried to paw at Mami lit up in me again. It happened fast, and Kelly never stopped chanting, but I grabbed the rock from beside her foot and hurled it at him in one quick, panicked motion. It clipped the top of the fence and bounced off his cheek. A painful, brief moment of shock passed between the three of us, everyone charged with the life-ending possibilities before us.

Julio growled and swung the gate open hard with his fat hand, poised to grab, or shake, or who-knew-what, to us. The contempt that seemed to bubble beneath all his interactions with Mami now appeared raw and naked in his eyes. One hand still balancing on the gate, he reached down to us on the ground, but Kelly sat straight up, digging fingernails into the flesh of her knee as she opened her mouth to scream, "*No!*," eyes shut tight, jaw wide, all her soda-stained teeth on display. Her voice high-pitched like an alarm, it rang out between the row houses and apartment buildings on the avenue, bouncing off of brick walls, clapboards, and screen doors. Momentarily deafened, I could vaguely sense the swishing of curtains being peeled back, the suction of window seals popping open as people peeked out from fire escapes.

Julio froze, cringing under the watch of the neighborhood. He backed away and closed the gate gingerly. Under his breath, he mumbled "cunts" in English, to make sure we knew how much he meant it. He glided down the block, one long stride after the other, trying to appear unbothered. A few beats after the dandruff-laden back of his head disappeared around the corner, and the normal chatter and traffic of the block resumed, we collapsed into a fit of nervous giggles.

"It worked!" I cried. "At least for now."

"You see," Kelly said, "I told you we were witches."

She reached over and slapped my hand.

"I got you."

I watched Kelly as she stood up inside the circle and pulled her overall shorts out from her behind.

"Come on, let's go over to the dugout," she said. "I think the Mets game is about to start. Isringhausen's pitching today."

"I can't believe we did that," I said, hugging my knees. "I mean, I don't know how much of that was really the spell, but *we* did that."

"You loved it," Kelly said, nudging me with her foot. "Embrace it, girl! You are powerful. And together?" she continued, shaking pebbles from her thigh.

She held out a hand to help me, but I pushed myself up off the ground on my own.

"Yes," I said, knuckling her shoulder. The loose strap of Kelly's overalls hung low off her chest, the metal buckle clanging against the copper button of her pocket.

"Together we're unstoppable."

SEPTEMBER 2006

The *New York Post* calculated that the Mets had a 98 percent chance of clinching the National League East, so Kelly and I piled into PJ Moore's early that night to watch the game, Mets logo glowing neon in the window beneath the elevated 7 Train. It was a Monday in mid-September, and I had my screen-writing class in the morning, but I didn't care. The Mets took priority—in Queens, when the Mets played well, you didn't take it for granted. Everyone else in Woodside seemed to feel the same way, as the bar was packed by six.

"I'll grab you a Smithwick's," Kelly said, rounding her hips out from beneath the table to make her way to the bar.

She had taught me early on that Smithwick's would garner more respect from Irish bartenders than Guinness, because everybody ordered a Guinness when they were at an Irish pub. Truthfully, I hated both, but never let on in front of Kelly.

We were lucky to have snagged a table by one of the few stained glass windows, next to the unused fireplace. There was a mural of John F. Kennedy along the far wall that led to the bathroom. The bar, situated on Woodside Avenue just before it merged with the main artery of Roosevelt, was only a few cobblestoned steps from the 7 Train, an express stop on the way to Shea. The neighborhood had seen a lot of change over the years, growing from an enclave for Irish immigrants to tight-knit pockets of community for Southeast Asians and Latinos. We were seated at the crossroads of Ireland, the Philippines, and Latin America to watch Los Mets win the division on their way to—hopefully—a World Series berth. It seemed only right.

I hadn't heard from Brian since we'd run into him at Shea a couple weeks ago, but he remained on my mind. I found myself sitting in class, thinking about his fingers on my neck that evening, or how his eyes danced in the light of the setting sun. And that wink—always as if his self-deprecation were an inside joke he shared with me alone.

Kelly came back and slammed the drinks down, sloshing Smithwick's over the lip of the branded beer mug and onto the carved wooden table.

"You'll never believe who's here," she said.

"Brian?" I asked, immediately regretting it.

Kelly frowned at me and threw a cocktail napkin my way in disgust.

"No, not fucking Brian," she said. She looked behind her and then leaned in against the table, the lace trim of her push-up bra peeking out from her V-neck T-shirt.

"Joey," she whispered.

I bent my ear toward her.

"Who the hell's Joey?" I asked.

"Shh." She pinched my lips. "Joey," she repeated, "Nicky Gargiullo's Joey."

I hadn't thought about Joey DiPrima since our eighth grade confirmation class. After that one particularly eventful St. Agnes's fair, we'd had to deal with him only peripherally through all the remaining sacraments our mothers forced us to complete on our road toward becoming full-fledged Roman Catholics. That first year after Kelly's letter was painful; the minute Mr. Sullivan dismissed us from religion class, we'd shoot out of the room and run down the stairs, avoiding all unnecessary contact. But as Nicky and his boys matured—Brian never went back to St. Agnes after that summer with the kiss—they gradually forgot and allowed us the mercy of fading into obscurity and irrelevance.

Behind Kelly's long, black ponytail, I could make out Joey laughing, posted up in the corner booth with a bunch of other ruddy-faced boys, silver chains still gleaming in the low lights of the bar. He was the only one I recognized from St. Agnes; no Nicky, I was relieved to see.

"What are they doing on this side of the boulevard?" I asked.

Kelly shrugged and sipped her beer, wiping foam from her top lip.

"Who knows," she said, bisecting her hair and tugging on it to tighten the ponytail. "They're not even Mets fans. Remember all that Yankee shit they used to wear?"

I nodded in their direction.

"They're wearing Rangers caps tonight."

"Who wears a hockey baseball cap?" she asked, frowning.

"They suck," I said with a shrug.

I noticed Kelly was ripping and rolling her napkin into tiny shredded tubes as she stared in their general direction. I caught the glint of Joey's earring—a diamond stud, just like Nicky's.

"You think they remember us?" Kelly asked, chewing on her bottom lip.

I swallowed a large gulp of beer and pressed myself against the banquette behind me.

"Probably not," I said. "I mean, maybe. They might remember *you*."

Kelly had gained elevated status among the white boys because of her freckles and rosy complexion, and the fact that her butt and hips, further accentuated by her swaybacked spine, filled out overnight in the seventh grade just in time for Jennifer Lopez to make it fashionable. I was always some strange brown girl who followed her around in the latest discount fashions from ABC Superstore that I somehow always immediately outgrew. We had done Secret Santa in religion class one year, before the S.W.A.K. letter. It was divided between the boys and the girls, and she received a Polly Pocket as a Christmas gift from one of them. I received a used, worn-down, blue plastic spinning top with what I hoped was a smeared chocolate chip on the handle.

"You think so?" Kelly asked, as her eyes lit up. She twisted the base of the beer glass between her hands. "Maybe I should go talk to him."

"You sure it's a good idea to get involved with them again?" I asked, recalling foggy memories of a party Nicky Gargiullo was at with us in high school during my dark period with Kelly. "After what happened?"

Kelly pursed her lips and adjusted herself in the chair.

"Joey never did anything wrong."

I sighed, remembering how he led the charge in mocking Kelly when she wrote her letter to Nicky at the fair.

"What are you gonna say to him, 'Hey, remember when I professed my love to your best friend in sixth grade?'"

Kelly cut her eyes at me and pushed away from the table to look up at the SNY pregame.

"You know it wasn't like that," she said, her eyes on the screen.

My shoulders involuntarily hitched up toward my chin, the memory of Timothy, and his lips, and his VIRGINIA IS FOR LOVERS postcard surfacing for a brief moment from the bedrock of our friendship, and I shook my head as if to rid him from it. I glanced at Kelly, guilt burning behind my ears, but she seemed to be lost in her own thoughts.

"Look," I said. "If you wanna go talk to him, go for it. I think he's a racist piece of shit who calls little girls wetbacks, but who am I to judge?" I smiled, raising my glass. "Maybe he's changed."

She turned to look at me, the fire in her eyes renewed.

"You think he'd fuck me?"

I choked on my beer.

"Jesus Christ, Kelly," I said, as I wiped my mouth with the back of my hand. Another memory of Kelly burying Timothy's boxers in the dirt flashed before me, but I blinked it away again. "I mean, only one way to find out, I guess."

She smacked the table and swiped her glass in one smooth motion. She stood, sending her chair skidding back across the hardwood floor as she walked away.

Minutes before the first pitch, I took out my phone to text Brian.

"Hey," I wrote. "You'll never guess who's here at PJ Moore's with us, watching the game."

I closed the phone and adjusted to slide it back into my pocket, when I felt it vibrate in my hand. He'd already responded.

"Timo Perez?"

I smiled at the blue-lit screen in my palm, remembering how excited and then how heartbroken Brian was the last time the Mets were in the World Series in 2000. It felt right, in a way, that he was orbiting back into my life when the Mets were hot and headed for October again.

People around me at the bar started hollering when Steve Trachsel took the mound for the Mets. The energy in the room was palpable, everyone hyped and ready for a celebration. I turned back to my phone and texted Brian, "Close. Joey DiPrima and some other meatheads from St. Agnes."

Pressing send, I wondered if Brian would care, if it would mean anything to him, calling upon the names of those Aryan kids he played CYO baseball with one summer. I tucked my phone back into my pocket and willed myself to focus on enjoying the glory of the Mets' clinching win.

❦

With every run the Mets scored, I checked my phone to see if Brian had responded. By the fourth run in the sixth inning, Mets up 4–0, I forgot about Brian, and Kelly found her way back to me, too, amidst the hooting and hollering in the bar. We embraced each other, jumping up and down, elated; we chanted that this was finally our time.

"They're giving out shots at the bar," she screamed over the television.

I followed her to the sticky edge of the dark wood bar and downed a burning shot of whiskey. Warm from the liquor, I looked up and over at Joey, whose hand was now firmly planted on the bare skin of Kelly's stomach where her shirt had accidentally hitched up. I watched Joey's eyes travel between the screen and his buddy next to him, never once acknowledging my presence. I liked nothing about their situation.

When the last Marlins batter of the game sent a fly ball to left field, the only sound in the bar, on the whole block, was the anxious gasping and shouting of fans that drowned out Cliff Floyd's easy catch and the end of the game. The Mets were officially the National League East Champions.

I picked Kelly up and swung her around, as she high-fived everyone in our radius. When I put her down, she dug her fingernails into the cool skin of the tops of my shoulders, and neither of us needed to say a word. For that brief moment, pandemonium all around us, it was just her and me, just the two of us shouting on top of the world, a world that normally never shook out in our favor.

The bartenders brought out pots and pans from the basement kitchen, handing them out to patrons, who proceeded to bang them together over their heads and out onto the sidewalk. Together, we were a cacophony of unrealized hopes and dreams, a smoldering fire that finally found some oxygen. Kelly handed me a wooden spoon, dried bits of onion stuck to it, and I pinged it against a stained skillet, following the crowd into the streets where cars slowed down to honk in solidarity, and people waiting for the Q29 bus stood with their hands outstretched, a receiving line of high fives. After living in the shadow of the Yankees for ten years, everyone seemed to understand this to be the big deal that it was for the Mets, for Los Mets, and for us.

Kelly hopped on Joey's back to ride him down Woodside Avenue with the crowd. Watching them, I wondered how the eleven-year-old versions of ourselves would have reacted if we had known that day was coming—not just the Mets, but that Kelly would one day ride Joey DiPrima down the block in public for all to see.

I bent down to pick up the baseball cap that had fallen off Kelly's head when she jumped, and when I straightened back up, I saw him.

Lagging behind the crowd, down Sixtieth Street, were Brian and his friend Pablo. He hadn't seemed to notice me yet, so I slunk back inside the shadow of a column outside the bar. I watched as he fist-bumped a few day laborers who passed by him, bouncing tool belts clinking from their waists as they walked, shouting, "Let's go Mets!" with the crowd. My heart skipped a beat as I took a step toward him.

"I didn't expect you to show up here," I said, throwing an orange-and-blue rally towel at him.

"It's another Mets miracle!" he said with a smile, referencing the 1969 team.

"So corny," I said, shaking my head.

Suddenly, Brian bent down and collected both of my legs, lifting me up and placing me over his shoulder. With his arms tight around my thighs, I beat my fists against his back, and he put me down. For the brief moment he held me up, though, I caught a better view of the sodium-pink streetlights, and the orange, white, and blue joy that was filling the street. I felt connected, I realized, to Brian, and to the crowd, part of something bigger, finally, part of some long-awaited recognition that I couldn't quite place my finger on.

Back on the ground, I straightened my shirt and made sure my breasts were still safely ensconced inside each cup of my bra.

"I don't know what it is with men and sporting events, but keep this barbarian impulse on lock, Brian," I said, hiking up my jeans by my belt loops. "I can stand on my own two feet, thank you very much."

Brian smiled at me and smacked Pablo, who seemed tired, on the shoulder.

"We don't have any noisemakers," Brian said, nodding at the pan in my hand.

Pablo looked around and picked up two white dinner plates

that a patron had left on one of the outdoor patio tables. He shrugged at us, eyes rimmed red from beer, and smashed them together with all his strength. The dishes shattered, naturally, shards exploding onto the gum-stained sidewalk. The three of us broke away laughing, when a high-pitched shriek startled us again from behind. The bouncer had somehow procured a whistle and was now pointing at us as he pushed past people toward where we stood amid a circle of broken ceramic.

"Move!" Brian shouted, grabbing my waist from behind and pulling me toward the rumbling overpass of the 7 Train.

Outside the diner on the corner down the block, I spotted Kelly making out with Joey against a red fire-alarm post near the curb.

"Kelly," I called out, "we're leaving."

She pulled apart from Joey. Her lips were raw and her eyes unfocused, until she saw Brian over my shoulder.

"You can go." She nodded.

I felt Brian step closer behind me.

"You sure you don't want to leave with us?" I asked, looking at Joey.

"Let's go to Rockaway," Brian chimed in, and I rolled my neck toward him.

"It's almost midnight!" I cried.

"So?" he replied, running his hands through his hair. I remembered how I used to pull it when we kissed, how I would grab a handful of hair and—

"You think the beach disappears with the sun?" he asked, that familiar twinkle in his eye.

"Okay," I said, waving my arms in surrender. "We'll go."

Before turning to follow Brian back to Pablo's car, I pointed at Joey and narrowed my eyes at them both.

"Kelly, you sure you good?"

She released her grip on Joey and stepped out of his embrace as if to protect him from me.

"Totally," she said soberly. "I'm fine. Don't worry about me."

"Okay." I squeezed her hand and turned to go.

"But you better be careful, too, you know," she called after us.

When I looked back I saw she wasn't talking to me but pointing a finger gun at Brian, one eye closed.

"I know where you live."

&

On the drive from the bar to Rockaway Beach, Pablo stopped briefly in Elmhurst to pick up his family's purebred miniature schnauzer to bring with us.

"He doesn't like to be alone too long," he explained, throwing the car into first gear.

The drive was exactly how I expected it to be on a Monday night in September: lonely, but beautiful with the crisp breeze blowing over the wild grass of the expressway and in through the open windows. We parked on 116th Street and walked past businesses already closed for the season to the wooden boardwalk along the beach.

Pablo halted at the aluminum ramp that led to the sand.

"You coming?" Brian asked.

"Nah," Pablo said, shaking his head. "Stanley's allergic to sand."

Brian and I shared a look and laughed.

"Why'd you even come then?" I asked.

Pablo set Stanley down on the boardwalk, the tags on his collar tinkling. He scratched at his nose and looked at us. He shrugged.

"I don't trust you two alone," he said.

"Yeah right, Pablo," I said, jumping onto the cold sand. "Like we ever needed privacy if we wanted to hook up."

I shot him a look.

"You of all people should know that," I said.

Pablo remained stone-faced as I turned, stumbling over the uneven sand. Brian laughed beside me as we walked toward the water, leaving Pablo with no one else but Stanley on the boardwalk. We took wide steps so our feet didn't sink too deep, but I felt lighter and lighter the farther I got from Pablo.

"I don't like him," I said, comfortably aware of Brian's body moving in unison with mine.

"Pablo?" he asked. "He's harmless."

Then he frowned, looking back toward the boardwalk.

"Well, I guess in some states he is considered a deadly weapon now," Brian chuckled. "Did you see those guns?"

He flexed his arm, and I laughed as the dry sand turned to the wet, hard-packed slope of the shore. The weather was still warm enough to get away with wearing flip-flops, and I was able to slip mine off easily. Brian needed to hold on to my shoulder for balance while he untied his Uptowns.

"Why'd you come out tonight?" I asked.

He looked up at me, his eyes genuine again, soft caramels melting under streetlamps.

"I wanted to see you," he said. "You remember. I told you so."

"Yeah," I said, as I cleared my throat. "Where'd you watch the game?"

"At a restaurant," he replied, straightening back up and hooking my arm to guide us toward the waves.

"A restaurant?" I asked. He never had very much money growing up, and I doubted college baseball was paying his bills. "With Pablo?"

"Uh"—he toed a shell in the sand—"yeah, he was there."

I leaned in to nudge him in the ribs. I noticed that his bicep was harder, more solid than I remembered it.

"And were there girls there?" I asked in a mocking tone.

"What?" he asked, deliberately cracking his voice to feign shock. "Of course not."

The roar of the waves grew louder as we inched toward the seam of the ocean. This time, he leaned his weight in toward me, pressing into the hollow of my waist.

"Okay, to be honest," he said, "a date went south, and I called Pablo to see if he wanted to swing by and catch the rest of the game. He's been a little off, you know, since he's been back."

"He's always seemed a little off to me," I mumbled, recalling that Pablo used to smuggle old *Hustler* magazines into our middle school cafeteria, where he charged kids a fee to borrow them— Brian, his best friend, always got them for free.

"Nah." Brian cleared his throat. "His dad has been sick, too, you know. After his mom and everything . . . it's been hard on him."

I eyed him in the dark and then glanced back toward Pablo, where he sat on a bench, calmly petting Stanley beside him. Pablo's mom had died of breast cancer before sixth grade, and I'd always assumed that he acted out as a vulgar, oversexed preteen and teen, in large part because of that unresolved grief.

"Besides," Brian continued, stuffing his free hand in his pocket, "I needed a ride home."

"Ah," I exhaled, throwing my head back, self-conscious of how the moonlight might grace the bones at the base of my neck. "The truth," I said, and Brian squeezed my arm tighter.

The water was ice cold on my toes at the shore. The shock sent me jumping back.

"Too cold, too cold, too cold!" I squealed, curling my fingers into Brian's forearm.

He laughed and pulled me away. In the moonlight, I could see the hair on his toes was slick, wet with the freezing ocean, but he made no sound, no indication that he was uncomfortable.

We turned to hike back up a bit and sat where the sand turned dry. We lay down and looked up at the night sky, the gravity of the ocean and the moon weighing us down, grounding my hips into the planet and filling my lungs with fresh air. I could only spot a few actual stars, but I was able to make out several planes soaring by, red blinking lights and deployed wheels, preparing to land at JFK. The game, the Mets, and the past all seemed so far away.

"We should be able to see more stars out here by the ocean, don't you think?" I asked the inky oblivion above us.

"Ambient light," he said.

I turned toward him and lifted myself up onto my elbow with an attitude.

"What you know about ambient light?" I asked.

Brian shrugged and pulled himself up to sit.

"The lights of the city are too bright," he said, peering above. "That's why we don't see any stars."

I watched him thumb a callus that had formed on his palm, training his eyes on his own hands.

"Not even out here," he said.

"Yeah," I said, studying his face before turning back up toward the moon. "You're doing pretty well, huh?"

In the corner of my vision, I could see him lean back onto his hands.

"What do you mean?" he asked.

"I mean your career," I said. "Baseball. School. St. John's ain't nothin' to sneeze at. You should be proud of yourself, man."

We were friends on Myspace, and I'd seen pictures he'd posted from playoff games over the summer. He'd traveled the Eastern Seaboard for baseball clinics, tournaments, and away games, and even though we hadn't actually spoken in a few years, from afar I was proud that he had left the basement apartment he grew up in under the sneaker-tied cables of Clement Moore Avenue and was really doing something with his life.

His face cracked into a smile, but a soft sadness remained in his eyes.

"I'm nobody," he said with a laugh. "On this team? I'm just a number."

I frowned.

"Yeah, and that number is the amount on your tuition bill," I said. "You got a scholarship, right? To play ball? And it's a pretty decent team, if what I've read is correct."

Brian tilted his head toward me, an intimacy.

"You reading up on me, Brisma?"

I slapped him in the ribs playfully with the back of my wrist.

"Look, don't go getting all gassed now," I teased, lying back down on the sand. "I'm just saying . . . you made good on your dreams. I respect that."

Brian lowered his shoulders down next to mine in response. I dug my toes into the cold sand and commanded myself to relax, to remember this moment, how the heat seemed to emanate from his solid triceps next to my own.

"My dreams weren't big enough," he finally said. "I got a scholarship, yes. But I know this is it for me."

He patted the sand beside him, and the granules he kicked up tickled my thigh. "I'm not gonna play professionally."

"How do—"

"I'm not good enough, Brisma," Brian said, cutting me off. "Point-blank, period."

He inhaled, his broad chest growing taller off the sand.

"And that's okay," he exhaled. "At least I can see myself clearly. Some other guys can't."

I recalled how often he fought—sometimes physically—to be seen by his mother, a tough woman who never showed up to any of his games, to feel the relief of her love instead of the eternal climb of insecurity. I wanted to hug him there on the sand, but after so many years of history stacked between us, I could only bring myself to offer a single curled finger of comfort against his forearm.

"You remember when we were kids?" he began. "You remember we used to spin your globe with a finger on it, and wherever it stopped, wherever we were pointing to, we planned to go there together?"

"Yeah," I said. "How embarrassing."

A silence hung between us like a ghost.

"You'll still travel," he said, sniffing at the air. "Go on book tours all over the world."

I groaned, a little embarrassed.

"Nah," I said. "I don't write stories like that anymore."

"No?" he asked, sounding disappointed.

"No." My lungs expanded, excited to share. "I write for TV now. Or, I hope to. I'm thinking of—"

Just then, he reached over and grabbed my arm.

"Did you see that?" he asked excitedly.

I squeezed his hand, afraid that he'd seen a shadow in the distance behind us, or the headlights of a cop car on its way to kick us off the beach, or worse.

"I think there was a shooting star."

"It was probably an airplane," I said, releasing my grip and relaxing back into the sand. "It's a busy night."

Brian turned onto his side and slid his hand down my arm to place it gingerly on mine. I froze, his hand on top of my clenched right fist, willing myself to remain calm.

"You reminded me of our first kiss," he said, "with your text tonight."

"What?" I lifted my head to look at him, but the moon had risen too high in the sky, and shadows contoured his face now; when he turned to look toward the boardwalk, I could see flashes of the whites of his eyes.

"That day at the fair with Nicky and Joey, and all those douchey CYO bros," he said. "That's when you kissed me. For the first time."

"Oh." I frowned. Brian and I had been through so much, so many other kisses, and more, that I hardly remembered kissing him as part of the drama that day at the fair.

"That's why I came," he said. "Tonight. Your text reminded me of that kiss."

"Well," I said, "I also got my first period that year at the fair, so you'll forgive me if it's not one of my top-ten most romantic memories of all time."

He laughed, his voice high and melodic, his chin up toward the moon.

"It was a pretty traumatizing weekend," I said, pulling myself up and dusting my hands free of sand.

"Not for me," he said quietly. He sat up, too, and inched over next to me, both of us resting our forearms around our drawn-up knees.

"Ever since that day," he said, "I knew that you were going to be a special person in my life."

This time, I laughed up at the moon, but nervously. My chest felt like it was filled with helium.

"Kelly was right," I said. "You are *always* spitting game, huh?"

I rocked forward onto my feet, without using my hands to get up, and stumbled a little finding my balance.

"You still writing poems out to girls in class? Slipping notes in lecture halls to Long Island girls driving their daddies' BMWs now?"

I offered my hand to help pull Brian up, which he took, the calluses on his batting hand gliding against my soft palm. I underestimated his weight and yelped, bracing myself against his frame to keep from falling backward. That close, I could smell the soap on the skin of his neck and the gel that he used in his hair. His other hand, I realized, remained on my hip longer than it needed to.

"No game," he said, his breath warm with cinnamon gum. "No lie. You are the most beautiful girl that's ever cared about me."

All the wisecracks my brain wanted to formulate got caught in my throat as I looked up at his eyes. His lips were parted, open and vulnerable. Leaning into his chest still felt like home, if I let it. *It would be so easy to fall back into this, into him*, I thought.

"Stanley!"

In the distance, I could see Pablo running after the trailing leash of a dog loose on the boardwalk. Stanley was poised to climb down the ramp we used to access the sand.

"Help!" Pablo shouted.

We broke apart and ran to try and save the dog from whatever anaphylactic fate walking on the sand might bring him. With every broad stride back, I tried to ignore the throbbing pulse between my legs, but I also couldn't help but feel safe with Brian there, running by my side. Some tiny, pathetic part of me wondered if maybe he and I were meant to be, after all, from childhood to college baseball. *This was poised to be the year for the Mets*, I thought. *Could it be for me, too?*

At the ramp, Brian ran full speed ahead of me, ahead of Pablo, to grab hold of the green leash. I tried jogging past Pablo when he grabbed my elbow.

"Brisma," he said softly, "it wasn't you I was worried about."

I frowned at him, trying to remember what he'd said on the boardwalk before. Pablo's eyes flicked toward Brian, who had by now caught Stanley. He inhaled sharply.

"It's Brian I don't trust."

I studied Pablo's face for the first time; it was smoother now, his acne scars faded by the desert sun. He had grown into his buck teeth, and a square jaw had emerged from his round baby cheeks. He looked stern, concerned. Like a cop.

I shook my arm free of him and rubbed where he had grabbed me.

"Okay?" I whined. "I'm good."

I picked up my pace walking over to Brian, who was rolling around with Stanley on the wooden planks, tickling his sides and rubbing his belly, safe and sound. *Pablo is the one*, I thought, hugging my elbows, *who I don't want to be left alone with.*

2000

The way that I first loved Brian was intoxicating and all-encompassing. We grew closer the summer after ninth grade, when the cut in Brian's stepdad's work hours meant they couldn't afford to continue sending him to Monsignor McClancy on the partial baseball scholarship he'd received, and he would instead be matriculating with us at our zoned high school that fall. Kelly and I spent every humid afternoon at Broadway Park together, watching Brian and Pablo play basketball with a few other boys they knew from I.S. 125. None of them were particularly good—Brian's sport was clearly baseball—but we enjoyed watching them peacock across the painted concrete, flexing their minuscule muscles beneath neck-worn T-shirts.

"Brisma!" he would often shout, acting as if he weren't purposely waving in such a way to flex his modest biceps. "This one's for you!" He had stretched out since our days at St. Agnes, when he was a short, chubby kid riding his skateboard down Clement Moore; now he was nearly a head taller than all of us, with a stubborn Adam's apple that bobbed in his throat when he spoke. Most times he missed his shot, but that only added to the charm. Parents were tickled by the manners he displayed (Mami was impressed with his *bendiciones* and *con permisos* at the house), teachers thought he was witty and self-aware despite mediocre grades, and kids of all genders were inevitably and inextricably drawn into his orbit, no matter what he did. He made friends and gained confidences everywhere, from the locker room, to the classroom, to the deli counter at the bodega.

It was this cocktail that did me in: the reflective heat from the asphalt of the park, the gloss-stained cigarette butts underfoot, and the elevator-drop pull of my stomach whenever Brian linked arms with mine or grazed the back pocket of my jeans as I walked to the piragua cart in the midday sun that turned my brain into a romantic kind of gauze, unable to think or function as anything but a sponge to soak up the blood pumping harder and louder through my veins whenever he was near.

Brian could charm anyone except his mother, it seemed, who was perpetually cold and unsmiling, at least to us; she never even shot so much as a warm nod in our direction. "Don't mind her," he'd reassured Kelly, Pablo, and me after she brushed past us and into his building's lobby one evening after work without a word. "She hates everyone equally," he'd said, "including me."

"You think Brian's cute?" I asked Kelly one afternoon, the air dense with weed and cigarillos wafting over from the handball court.

"Nah," she said, flicking a Marlboro Red with her thumb, the chipped lavender polish revealing calcium stains on her nail.

"I'm not really into that basket-maker type," she said, her hooked fingers piercing the cloud of smoke around her in air quotes.

I shoved my shoulder into hers playfully.

"Girl, you are that basket-maker."

"What?" Kelly said as she exhaled, bringing the cigarette to her collarbone. "Cuz I'm half Colombian? Please. You know I like white boys."

I let it slide, this strange declaration, though it sat in my belly like the knot of an ulcer beginning to form. I pushed away playground memories of Kelly claiming my ashy knees and elbows were dirty against her pink, knobby joints.

We had cut a ton of classes that June at the end of ninth grade and rode the F Train into the Village every chance we could. Kelly got a tattoo on her rib cage at a St. Mark's tattoo parlor owned by a friend of Frances's. Sometimes I thought she got the tattoo, a trinity knot small enough to be concealed by her bra, out of jealousy; I wore a cup size three times larger than hers. She claimed she chose it not for Frances, but after her father got an identical one on his wrist that he'd kiss anytime he missed Kelly and Patrick during one of his Colombian sojourns. I didn't like it: the father, the son, and Kelly's lonely ghost, eager to ink a family that was never there into permanence. But she used it as an icebreaker, a ploy to flash her breasts at older Catholic prep-school boys waiting to transfer buses home from the Queens Center Mall. I'd usually tag along on the dates she scored, for safety.

Whenever I tried to talk to the inevitable buddy those Catholic schoolboys would bring along on those clandestine hookups, the friend would only ever ask questions about Kelly.

"Why doesn't she have a boyfriend?"

"What does she look for in a guy?"

"Have you two ever made out?"

They were usually uncomfortable in her mildewed basement, where most of the hookups occurred. Those boys were used to finished basements with wine coolers and backyards with shiny red grills and green grass, not the train tracks and the tall, littered weeds of our dugout.

Our time spent with Brian and Pablo at Broadway Park was a welcome reprieve from the weight of holding up my end of conversations with white boys who never really saw me. At the park, I could relax and feel safe in their universe, the thin slapping of blue rubber handballs—*sock!*—and the buoyant bouncing of worn-leather basketballs—*ping!*—a siren song of sorts for a galaxy of kids no one bothered to think too much about outside of a police blotter.

"So Pablo is a no then, too?" I asked, nodding toward Pablo, whose deep tan never quite masked his pockmarked face.

Kelly raised her eyebrows, considering him for a moment. The extent of any sexual tension between the two was relegated to the pool table at Golden Q, where they'd try to best each other, head-to-head, on rainy days after school.

"I'm not against the idea," she said, as she shrugged.

I crossed my arms against my chest, glancing down briefly to make sure I wasn't spilling out of my tank top.

"You ever wonder what this white-boy obsession is about?" I asked.

Kelly dragged on her cigarette and exhaled before answering with her chin held high.

"Not even for a second."

We chain-smoked and shot the breeze like that until the streetlamps turned on. Brian and Pablo gave us rides home on the pegs of their bikes. As cars whooshed by us on our ascent up the hill, I held on to Brian's shoulders, where the sun had pinched his skin tight, and inhaled his combination of sweat, cheap gel, and sprinkler water that had dried his straight black hair hard and felt my heart break—for him or for me, I wasn't quite sure. I knew, balancing on those pegs, that I wanted to be by him, to be associated with him. I felt proud holding on to him. He was my ticket, I sensed; I just didn't know to where.

✌

We started dating the weekend before the Fourth of July. The fair at St. Agnes was exposed to have been a drug front; the rector was allegedly using it to launder money he made selling amphetamines out of the rectory. In response, the church held a dance to help recoup the funds that had been spent by the dismissed Father Michael. The theme was Summer's Bounty, despite most of us never having even set foot on a farm. Pablo had jokingly convinced me it was a costume party, so I was the only person in our grade to show up in costume. I wore a black-and-orange patterned T-shirt with wings over my shoulders as a monarch butterfly.

Kelly had left my side to grab us some sodas when, much to their amusement, the white boys found me.

"Nice outfit, butterfly," Joey DiPrima growled. "You lookin' for somewhere to land?"

He patted his lap and his boys snickered.

Brian was no longer among them, the fracture of their racialized social strata already straining their tenuous friendships; not only did the white boys have to look past the fact that Brian was Latino, now he was enrolled in the poor high school in the ghetto instead of one of the prep schools like them. It was too much for their friendships to handle, and so he began hanging out more with Pablo, who'd come here as a kid from Manila and whose dad was so religious he forced Pablo to wear black with him in mourning for all of sixth grade after his mother died.

In the gym where the dance was being held, I could just make out Brian and Pablo playing Bullshit with a deck of cards on one of the benches along the wall. I barely entertained Joey's remarks and waved the group off as I quickly slid off the wings and balled them up in my hands. I eyed the nearest exit and squeezed the box of cigarettes inside the waist of my leggings. I climbed the stairs to the balcony over the gymnasium and out onto the fire escape. Brian followed.

"I like your outfit," he said.

"Please," I replied, gesturing inside to where Joey was probably still flapping his wings, making fun of my outfit. "I don't need you to taunt me, too."

"No," he said. "I'm serious. I know Pablo was trying to prank you, but I think you look cute."

I froze, wondering if I'd heard him correctly.

"Cute?"

"Yeah," he said, gingerly picking the wings out of my hand. "Wholesome."

"Oh," I said, remembering a debate in the park last week about who on *Dawson's Creek* Pablo and Brian deemed to be fuckable or not.

"So not fuckable, then?" I asked.

He laughed.

"You don't wanna be fuckable," he said. "Guys don't marry fuckable."

I flicked my cigarette and made a show of looking around the fire escape.

"Who the hell's getting married?" I asked, palms to the sky. "We're teenagers."

"All right," he said with a smile, hands up in defense. "I take it back. Not wholesome, then."

He grabbed on to the iron handrail of the fire escape, and I smiled, feeling his warmth beside me, as I looked out onto the lights of the boulevard.

"Whoa," he said, as he elbowed me. "Talk about fuckable."

He pointed to an open window at the back of one of the cheap motels that littered Queens Boulevard a block over. Inside, a woman was bent over the radiator, a man wearing only a white T-shirt behind her.

"Oh my god," I laughed. "This is a church! Don't they know this is a church?"

Brian smiled and raised his eyebrows, lips curling mischievously.

"Is this offending your . . . *wholesome* sensibilities?"

"Dude, it's offending my human sensibilities. They're in front of a church!"

He shrugged and leaned forward to get a better look.

"Aren't you curious?" he asked, mouth open, his tongue poking at his bottom lip.

"Don't be a perv," I said, covering his eyes with my hand. "Let's go."

My cigarette had burnt out between my fingers, so I reached for my Zippo to light it again.

"You shouldn't smoke, you know," he said, following me.

"Yeah, yeah," I said and rolled my eyes, but my stomach was burning with delight. "Ruins the wholesome fantasy, right?"

I balanced the cigarette between my teeth as I brought the lighter to my mouth.

"I read that after five years, though, if I quit, my lungs will turn all pink and pretty again."

Before I could relight the butt, Brian yanked it out of my mouth, a flake of my dried lip stuck to the orange filter. I attempted to cry out something about the price of cigarettes, but he drew his face close and pressed his soft lips onto mine.

He tasted of tangerines and Winterfresh. When he pulled away, I noticed for the first time the beauty marks that freckled his heavy lower lash line and how the orange glow of the courtyard lights reflected off the irises of his eyes like butterscotch.

"For me?" he asked. "Don't smoke. For me."

OCTOBER 2006

"Exterior. Inner city." Tyler, a white boy in my screen-writing workshop, read aloud from one of the desks arranged in a circle in the classroom. "Omar kneels down to lay the bloody knife on the asphalt and looks up at Dimebag."

I adjusted myself in my seat, the seam of my jeans biting into my thighs, as I braced for the end of the scene. I'd been given the part of Dimebag to read, while Hye-Jin, my closest friend at Hunter, read for Omar.

"I'm not saying this." Hye-Jin shook her head at Professor Acevedo.

Professor Acevedo scratched her ear. "Yeah, I don't think—"

But Tyler sat up in his seat and read Omar's line for Hye-Jin. "Me mash up any bomboclat 'cross your path, son."

"Oh," I found myself saying quietly, turning to meet Hye-Jin's eyes next to me. Her chin was tucked into her fist, her shoulders narrow and tense like mine.

"DIMEBAG." Tyler turned the final page to close his script, nodding to me for my line.

"Word," I read, scanning the room. "I gotchu."

I wondered if Tyler had ever met anyone actually convicted of a crime. I thought about Frances, surrounded in her living room by stacks of neon-colored flyers promoting her fake charity for victims of Hurricane Katrina, complete with stenciled praying hands on them. I remembered how she gleefully told me and the boys Kelly brought home about her genius plan.

"Those people don't need the money," she'd crowed. "They're dead!"

Her laugh, like gravel being shoveled against concrete, still echoed in my memory sometimes.

Professor Acevedo cleared her throat in the classroom. Her heels clapped against the linoleum as she sat up in her chair.

"Let's open the floor to feedback. Remember," she said, as she held up a finger, "we start with the positive."

In the silence that filled the room, I realized my face was still screwed into the deep frown that had grown during the workshop. Tyler's scene was filled with stereotypes about the "inner city" and gross caricatures of Black people. In the room, the only people of color were me, Acevedo, and Hye-Jin. I'd seen plenty of photographs of my grandfather, who'd died before I was born, and despite his clearly broad nose, bronze skin, and wavy hair, Mami refused to acknowledge it.

"I don't know what you mean," she'd say. "Somos boricuas. We're all a little Black."

I could never form the right words to explain to her how this felt like a reduction—how it felt like the mortar that held me together was dissolving into a solid, seamless wall she could never see, only bump up against in the dark.

"What was that?" Hye-Jin whispered, when a redheaded girl began praising Tyler's ear for dialogue.

I raised my eyebrows. "Felt like a drive-by white-ing."

Hye-Jin smiled an upside-down smirk and shook her head.

"Not your best," she said.

"Hye-Jin?" Acevedo asked. "Anything you'd like to share?"

Hye-Jin had grown up in Jackson Heights, the neighborhood over from Kelly and me. We didn't know each other, though we took out books from the same library and were both treated to the Kitchen Sink at Jahn's Ice Cream Parlor on Thirty-Seventh Avenue on special occasions. When she was fourteen, her parents upgraded their Corona bodega for a chain of laundromats near Fordham and moved to Riverdale, where she attended Bronx Science High School. To her parents' dismay, she chose to attend Hunter College, a city school, and turned down a biology scholarship to Boston University; she'd scored an editing job at Manhattan Neighborhood Network her senior year, and her dream was to someday work for IFC. She was taking Acevedo's class to develop a better sense of plot and action, which she hoped would help her visual storytelling.

"Sure," Hye-Jin said, pushing herself to sit up tall in her seat. "I thought his spelling was strong."

Acevedo blinked.

"And the setting was . . . vivid."

The redhead tooled the eraser head of a number two pencil against her scalp. I watched Acevedo cross her nylon-stockinged legs.

"But I'm sorry." The words rushed from Hye-Jin. "The dialogue is contrived and racist, and you've really just got to reconsider your whole script, dude."

Hye-Jin folded her lips between her teeth.

"Racist?" Tyler exclaimed, red apples of shame rushing to his cheeks.

"Remember," Acevedo said as she held up a palm, "no speaking until the end of the critique."

"I can't defend myself?" Tyler whined.

Acevedo looked at Tyler, for what I realized was the first time since he began. "No."

"But I've done my research!"

Acevedo stood up to try and wrestle back control of the workshop.

"You researched Jamaican patois?" I asked, giving up any hope of being able to lower my eyebrows from their dubious perch.

"Wait—" Acevedo tried, but Tyler kept talking.

"*Belly* is, like, my favorite movie, okay?"

Acevedo, Hye-Jin, and I all let out an exasperated sigh, while a few others in the class giggled or kept their eyes trained on their desks. Acevedo looked up at the clock on the wall, BROTHER printed on its face, staring at us.

"We are just about out of time," she said, tapping her wrist. "Why don't you all pass over your annotated copies of Tyler's script, and he can use that feedback at home for consideration as he revises his scene."

As everyone passed over their copies of Tyler's script and packed up their own books to leave, I snuck my phone out of my back pocket. Mami had sent me a realtor.com link to a two-family house in Ozone Park that was about to go into foreclosure. "Come w/ me to see this?" I started to type a response, then deleted it and opened my text window to type a new message.

"White boys out here wildin in the TV/Radio dept. You don't even know."

I scrolled to Kelly's name and clicked send. She'd be starting her shift soon as a bartender at Riviera, a strip club in Astoria. Kelly enrolled at LaGuardia Community College the same time I started at Hunter, and the gig helped her pay the balance on her tuition bills—Frances was not only no help to her, but a drain, especially after she was sent away. I was proud of Kelly's hustle: night school, a real job, a side hustle, all to not miss a beat, starting college with the rest of us. She didn't let the messy shrapnel of Frances's life define her.

"That was insane," Hye-Jin said, standing up to pack her bag.

I looked to the front of the room where Acevedo was behind her desk, reaching into her bag and pulling out a bright green folder.

"I know," I said. "But I'm used to it."

I turned back to my phone and copied and pasted the text I sent to Kelly into a new message to Brian. But then I added, "Wanna grab dinner Friday night? Mets are traveling to LA for Game 3. (Let's go Mets!)"

I pressed the worn green send button and tucked it back into my pocket. I felt a thrill imagining the team flying to LA, disembarking into the dry heat, palm trees lining the roads that welcomed them. I imagined me, Brisma, driving down Sunset Boulevard, windows down, the sun warming my elbow on the car door on my way to my fellowship. I'd daydreamed about this future often, especially in Acevedo's classroom, but this time when I turned my head, Brian was sitting shotgun.

"We're all used to it," Hye-Jin said, hoisting her bag onto her shoulder as we walked toward the door. "Doesn't make it right. In the mood for coffee before your next class?"

I opened my mouth to say yes, when Acevedo called out to me.

"Hey, Brisma," she said, one curling finger in the air. "I printed off something else for you."

She handed the thin stack of papers from the green folder to me. At the top of the first page was a familiar, colorful peacock logo.

"Another application? For NBC?"

Acevedo fanned out her fingers on both hands and smiled. "Best to cast a wide net."

Hye-Jin poked her head in between us to look at the papers.

"*Another* application?" she asked.

"She's already applied to ABC and a few others," Acevedo said with pride.

I felt my skin turn hot as I folded the papers in my hand and hooked my arm around Hye-Jin's shoulders to usher her out.

"Thanks, Professor. I'll take a look at this tonight."

I dragged Hye-Jin to the escalators of the West Building. The floor-to-ceiling windows in the common areas around the elevator bank gave us a wide-open view of Lexington Avenue and the more commutable areas of the Upper East Side. I often felt like I was attending college at Madison Square Garden, or worse, in the doldrums of the Manhattan Mall. I was acutely aware, especially with Brian and his baseball-playing, frat-hopping antics back in my life, that I was not having the quintessential college experience.

"Writing programs," I explained to Hye-Jin, "to get your foot in the door more than anything. But who knows? It's a crapshoot."

"Nah." Hye-Jin punched my shoulder as we rode down to the ground floor. "You have awesome ideas and your scripts are flawless."

She clutched her chest. "That baseball psychologist drama you turned in last semester?"

"That's the spec I submitted!"

"Girl," she said as we stepped off the escalator, "you're a shoo-in."

I smiled. It felt nice not to have to shirk my ambitions for the sake of someone else. I checked my phone to see if either Kelly or Brian had texted me back and saw that Brian had.

"Sorry, boo. Hooking up Coach w/ a connect for new jerseys in Bridgeport. No choice. Next time."

I clapped my phone shut and sighed. I pushed my way through the revolving doors to the street, where I was greeted by the sweet, vanilla scent of nuts roasting in an open cart. I turned to Hye-Jin, who was already fishing out her MetroCard on reflex.

"How about this?" I asked, patting her arm. "When I'm show-runner someday on a wildly successful drama, I'm calling you in to be my editor."

Hye-Jin stuck her hand out.

"Deal."

2000

My father rang our doorbell on a freakishly hot Saturday in September when Kelly and I planned to go to Macy's for free AC and a shoplifting spree. He acted, after eleven years, like he'd just returned from a quick overnight trip to D.C. I hadn't seen him since I was three, when he'd flown to Puerto Rico one morning without telling me or Mami. With the exception of a phone call around Christmas each year, I hadn't even talked to him all that much. I only had a few fuzzy memories of him in checkered chef pants and thick rubber clogs. Last we knew, he was living in Miami and driving trucks for Hostess cross-country.

Mami opened the door, her hair still wrapped from the night before.

"Lord *God*, almighty," she said.

"Oh." He smiled, revealing striking white teeth I knew better than to trust. "That's not necessary," he said. "You can just call me Eddie."

He stuck his right hand out as if they were meeting for the first time.

"We made a child together. Remember?"

Mami slapped his hand quick with the back of hers.

"Listen," she hissed through her teeth, "you don't gotta be reminding *me* who had whose baby, okay?"

I bit my lip as I watched them from behind the hinge of my bedroom door, eyes widened in fear. Yet still, Mami stepped back against the wall to welcome him into our hallway.

"Brisma!" she hollered, though she must have known I was spying on them. "Come see who the Twinkie truck brang in."

I was terrified and excited as I bounced from behind the door in one sweeping leap, stopping just short on my toes where my father stood. I didn't know whether to hug him or shake his hand. He was still a stranger to me.

"How ya been, Brisa?" he asked, scooping me up in a hairy embrace, his chest heavy with Drakkar Noir. I frowned as I pulled away.

"Nobody calls her that," Mami said, opening the fridge.

"Why would they?" I asked, looking between them.

"That's your name," he said, maintaining tense eye contact with Mami, as he slid off his jacket.

Turning to me, he grabbed my shoulders and lowered his head to be face-to-face.

"Your name was supposed to be Brisa," he said, waving his hand like a magician or a car salesman. "Like the sweet Caribbean breeze that brought you into our lives."

Mami sucked her teeth. "Listen to this," she muttered under her breath, as she slammed the fridge shut.

He coughed and straightened up.

"He means sea breeze," Mami said. "Too many sea breezes brought you into our lives."

He raised a brow at her, fingering the mal de ojo pendant he wore around his neck. "But the city made a mistake on your birth certificate, and your mother never did anything about changing it."

"Mira eso," she continued, as she flicked the cap off a Heineken bottle, his favorite, that she perpetually kept stocked in our fridge for precisely this hypothetical occasion.

I expected a long tirade to follow, the way she'd set me straight whenever I dared talk back to her, but Mami bit her lip, sliding a coaster down in front of him to place the Heineken bottle on.

"Other *things* were on my mind," she said, stopping short at the kitchen table where his jacket was thrown over a chair.

That should tip her over the edge, I thought. She hated when I left my clothes around the house. But Mami just picked it up without a word, smoothing it against her chest, before hanging it on the coatrack behind our front door.

It didn't sit well with me that he'd been in our house for less than five minutes and was already passing judgement on what she did or didn't do in raising me. I wanted to stand up for both of us.

"Why are you here?" I asked, when Mami slipped behind her bedroom door, a bobby pin already clenched between her teeth as she undid her silk wrap. She'd invested in a Japanese straightening perm that summer and no doubt wanted to seize the opportunity to display the magic all that formaldehyde had worked on what she referred to as her "pelo malo."

He looked at me with wide, round eyes and an open mouth, the question clearly a threat to him.

"Because I'm your father." The word in his mouth, *father*, was laden with shame—his or mine, I wasn't quite sure.

"I wanted to see you, Brisa." He repeated my almost-name and set the sweating beer down on the table.

I screwed up my lips at him.

"You're so grown already," he said, looking at the door Mami had disappeared behind for confirmation. "I bet you've got all the boys after you."

I wrapped my hands around my elbows and shifted my weight, saying nothing.

"Hey," he said, playfully punching my arm as he reached around into the pocket of his hunter-green JanSport backpack. "Look at this."

He fanned an envelope open, revealing a set of pin-striped tickets.

"Two tickets to the Yankees game today!" He smiled again with his too-white teeth. "You and me."

I looked at him and then at Mami, who was gliding back into the room in a form-fitting dress with her hair laid down, all black silk and shine.

"You're not going to work today?" I asked, expecting to see her usual pastel scrubs.

Mami snapped her purse open and closed at the table, as if to check on something, before smiling smugly at my father.

"I have a Mary Kay meeting before my shift."

I rolled my eyes and turned back toward the Yankees tickets.

"I'm a Mets fan."

"Brisma," Mami clucked, as she slipped the coaster underneath my father's beer.

He laughed, lifting his Yankees cap to pass a hand over the tight curls that hid beneath.

"I really have been away too long, then, huh?"

He tucked the tickets back into his zippered pocket.

"Come on," he said. "It'll be fun. We can catch up over hot dogs and ice cream."

I thought about Kelly and how we were supposed to go to the mall that afternoon to lift a bikini from the clearance rack at Macy's. Mami hadn't let me buy a string bikini over the summer ("¿Como una sucia?" she'd asked), and Frances had taught us that it was easier to get away with stealing the merchandise that stores were already trying to get rid of at the end of the season ("Less of a chance they'll prosecute," she'd said). I was never as comfortable as Kelly or Frances was shoplifting, but I went along with it because I didn't want to give her another reason to think I was immature. I narrowed my eyes and tried to summon what Kelly would do in this situation.

"I already have plans," I told my father, standing in our foyer with his worn-out backpack crumpled at his feet.

"Brisma!" Mami repeated, sterner this time.

"What?" I shot back. "It's true! Kelly and I—"

"Kelly and you, nothing," she said. "You see Kelly every day. This is your father."

She said the word now as if it was supposed to carry some weight, as if I was supposed to treat it with some reverence.

I looked at him with his dark, Homer-like stubble around his mouth and his sweat-stained T-shirt doused in cologne.

"So?" I shrugged, knowing I was provoking her.

"Brisma!" Mami shouted, smacking the table so hard that his green bottle rattled against her ceramic coaster, a castanet of pent-up fury.

"You have ten minutes to get yourself ready," she said, pointing a red fingernail in my direction. "And then you are going to the Bronx with your fatherwholovesyou."

She ripped a paper towel off the rod.

"And for Christ's sake, comb your hair."

⁓

The stadium was crowded, of course—more crowded than Wednesdays at Shea when Kelly and I traded in empty Pepsi bottles for free seats in the bleachers. My father's seats were just as bad as those, though, as high up as possible and behind the left field foul pole. The still-summer sun beat hot on my scalp as I waited for him to return from grabbing hot dogs and beer from the concession stand.

It was only the second inning, but the crowd was already rowdy, riled up at the prospect of the Yankees clinching the division. They'd lost their last six games, but the people in the stadium still had faith the team would come through. "Greater expectations," Brian had joked. I felt uncomfortable, surrounded by testosterone-fueled yuppies shouting over my head at the field. I missed having a backpack of snacks to rifle through and Kelly by my side to rank the hotness of players on the visiting team.

For a brief moment, I wondered if my father had abandoned me there, brought me all the way to the Bronx just to disappear again, following a new, random woman onto the 4 Train and away from me.

Just then, I saw him turn up the concrete steps, carrying a plastic basket of food, his hot dog already half eaten.

"Everything okay?" I asked.

"Beautiful." He smiled, scratching the tip of his nose. "Here's your dog."

He sat down heavily in the seat next to me, shaking the row. I had forgotten how much physical space his broad, six-foot frame took up.

"Hey," he said, as he knuckled the back of my hand. "You ever have a dog?"

I ripped open the one packet of ketchup he left for me in the tray.

"Like a puppy, I mean."

"No," I answered, squeezing the sauce between my bun. "The landlord doesn't allow pets. You don't remember?"

He winced, as if he wished I hadn't acknowledged that shared past, that he'd ever lived in that apartment with us or that we were ever a family, the three of us a unit.

"So tell me about your life," he said, as he wiped his palms on the thighs of his faded jeans. "How's school? You like it?"

"No," I answered, swallowing a mouthful of bread. "But who does? It's high school."

He laughed, and when he tipped his head back, I saw that there was a dark gray gap in his perfect white teeth, a glaring void amidst what must have been expensive dental work. I was reminded of a Japanese word for something like that, a word I'd learned in art class last year: *kintsugi*. The imperfection of a piece of pottery, a crack or a hole filled with gold, and it was this imperfection that made it perfect. Mami had an emergency gold bridge put in her mouth when she broke a tooth eating a green apple from my free lunch during a fourth-grade field trip to Alley Pond Park. She finished paying it off last Easter.

"Ain't that the truth," he said with a chuckle. "High school's the worst."

Mami told me he'd dropped out of high school to work at a restaurant on the Lower East Side, near where he'd grown up in

Alphabet City. Mami had gone to community college after he left, to get her nursing degree.

"You have friends?" he asked, taking a swig of the Heineken draft he'd purchased in a novelty Yankees cup. Mami never let me buy any souvenir cups from games, or the circus, or Six Flags.

I frowned at him.

"That's kind of a stupid question," I said. "Of course I have friends."

"I'm trying to get to know you, B," he said, tugging on his earlobe.

"Well, first things first then," I said, brushing crumbs off my lap. "My name is Brisma. Not B. And definitely not Brisa. Got it?"

I felt proud acting so ballsy and wished Kelly were there to see it.

"I don't do cutesy nicknames."

He stared at me, a bit shocked, with raised eyebrows and a slackened jaw. I stared right back at him, refusing to lose this game of chicken, until he clapped his hands together, breaking the spell.

"You got fight," he said, as he pointed at me. "That's good." He wiped his top lip. "If you're gonna get anything from your mother, God help me, it should be that."

I was pleased that he drew this comparison between Mami and me, and again, I wished that Kelly or Brian were there to see me taking charge. So often, I felt like the wallflower in *The Kelly Show*.

"So," he continued, producing an open bag of sunflower seeds from his pocket. "Any boyfriends?" It was the bottom of the fourth, and he trained his eyes on the batter's box.

"Plural?" I asked. "As in, more than one?"

He turned back to me, placing a hand on my forearm.

"Mira, you're fifteen," he said. "A baby. It's no time to get serious with any one boy."

I wanted to rip his hand off my arm, the heat of it raising my temperature, stoking my anger. I felt confused by this reversal of how I'd seen every TV dad act toward his teenage daughter. What was this?

"Well," I said, "I have one. A boyfriend. Singular."

He chuckled, turning his attention back to the field.

"And where is he today?"

He sprinkled a handful of seeds into his mouth. I wanted to kill him. Why was I here?

"I don't know," I stammered, annoyed. "Probably hanging out with friends. Playing ball maybe?"

"Oh," he said, as he spit a seed in my direction. "An athlete?"

"Yes," I said proudly. "He just got on the varsity baseball team, actually."

"Impressive," he said with a nod, wiping the palms of his hands together. He leaned in toward me.

"And you think he's not out there chasing the skirt of some hot blonde right now?"

He reached for his beer, and I was tempted to ram the novelty cup up into his nose, anything to break the smug look off his face.

"Why would you say that to me?" I held back from cursing at him. In my head, I heard Mami's voice telling me, *He is your fatherwholovesyou.*

"Why am I even here right now?" I asked. "Why are you?"

People had quieted down around us and taken note of my raised voice.

"Shh," he said. "Cálmate."

I bit my tongue and focused on the field. "What do you want?" I asked.

He cleared his throat.

"I just want to make sure"—he fingered the plastic rim of his cup—"you're good."

He took a quick sip.

"I want to make sure you're gonna be good."

I looked at him, lifting my shoulders expectantly.

"I have been good, no thanks to you," I said.

"No," he said, wiping his mouth with the back of his hand. "No doubt."

On the field, David Justice had been fending off foul balls in the batter's box on a 3–2 count for a while. The game felt so far away from us, we could have been watching it on a television screen instead of inside the stadium.

"The thing is," he started, "I didn't say goodbye last time."

I squinted at him, not sure if I'd heard him right. With a loud crack, Justice hit a heater down the middle with such power there was no question it'd soar out of the park. The stadium erupted. The Yankees scored the first run of the game. My father didn't break his gaze from me.

"Last time?" I shouted over the crowd.

A vendor turned up our aisle selling ice cream inside tiny Yankees batting helmets. My father reached for his wallet.

"You want an ice cream?" he asked, changing the subject.

"No," I said flatly.

He sighed and clasped his hands as the Jumbotron tried to keep the audience riled up.

"I'm moving," he said.

"Okay?"

"I mean," he said, "I'm leaving the country. To Argentina. I'm moving to South America."

I laughed. I wondered how many stamps he'd already collected on his passport in the time apart from us and tried to imagine him sitting on a plane living like un jetseter, as Mami would say, instead of behind the wheel of a Twinkie truck. Mami didn't have a passport and neither did I. I had never even seen a U.S. passport in real life.

"Okay?" I repeated. "For a woman? A *hot blonde*?"

He cleared his throat again.

"She's someone special," he said, and the inside of my guts turned to lava, as it was clear this meant that we were not, that I was not, ever *special* enough.

I shrugged and let my empty hands fall to my lap with a slap.

"Congratulations," I said, fighting back the angry, threatening lump in my throat. The sun overhead felt oppressive then, and I felt my chest flush from the heat and the rush of adrenaline. I didn't even really know him, this man sitting next to me who was my father, but that didn't matter as much as the fact that he would never be the man I wanted him to be.

We watched Jorge Posada fend off a few foul pitches on another 3–2 count in silence. I became very aware of my own physical space, how my body felt abuzz with the mounting desire to get as far away from him as possible. I sensed my energy was too angry, too volatile for even Yankee Stadium to hold.

Just then, Posada's bat sent a ball deep into right field, immediately following up Justice's home run with his own. The crowd rose to its feet as the Yankees took a 2–0 lead, and the emotional release of tens of thousands of people packed into the stadium coaxed tears to fall from my own eyes. I wiped them quickly and stood to push my way past my father.

"Thanks for the hot dog," I shouted over the crowd.

"You can't leave," he said, gesturing toward the diamond. "It's only beginning to get good!"

"It's a lost cause," I muttered, tugging at my low-rise jeans. "Besides, I've taken the subway home from here before," I lied. "I'll be fine."

He looked at me with somewhat sad, but mostly relieved, eyes.

"Okay," he said, stepping over to hug me awkwardly in the concrete aisle where people were piled up behind us, attempting to exit for the restroom, for more beer, for food.

I pulled away from him and saw a flash of dejection in his eyes. *Good*, I thought, despite a flare of guilt in my chest.

"Goodbye, Brisma," he said.

"Uh-huh" was all my anger allowed me to say, my mouth unable to form words as I turned to leave, determined to keep any more tears from falling in his presence.

∽

Mami had already left when I got back from the Bronx. Having eaten only half of the hot dog my father bought me, I heated up a plate of leftover rice and beans in the microwave and sidled up to the living room window overlooking the avenue to eat it. I liked sitting there best, with a view of the neighborhood, my feet propped up on the boxes piled against the radiator of Mary Kay cosmetics that Mami had started selling at work. It was the latest in a line of side hustles to dig herself out of the debt my father had left her in.

Across the street, I spotted Brian walking down the concrete stairs to Kelly's door. I knocked on the screen window to try and get his attention, but stopped short of calling his name. Figuring I'd be able to salvage what was left of the afternoon by catching up with both of them, I sprinted out the door and down my own stoop, but once my sandaled foot hit the pavement, I heard my father's voice in my head. What were they doing together? They rarely hung out alone, if ever. Even when it was a bunch of us at the park, Kelly was much more likely to wrap Pablo's arm around her or jump on his back for impromptu piggyback rides, not Brian's.

I marched across the street, shaking my head to rattle my father's words out of my ears: *"You think he's not out there chasing skirts?"*

Not Kelly, I chanted to myself, a prayer. *Not Kelly*.

The front door to her house was unlocked, as usual, and the screen door whined on its hinges when I opened it. Inside, I was greeted by the same smells that always sat in her hallway: ferrets and butter, but there was something else, too. The beach. No, the dampened insides of a sandy beach tote. SPF.

"Kelly?" I shouted. "Brian?"

The house felt empty, as my voice echoed off the stenciled walls. From a cage in the living room, one of the parakeets flapped its wings.

"Hello?" I called out.

My ears adjusted to the weight of the silence in the entryway, and I realized I did hear something beneath the clock ticking at the top of the stairs. I heard what sounded like a cord, like a venetian blind cord bouncing in the breeze. The breeze. Something was off.

I stepped toward the stairs, which I realized now were brighter than usual, and looked up. The rickety ladder that led to the roof was hanging from a small door cut into the ceiling on the second floor. While I'd noticed this door many times throughout our childhood, I had never actually seen it opened.

"Hello?" I called up, but on the ground floor, I was too far away from anyone who might be on the roof to hear.

I walked up the stairs slowly, my toes extending over the soles of my sandals and sinking into the mold-green carpet. On the landing, I turned to examine the ladder closely. It was made of red rope, except each rung was encased inside what looked like tiny bullets of metal to climb on. It didn't look like it could hold me, but I was propelled by the pit in my stomach to test its limits and follow Brian, who must now be on the roof. I pulled the ladder taut and tested one foot on the nearest plank. It would have to do. I climbed up, cursing under my breath.

The sun bounced off the silver-painted roof, and it took a moment for my eyes to adjust to the scene before me. Brian, who I'd seen only moments ago bounding down the stairs, was now shirtless, revealing a tank-top tan still on his torso from the summer. Kelly was lying facedown on a purple beach towel I knew well from our bus rides to Rockaway, when we'd use it to keep our bare thighs from sticking to the hard plastic seats of the Q53. Now, Kelly's bare breasts lay against it, a red bikini top sitting crumpled and off to the side. Her raven hair was piled up messily on top of her head in a way that always seemed chic, yet whenever I tried it, I looked like a pineapple. Her string-tied bottom was pulled between her plump cheeks, giving the appearance of a thong.

Brian was kneeling on the silver-painted roof, applying lotion to her glistening thighs. Her body narrowed at the waist in such a symmetrical way that it reminded me of Veronica from the *Archie* comics. Watching them, I felt angry, and envious, and excited, somehow; it was a little like how we felt when we jetted to the door after hearing the crunch of metal on the block to find out whose car had been hit.

I was tired of always being the Betty to her Veronica. I was ready to fight.

"Are you kidding me?"

Kelly jerked her head around, trying to cover her breasts with her right hand, but her pink areolas weren't fully covered by her forearm. They were barely distinguishable from her pale skin, and though I'd seen them countless times before, it was different with Brian standing shirtless between us. In a flash, I thought of all the times Brian had taken my dark brown nipple into his mouth and wondered if he'd been longing for Kelly's *Playboy*-approved tits all along.

"What are you doing back?" Kelly asked, stringing her triangle bikini top around her neck and under her thick hair, which had now spilled across her shoulders.

"I got on a train the hell out of there. Sorry to spoil whatever fun has been going on around here."

"Did something happen with your pops?" Kelly asked, ignoring Brian's presence on the roof with us. I resisted the temptation to answer her, to follow her down that road of questioning and dump my nightmare experience on Kelly, who had always understood the kind of jerk my dad was.

"What do you even care?" I spat at her.

I looked at Brian standing frozen off to the side, white goop still coating the webbed skin between his fingers. I wondered how the calluses on his batting hand felt against Kelly's bare ass, and whether she traced them, too, like I did during days we spent burrowing into each other in his twin bed when we were supposed to be at school. I stepped closer and saw what I realized was excitement in his eyes: at having been caught, or perhaps at the potential for me to join them in whatever they were about to do. I hated him in that moment and fought the same violent impulse I had with my father just a few hours before. I wanted to rip his eyelids down like a curtain, to shut out the mischievous twinkle that pierced me like glass.

"We're just tanning, Brisma," Kelly said.

She finally tied the string of her top into a knot and leaned back onto her palms—exhausted, like she knew this was coming and wanted to just get it over with. Brian shifted on his heels, the first perceptible movement I'd noticed, and pinched the hem of his shorts down his leg.

"Tanning?" I shrieked. "His hands are *inside* your ass!"

Kelly rolled her eyes.

"Grow up," she said, pulling her legs underneath her to stand up. "Nothing happened."

"How is *this* even happening?"

Brian cleared his throat to speak. "She invited me over just to chill. To see her new bathing suit."

I felt the tendons behind my eyeballs strain, as I turned to face Brian.

"And you came?" I asked.

"I didn't!" Brian protested. "I swear!"

I sucked my teeth and turned back to Kelly.

"Why would you even invite him over like that?" I asked Kelly. "My boyfriend."

Kelly slid her painted toes inside platform flip-flops that sat at the top of her towel. Her belly was soft and dotted with terry-cloth impressions from lying down so long on one side. She grabbed her pack of cigarettes from the ledge but then balled her hands into fists at her hips. She shook her head in my direction but kept her eyes lowered.

"I don't know," she said. "I'm stupid."

I stood there enraged and heartbroken. The heat from the re-flective roof cooked the undersides of my feet through the thin soles of my sandals, and I tried to focus on that pain to keep from physically attacking the both of them. Kelly's moment of vulner-ability confused me—was it genuine or was she manipulating me?—but the vision of the two of them together, under that sun, imagining his thick lips on her pale breasts, assaulted me again, and I screamed at Brian with the only argument I could articulate in that moment.

"But she smokes!"

They both looked at me.

"She smokes," I repeated. "You don't like girls who smoke."

Kelly spun the wheel on her lighter self-consciously, as if she was embarrassed for me, and that made me want to eviscerate her.

"You *are* fucking stupid," I said, egging her to look up at me. "And a slut."

There was a flash of rage in her eyes, but she squared her jaw immediately to conceal it. Like my father, there seemed to be some relief in her posture, like something she'd feared for a long time had finally come to pass. Coolly operating on autopilot, she tapped the bottom of the pack of Camels against the inside of her wrist.

"We are done," I continued. "Don't call me, don't come to my door. We are never speaking again."

She slid a cigarette out, looking past me toward the boulevard. Brian wiped the lotion off on the fabric of his shorts and tried to come after me, the bottle of Banana Boat still in his left hand.

"Back off," I warned him.

He took another step, and I punched the bottle out of his hand, my knuckles against the half-filled plastic creating a satisfying crack before it shot through the air and landed at Kelly's feet with a *splat*, leaving a violent starburst of white lotion across her legs and the ledge of her roof.

"Good," I said, turning on my heel to make my way back inside.

At the top of the ladder, I pointed between the two of them, my fist a metronome of guilt and shame.

"I hope you're happy."

On my way down the ladder, my big toe got caught in the rope, and I tripped, falling four planks to the landing below. The force of my weight shook the second-floor landing, and I heard Kelly above try to stifle her cruel, nervous, hyena laughter. It reminded me of the St. Agnes fair, when we ran away from the boys, soaked in soda, and blood, and piss. It had felt wild and free then, when I was on the inside of it. Both of us feral and uncontained. Unstoppable. Now, I felt like it was a cackle of evil, of something deeper and uglier than I'd ever understood.

I scooped myself up off the carpet in anger and shot down the stairs and back across the street to my own house, where I finally allowed the pressure that had been building behind my eyes all day to escape, salty tears that burned as they slid down sun-crisped cheeks.

OCTOBER 2006

The four of us—Kelly, Brian, Pablo, and I—convened at the bar at the Cuckoo's Nest in Woodside to watch Game 7 of the National League Championship Series against the St. Louis Cardinals. Sitting on the edge of our seats, all in a row, necks craned to watch the flat screens above us, it felt as if our shared history had been rewritten—as a fandom, as a borough, and as four kids of color who never quite felt like they fit in anywhere—and we were eager to lean into our new stories. As if the past twenty years were simply a prelude to this Mets comeback, to our comeback.

Kelly was nervous, cracking peanut shells with the fatty bottom of her fist on the bar top. We'd watched all the other postseason games at PJ Moore's down the avenue, but they'd made the mistake of charging a cover to watch the games, so we boycotted them on principle.

"They're just trying to make a buck on this," I'd complained to Kelly, as she dragged me by the sleeve of my David Wright jersey to Cuckoo's Nest on the corner. "Wouldn't you?"

She'd stopped in her tracks and whipped her head around.

"Absolutely not."

Frances had requested an increase in the allowance Kelly deposited into her commissary account each month (for Claritin and the low-sugar Welch's Fruit Snacks she claimed were necessary now that she was diabetic), which meant Kelly had to drop a class and work an extra shift at the Colombian bakery on Broadway.

"I don't like this," Kelly said, as she shook her head and muttered into her brown bottle of Coors. The game was close, tied at one going into the sixth inning. "We shouldn't have changed bars. It's bad luck."

"You gotta believe, ladies!" Brian roared, reaching around me to pat her on the back. It was exciting to feel his arm around me for that moment, but I also felt a pang of jealousy. *Old habits*, I thought.

"I don't know," I said, leaning forward to block the eye contact between Kelly and Brian. "I kinda prefer this place."

The bar was brighter than PJ Moore's, the front facade a wall of windowed doors that the owners opened on warm nights to let light and fresh air in. I inhaled, the air slightly metallic with beer and melted cheese.

"More room to breathe here," I said.

Brian sat to my right and Pablo on the other side of him. I hadn't had a genuine conversation with Pablo in years, and when we did talk, there was a charged tension between us that still lingered from our high school days.

But that night, the four of us left all our baggage at the door. We were the children of immigrants, Latin American and Southeast Asian, and watching the majority Black and Latino players on the team, on our team, fight on a national stage felt like a win for us.

On TV, Pedro Martinez waved to the camera from where he sat in the dugout, his pitching arm in a navy blue sling post-surgery.

"Ugh, I miss Pedro," Kelly said.

"Me too," I said. "Shame he can't play, right?" I elbowed Brian.

He seemed startled, not paying attention.

"Well," he said, as he swallowed his beer, "he's pitched in plenty of playoff games. He probably doesn't care one way or the other as long as he's getting paid."

"Hey," I said, leaning my hip into his. "How'd your road trip go last weekend?"

Brian inched away and tossed a peanut into his mouth.

"Boring." He chewed and I watched his jaw clench and unclench, never turning to look at me.

Despite his gregarious start to the evening, slapping high fives with strangers at the cocktail tables along the wall, I thought Brian was acting a little weird. He wouldn't drain a glass of beer without signaling for his next before he was halfway through. His eyes were jumpy, bouncing from the screen, to the bartender, to the street outside. He seemed scared, as if he expected an attack at any moment. But we were all a little on edge, with a World Series at stake.

That was when, from the back of the bar near the bathrooms, we heard a rumbling coming toward us. A scrum of sneakers, and fists, and orange hoodies tumbled past our backs, a brawl among white boys with ruddy cheeks. Irish kids from the right side of the Long Island Rail Road: Maspeth, Glendale, Middle Village. This was the closest they'd ever come, I thought, to actually riding the 7 Train: drinking at a bar beneath its shadow.

Brian immediately hopped off his stool and wedged himself between the two main fighters.

"Not during the game, boys," he said with the authority and experience of a college locker room, as if they'd listen to him, as if his time in the catcher's box made him forget who he was, or who he wasn't. My throat tight, I reflexively reached out toward Brian, as if to reel him in, but touched nothing but air.

"Who the . . . ," the sloppier one said, frowning at Brian, confused. He wore a silver chain from which a St. Anthony medallion swung as his two buddies held him back by his elbows.

"Someone get this fucking spic out of my face," he said, nodding to his friends.

His slur broke the dam of tension in the room, and it seemed as if everyone in the bar rose to their feet in response. I knelt on the black pleather padding of the barstool, while Kelly climbed onto the bar itself, still holding her full beer, screaming at the sloppy kid.

"You don't belong here!" she said, pointing with her free hand.

"Get your ass out of here!" I threw a crumpled napkin at him as Brian ducked his punch.

Pablo, I noticed, sat coolly in place, his back to the melee. He lifted the tall, shapely glass of Blue Moon to his lips and took a sip, careful not to knock the orange wheel wedged onto the rim. He set the glass down gently on the felt coaster and wiped his upper lip with a green napkin square from behind the soda gun. I saw him take a deep breath with his palms flat against the curved edge of the bar, watched his broad chest grow inside his gray ARMY T-shirt before he pushed off and stepped into the action.

Amidst the chaos, the diminutive Pablo, no more than five feet six, reached up and grabbed the racist prick by his flushed neck and walked him confidently out the front door. There was no emotion on Pablo's face that I could discern, not fear, or anger, or any of that old-school, jumping-to-your-boy's-defense hype. He was trained to handle this. And no one, not even the sloppy dude's buddies, put up much of a fight. They followed, as did most of the bar, out onto the sidewalk to watch as Pablo deposited the instigator, with an audible plop, facedown on the sewer grate on the sloping corner.

The kid's lip burst open against the concrete, and he looked back up at Pablo, a thin line of blood spilling down his chin.

"There's no need for that kind of language here," Pablo said, rubbing his dry hands together in the cool, October night.

"We're here to watch the game," he said, as he thumbed the air back toward us. "If you're not, you gotta leave."

"You must be," the kid said, wiping blood off his lip, "out of your mind." He sat up and squinted into the awning lights of the bar. "No chink is gonna manhandle me or tell me how to live my life."

The bar erupted behind him with jeers, and plastic cups, and more than a few pieces of cutlery bouncing out onto the pavement in his direction. Pablo cracked his knuckles and squatted down, bringing his face close to his bloody lip.

"You have a life thanks to this chink," he said, tenting the chest of his T-shirt between pinched fingers to show him the word ARMY.

When it looked like it finally registered on the guy's face that he'd been thrown out of the bar by a veteran, Pablo palmed his sweaty forehead like a basketball and mushed him back toward the sidewalk.

Everyone watching cheered Pablo back into the bar. Several bros in orange-and-blue sweatshirts reached out their hands to shake Pablo's.

"Thank you, man," we heard.

"What a hero!" a girl shouted from the back.

"Thanks for your service, bro."

"Sir." A middle-aged white man nodded.

Brian, who'd managed to avoid even a scratch in the larger fight, weaved through the crowd and put his arm around Pablo, who remained quiet and, from what I could tell, kind of embarrassed.

"We're not paying for drinks all night!" Brian said, as he patted him on the chest. Pablo winced a polite smile in his direction without raising his eyes to Brian's. Something else seemed off—some imperceptible shift in their dynamic.

"All right, all right," Pablo said, swiveling back onto his seat. "Game's back on."

From beginning to end, the fight had gone down in the space of a commercial break.

I maneuvered myself back onto the high barstool, never once taking my eyes off Pablo. He was a totally different person from the acerbic kid we grew up with. He had humility. He seemed to be in control; there was a steadiness in him that I hadn't seen since his mom died, when he tried so hard to be strong for his dad outside St. Agnes. I was in awe of him, and yet I still distrusted him. I didn't want to have to forgive him for who he used to be, even when I'd forgiven everyone else. But he was a fifteen-year-old kid back then, a boy whose thoughts were preoccupied by all sorts of terrible teenage stuff like porn, and apple bongs, and squeezing the glow out of lightning bugs for fun.

An older white guy wearing a chrome-plated whistle around his neck patted Pablo briefly on the back and slipped a shot of Jameson in front of him.

"Very classy," he said through his gray mustache, winking.

I hated when people—but especially white men—called people classy. It almost never had anything to actually do with class; to me, it always sounded like racially coded language, like, "good boy, playing by our rules," or "how lovely that you know your place." Sportscasters loved to call out when a player acted with an abundance, or a lack, of class. Throwing your bat after a hit? Not classy.

Getting kicked in the face by an opposing teammate's cleats and shaking the dude's hand after? Classy.

I rolled my eyes, and Pablo caught me.

"What is that for?"

"Oh." I cleared my throat. "Not because of the free drink," I said. "Or because of you."

I slid my hands around the sides of my own chilled beer. "I just hate when people use that word."

"What word?" Pablo asked, one thick eyebrow raised.

"Classy."

"Me too," he said, relaxing his shoulders a little. I was surprised we were on the same page.

"Carlos Delgado would never be called classy," he said.

My face broke into a wide smile.

"Exactly!"

That Pablo agreed with me so readily shocked me. Kelly and I had protested the war in Iraq, wearing duct tape around our jacket sleeves and walking out of fourth period history to march on midtown. And Pablo had fought in Fallujah, yet here he was, also admiring an activist I looked up to?

"Fuck," Brian muttered, bending forward between us to grab my hand with both of his. He nodded up at the screen. "Look!"

St. Louis was up, and Pérez had already let one on base. I tried to ignore the electricity I felt from Brian touching me and concentrated on the screen above me.

The Cardinals batter hit a rocket that was sure to go out of the park. The whole bar groaned in terror, the seconds it took for the ball to reach the outfield feeling like an eternity for every one of us.

Kelly clutched my left arm on one side of me, while Brian's sweaty palm pressed against the back of my right fist.

But then, like a burst of light, Endy Chávez, playing in left field, leapt up at the wall and, reaching with his glove, yanked that ball from out of the stratosphere. A lightning-fast throw to second base and then to Delgado at first (Chávez–Valentín–Delgado, a Latino lineup threatening to kick this team out of Queens and back to Missouri) resulted in a jaw-dropping double play from the outfield that retired the side and kept the game tied.

We all screamed. Brian grabbed my face in his hands and we screamed, both of our mouths wide in joy and disbelief. Just past him, I could see Pablo smiling his big, toothy grin up at the television in awe. Our histories really didn't matter, then: this moment of grace, of elation, transcended all the roles we ever found ourselves in.

"It is a miracle!" I said.

"See," Brian shouted, leaning in to kiss me quickly on the lips, tight and closed, like an aunt.

"I told you," he said, as he shoved a finger at the bones in my chest, tapping twice. "You gotta believe!"

When he kissed me, my ears flushed with heat and blood, and I couldn't make out sound for a few seconds while I looked around at the cacophony playing out before me. It was pure joy, that moment, the temptation to believe it was finally our time. Not just our time to be validated as Mets fans, perpetually in the shadow of the Yankee dynasty across town, but our time to be seen, to have access, to come into our own. Our time to excel, to succeed. I wanted to jump into Brian's arms at that moment, to wrap myself around his torso and run away to live in a ranch house on Long Island with him, two kids who made it out of the hood, playing catch on a green lawn with our future children.

"This is it!" Kelly said, punching me on the arm, smiling.

"Can you imagine?" I asked, hoping she hadn't seen Brian kiss me. "We're so close!" I knew better than to invoke the words "World Series."

"Don't say it," she said, wagging a finger at me. "I'm going to the bathroom, but we still got three and a half more innings."

She began to snake her way to the bathroom.

"I'll come with you," I shouted after her.

Waiting on the line, commercials for hair-growth systems reflecting bald heads in the mirror behind Kelly, I tried to ferret out what she might have seen.

"It's cute to see Brian so excited," I said.

Kelly pursed her lips at me.

"What?" I asked.

"Don't be so desperate," she said. "It's not a good look."

"I didn't mean anything by it," I said. "Just that I know he's been a huge Mets fan since he was a kid. It's cool to share this night with other people who get it."

Kelly shook her head.

"You're always jumping the gun," she said. "We ain't got shit yet!"

"Damn," I said. "Such a Debbie Downer tonight."

"That's funny," she said, as she pushed open the door to the stall that had just cleared out.

"What is?"

"Brian called me the same thing last week."

"Oh yeah?" I asked.

"Yeah, when I told him there was no shot in hell we'd ever hook up again."

I stared at the stall door reverberating in the frame, as Kelly slid its lock in place.

"Again?" I was only able to parrot the word back to her.

"Oh, you know," her voice rang out. "Like when we were kids."

The stall at the end of the room opened up, and I slipped into it, furious that our conversation had been cut short. I wasn't about to yell out my jealous line of questioning from one end of the bathroom to the other. I commanded myself to pee, but I was too upset to concentrate. All the times Kelly had competed with me for the attention of anyone—the waiter at Mark Twain Diner, the boys at the St. Agnes fair—came rushing back to me. I wished then, staring at the mildewed grout of the bathroom floor, that instead, she would just once be happy to let me have one thing all to myself. Why couldn't she not elbow me out on this one thing? Weren't we past that?

When I walked out of the stall, Kelly was already drying her hands and using her paper towel to open the door back into the bar.

"Wait a second," I called after her. "Wait for me."

I reached above her to hold the door open for us. "What were you saying before?"

She shook her head without looking at me. "It's not important," she said, pointing up at the glow of the tilting screens that lit the path back to our seats. "Look," she called over her shoulder. "The game's back on."

"Yeah, I know, but—"

She placed a cold finger over my lips, her mascara clumpy on wide eyes.

"No jinxing, remember."

I sat back in my seat, keenly aware of the wooden rods on the backrest digging into my kidneys. I was uncomfortable and upset. I felt like all the hairs on my body were on fire and swaying in attention from side to side, from Kelly to Brian on either side of me. For possibly the first time in my life, I felt a closer kinship to Pablo than to either of them. He felt like the more mature island here in a sea of childhood jealousy.

We watched the top of the ninth in silent horror as our relief pitcher gave up two runs. I could feel everyone praying to their gods, to their lucky underwear, to their rosary beads, to all manner of energy in the universe to keep the Mets alive in this last game of the series, to at least let them tie the game in the bottom half of the inning. But still, I worried Kelly had irrevocably changed the vibe of the game; she had tempted the vibrations of the universe into misalignment, and this could only spell bad news for us and the Mets.

And then the Mets' José Valentín hit a fly ball that got him to first base. That was a start. There was hope. Endy Chávez—Endy! Endy, of the new Greatest Catch of All Time—came up to bat and hit a line drive that put him on, too. Paul Lo Duca, the catcher, was walked on to load the bases with two out.

I was no longer at the Cuckoo's Nest but at Shea Stadium, zeroed in on the next batter: Carlos Beltrán, fellow Boricua and highest-paid player on the Mets for two years running. He was our last shot. If anyone could save us, it should be him.

But Beltrán struck out. Looking. No foul tip on the end of the bat. No swing and a miss. Possibly the single most pressure-filled moment of his entire sports career, playing for a team that hadn't won a World Series in exactly twenty years, and Beltrán choked.

He choked, and as the St. Louis Cardinals stormed our field to celebrate their win that granted them entry to the World Series, Beltrán coolly shrugged and rested his bat against his thigh, unlacing his batting gloves while he looked on. No more emotion than that.

But there was plenty of emotion to spare in the bar. Bartenders threw rags at the flat screens above them, grown men pawed at their tear ducts with the curve of hairy knuckles. Brian had buried his eye sockets deep into the crook of his folded arms on the bar top. Pablo sat in a stony silence, the bright colors of the upbeat commercials for car insurance dancing in the pools of his dark irises.

"What the fuck was that?" Kelly asked. Her orange-painted fingernails were frozen like claws at each of her temples.

"What did you expect?" I replied, more anger in my voice than I'd intended. "We choke," I continued as I slid off the stool. "We always choke. The Mets will never win shit."

I punched my fist through the arm of my black hoodie and tugged it on over my head through the tight neck hole. It stung smoothing out the large blue font printed across the front of the sweatshirt, NEW YORK METS 2006 NLDS CHAMPIONS, as I pulled the hem down to my waist.

I took one last swig of my beer and slammed it down on the coaster, startling Brian out of his grieving pose at the bar.

"Let's go," I told Kelly. She looked briefly, almost imperceptibly, at Brian and then back at me. She was calculating something.

"You're leaving?" Brian asked, his fingers grazing the bare patch of skin at the nape of my neck. He began to massage it.

"Naw," he said, seemingly back to his usual self. "It's too soon. You're in shock."

He slid the stool I'd been sitting on out again, as if to invite me back. "Stay. Have some consolation scotch with the rest of us. On Pablo, remember?"

"No," I said, shrugging him off. "Staying here will just make me feel worse. Plus"—I swung my bag onto my shoulder—"I've got to finish some follow-up work on an application tomorrow."

"A job application?" Brian asked.

"Yeah," Kelly interjected, licking juice off her thumb from a free round of lemon-drop shots.

"Didn't you hear?" she asked, her face a mix of bemusement and pride. "Brisma's going to be a big Hollywood writer."

She threw back the frosted vodka shot she'd been holding in the balance between us.

"Wait, you're *leaving us*?" Brian asked and reached for my waist. "You can't do that."

I knew it was a line, but I liked the way it made me feel anyway. I liked his calloused hand on the belt loop of my jeans. I liked that he rested it right above the curve of my ass, as if he wanted to protect me, to keep me for his own.

I wondered what Kelly would do in this situation, always Rizzo from *Grease*, making men eat out of the palm of her hand. I cupped Brian's cheeks and gave him a squeeze before reaching for and downing my own vodka shot.

"Kelly's exaggerating," I said. "It's just an application. There's a million-to-one chance I'll get it."

"Well," Brian said as he held my hand, "that's dope, anyway. I told you you'd make it big someday."

I was embarrassed by his sincerity and took a step back.

"I haven't done anything yet," I said and turned to Kelly. "You coming or not?"

She checked Brian again before reaching across and taking Pablo's shot for herself. Her eyes were half-lidded and up to no good. It was a look I'd seen many times before. She shook her head at me.

"Nah," she said. "No way. I've got a long way to go to numb the pain of this one here tonight."

I shrugged and turned to leave when Pablo slid off his stool and stood tall beside me.

"I'll walk you home," he said.

"Oh," I said, as I grabbed the strap of my bag on my shoulder, "that's not necessary. I'll be fine."

"It's late," he said, putting on his jacket, "and you're on my way." He looked at Brian and Kelly, who were up on their tiptoes, balancing on the footrest of the stools to scope out the bottles available behind the bar.

"No point in staying here," Pablo said.

That's what I was afraid of. Looking at the two of them laughing and well on their way to a blackout, I fought back pangs of jealousy. Things had been over between Brian and me for years; Kelly and I had moved on from our fight a long time ago. No one belonged to anybody. We were all free agents. So why did this still bother me?

My head dimly ringing with the phrase "girl code," I turned back to Pablo.

"Sure," I said. "What the hell."

2000

Brian had to fight for women to love him his whole life. That's what he told me when I finally agreed to hear him out in the park one evening in late October, after the drama with Kelly on the rooftop had died down. A peace talk, he'd called it.

He confided in me that his mother first started throwing fists when she began dating Ivan in '96. They'd been dating in secret, or at least secret from Brian and his brother, and then one day, Ivan moved in and started telling him how to cut his hair, clean his room, hang his towel. Ivan demanded Brian get dressed in their windowless bathroom after a shower, skin still wet beneath the thin fabric of his boxers. Ivan would thumb the elastic waistband of Brian's Fruit of the Looms and say, "Nobody wants to see that."

His mother, Griselda, never took Brian's side. When Ivan was at work, doing security for an office building on Wall Street, Griselda would come at him, fists in the air like a windup toy. She would not stand for Brian breaking Ivan's rules, she said. She wouldn't let him ruin this for her.

When it grew to be too much, he'd take refuge at his aunt Mel's house in Sunnyside. She'd fix him a plate, and ask about school, and give him books of poetry she thought he'd like. But even that he had to hide from his mother because Griselda had been estranged from Mel for years.

"Mel is gay," he explained to me. "And really, more like a guy. Maybe that's why we get along. But it drives my mom nuts."

He laughed sadly, the way I'd already grown familiar with laughing at my own pain, because what other option was there?

"She's petrified I'll turn gay if I spend time with Mel," he said, rolling his eyes. "Can you imagine?"

I placed my hand on top of his and scooted over on the park bench, the sun setting behind the turning leaves, brilliant bursts of yellow that curled brittle and dropped to the glittering blacktop.

"You made me feel good enough," he told me. "Safe. And not something I had to hide, like Mel. It just seemed easy, and"—he licked his lips—"I think maybe it scared me."

Brian's story worked. I felt special that Brian was confiding in me, and I felt like I had a responsibility to take him back. If I could easily offer my love to him, then maybe it would fix him, fill the hole in his heart, show him that he didn't have to fight to make every woman in his life love him. I would fight so he didn't have to.

Taking on this mantle, it was easy for me to forgive Brian and not Kelly. She had her pick of boys; when she was done with one, there was always another IM'ing her to ask if he could come over. She didn't need to go after Brian, but she did. He didn't just magically appear on her rooftop that day; she invited him. She couldn't stand to let me have one thing all my own.

Brian and I had a good stretch after that autumn night talking in the park. He volunteered to repaint our bathroom, much to Mami's delight, after the pipes burst over the winter. On dates we went to the movies and then to Barnes & Noble, where he'd read me poetry Mel had introduced him to, from Sandra Cisneros and Langston Hughes, sitting shoulder to shoulder on the carpet. When I finished reading a new novel, I'd leave it for him in his locker, highlighted and annotated, with an inscription on the title page that always ended with a smiling heart. He begged to read the next installment in the serialized story I'd begun writing about two brothers solving mysteries along the LIRR tracks in Queens. He wrote letters to me during class that he signed "Your #1 Fan," and he slipped them inside my backpack when we passed each other in the hall in between periods.

But as hard as I tried to ignore it, he was exactly the type of mujeriego to write letters to all the girls. Eventually, Brian was back to chatting up every girl he met: the cashier at White Castle, the instructor in biology lab, park workers doing community service, fans in the stands at his baseball games. I could never keep enough tabs on him. It was exhausting. And then he started telling me about those other girls, girls who purportedly hated me, girls in neighborhood gangs called the Spades or the Hearts or some dumb alleyway-gambling name, who had threatened to beat me up because I was dating him. For a while, it excited the both of us, perversely. For Brian, that he could get multiple girls to fight over him; for me, that I was with a boy who other girls seemed to want so bad. It was the way I felt riding his pegs up our block, times a million.

The truth was, I felt that he had chosen me. Between Kelly and me, and all the other girls on the periphery, he had chosen me. And all I'd ever wanted was to be chosen.

ço

Brian introduced me to the Nuyorican Poets Café on the Lower East Side during the spring semester of our sophomore year. I snuck out one May night, early buds shivering on otherwise bare branches underneath the streetlights, not all of the chill yet out of the breeze that blew down the boulevard. Kelly and I had always intended to go to a slam night together, but I hadn't returned any of her calls or emails since that day on her rooftop. By Christmas, she stopped trying. With a nagging twinge of resentment and guilt, I watched the electric candles in her top-floor windows glow all season long, until finally, Kelly packed them away before Saint Patrick's Day, and her blinds went dark again. I still couldn't forgive her for trying to steal Brian from me.

Brian met me at the Roosevelt Avenue Station to ride the F Train to the last stop in Manhattan. He took my hand as we climbed a rickety set of wooden stairs hidden behind a heavy velvet curtain at the entrance of the brick-walled club and opened his palm toward the empty balcony where two folding chairs sat facing the stage below.

"Who did this?" I asked.

He winked his long, thick eyelashes and tugged my arm toward the seats.

"I know someone," he said, nodding in the direction of the dark DJ booth. That was enough to send my stomach into somersaults; at sixteen years old, no one we knew really *knew* anybody like that. And here he was, this boy I thought I knew from the block, claiming to be in with those Manhattan kids, with a Puerto Rican Loisaida crew I imagined were the type my father used to ride with back in his day.

"No way!" I teased, bending down slowly to slide onto the metal seat, hoping he'd catch an appreciative glimpse of my butt in the tight Polo jeans I'd gotten at Jimmy Jazz. "Who you think you know?"

An older man walked by in a pageboy hat that framed dark, under-eye circles and skin tags on his mustachioed face.

"Eh, papi." He held out a hand to shake Brian's.

"Patrón," Brian said, pulling the hand to his chest for a hug.

"And who's your beautiful friend?"

I smiled up at him, but he wasn't looking at my face.

"Don't worry about it," Brian said, standing to block me from his gaze.

"Well," the man said, as he rubbed something between his thumb and forefinger—a rolling paper, from the sound of it— "enjoy the show, okay? Disfruten, you two."

"Bendición," Brian said, his blank face belying an old habit. A warmth curled up against the inside of my ribs at how easily Spanish danced off his tongue. I felt safe when he spoke it, welcomed in a way I hadn't felt before. Because I had never become fluent myself, his Spanish felt like a passport to a world that shunned me; he was the acceptance I craved.

The man clicked a blessing under his tongue as he turned and disappeared down the tight stairwell at the back.

"Who was that?" I stood up behind Brian.

"Someone I know."

"Why are you being all cryptic and shit?" I needled him in the ribs over his cheap, polyester soccer jersey. "Tell me."

I caught him rolling his eyes as he slipped off his jacket and took his seat. That was all I needed to feel like I'd been slammed in the chest, his eyelids iron doors on my heart. I could not stand feeling dismissed by him and was willing to do anything to stop it.

"Sorry," I said. "I didn't mean to push." I sat down in my seat next to him. "This is really cool, what you did. No one's ever done anything like this for me before." I slid my hand on top of his closed fist.

We watched below as the line of people outside began filling in the chairs surrounding the small stage. It grew so crowded that people began sitting cross-legged on the floor along the aisles and at the foot of the stage. There were people crammed into every available space on the floor, a carpet of humanity, of poetry. I'd never before seen people—certainly not people who looked like us—come together to support or enjoy literature in any form. Reading was a punishment prescribed by our parents. I'd always understood the arts to belong to wealthier, whiter people; art for us was an old paintbrush shared between two kids' watercolors, before the program was stripped from our curriculum due to funding. Sitting in this buzzing room full of kids of color, I envisioned for the first time a world in which maybe I could write for a living, as a career.

I felt Brian's muscles relax under my hand, and he opened his fist to clasp my fingers. I looked at him tentatively. Maybe he felt the same excitement, the same promise I did.

His eyes only flicked toward me once, quickly.

"My aunt," he said. "Okay?"

I looked behind me, at the DJ booth, where the same freckled guy now stood with oversize headphones on instead of his pageboy hat. He was bald, I could see, but it looked by choice, like he shaved his head.

"What about your aunt?" I asked.

"That was Mel." He scratched his nose and glanced toward the DJ booth, too. "She—he—is the DJ here."

Brian looked at me, the overhead lights dimming and the spotlight flashing over his face as the lamp swiveled toward the stage.

"She is a he," he said. "Now."

"Oh," I said quickly, loudly. The audience had quieted to a low hush as they waited for the emcee to step onto the stage.

"But we're still mad close, despite"—he licked his lips—"everything."

I shrugged exaggeratedly, eager to make him feel comfortable, to let him know I wasn't judging him, that I would never judge him.

"That's cool," I said, stiffening my spine against the back of the chair.

A tall woman with braided hair took to the stage and the crowd hollered. I applauded automatically, but felt Brian still beside me. I brushed up against him and rested my hand on his thigh to try to communicate to him all that I was feeling that I didn't have the words for. I wondered if this was a test, if he'd shared anything about Mel with other girls before.

We tried to sleep together for the first time that night.

I wanted to prove to him I'd be there for him, that I could make him feel all the things he was missing. That I could make him feel like the man he was afraid he'd never become. But it was too painful, and we were too clumsy to understand how our bodies worked best. He curled up away from me afterward, a little spoon.

It was the only time we went to the Nuyorican together. After that night, he stopped reading me poetry and leaving me notes in my backpack. I thought about that night often, wondering if I'd failed his test, or if it was inevitable for us since that afternoon on Kelly's roof.

შ

We were in this off-again dip of our volatile on-again, off-again relationship when the Twin Towers fell, yet he was the first person to check in on me. The night before, I'd told him I was cutting class to go to the city and camp out for tickets to Destiny's Child with a friend from history class. Tickets were going on sale that morning at ten, and I didn't want to lose out if they sold out quickly. He hated when I cut without him; I suspected it was because he wouldn't have me for an audience to parade girls in front of. My friend canceled on me at the last minute, so I went to school instead.

Brian had been in chemistry class, on the top floor of our school, where he had a clear line of sight to the plumes of dark smoke that billowed from the edge of the Manhattan skyline, as if the island itself were one long, burning cigar. In the commotion, he ran down to my English class on the second floor and tapped his house key lightly on the back door, which was near my seat—our usual signal to sneak out and hook up during class. I could see the relief in his eyes when I turned to face him.

He brought me to the back staircase that led to the fourth-floor girls' gym and locker room, a tiny, seldom-used, attic-like stairwell that many couples used as a make-out spot. Without a word, he pressed me up against the window, fortified with a steel cage for our protection, to keep us from falling—or from jumping. In the red glow of the EXIT sign, his breath wet on the hollow of my neck, he blinked hot tears against my jaw. We stood like that for some time, just the two of us clinging to each other, letting our hearts beat together against each other's rib cage.

"Don't do that," he whispered.

"I didn't," I said immediately in response, though I wasn't quite sure what I was responding to.

"Don't leave me." He rubbed his nose against the soft skin under my ear. "I can't lose you."

I loved him in that moment, beyond the Nuyorican Poets Café, beyond the little boy on the CYO baseball team, beyond the finger-banging in the back of the Elmwood movie theater. I loved him because he gave me what I'd been missing my whole life: a man who needed me, who feared a life without me in it. I loved him, and I feared him a little bit, too, but I didn't know if there was a difference then, and certainly not on that day, when it felt like nothing about our future was safe or guaranteed.

I buried my fingernails in the flesh of his shoulder blades and tried losing myself in the rhythm of his lungs filling with air and emptying again. I wanted to stop time and hide inside the protection of his body.

"Is this the end of the world?" I asked, my voice sounding smaller than the screaming inside my head. My mind raced with images of horsemen, and brimstone, and something about the numbers 666 being carved into the foreheads of the damned. I wished I'd paid more attention in religion class; I wasn't sure what was actually the Bible and what was the horror aisle of Blockbuster Video. I thought about the summer Kelly tried to convince me that we were witches and how wielding that false power felt so important to us then, and so silly in the face of true catastrophe.

He pulled apart from me, the warm sweat on our chests cooling and evaporating in the dim pink light of the stairwell. I studied the space on his forehead between his eyebrows but found nothing there that indicated the apocalypse.

He frowned, and I could tell he was cycling through platitudes, trying to find something appropriate for the situation, something that would calm us both down. There was nothing smooth about him in that moment; he was all frayed ends and fright. I felt privileged that he was allowing me in to see him that way.

He sighed a little, sounding like a small dog in a thunderstorm, and grabbed my neck to pull me in and kiss the spot on my forehead that I'd been studying on his. In his embrace, I wondered if there was something telepathic between us, if he was thinking of the book of Revelations, too, if he understood something about the world I didn't. I closed my eyes and squeezed him back. And like a shaking dog, he was my weighted blanket. His presence calmed and secured me when the world felt like it was crashing down around us.

OCTOBER 2006

It was quiet as Pablo walked me home through the residential streets that snaked up the hill from the bar, the air heavy with dejection after this latest in a long string of heartbreaking Mets losses. The pavement glittered under the streetlamps; only a few curtained windows glowed yellow from their boxes inside brick, two-family homes built in the '50s, few people still awake, perhaps watching the slow-motion replays of Carlos Beltrán ending the game with his called strike three.

"Can't believe you *chose* to leave, after playing the role of knight in shining armor back there," I said, jerking a thumb down Woodside Avenue toward the bar. "You could've drank your sorrows away without spending a dime."

"Ah." He waved. "I'm over drinking like that these days."

I raised an eyebrow at him.

"You are?" I asked, turning to look at the sidewalk ahead. "Huh."

I kicked a folded coffee cup into the gutter.

"When we ran into each other at Shea over the summer, I hadn't realized you were such a changed man."

"Yeah," he said. "I suppose I am."

He stuffed his hands in the pockets of his jeans. They fit him, I noticed, like they were supposed to. Not like he used to wear them, baggy and bunched in a heap on top of unlaced white Uptowns.

"I've grown up," he continued. "I'm not the same dumb kid that thinks he needs to be a dick to everyone he meets anymore."

I laughed, the familiar mixture of bitterness and self-righteousness I usually felt around Pablo rushing to the surface. I was nervous that this was the closest we'd ever come to acknowledging the events of that night at his party five years ago.

"Well, you *were* a dick," I said, pulling the drawstrings on my hoodie taut around my neck. "No doubt about that."

Pablo rested a hand on my shoulder to slow me down so I would look at him.

"Brisma—" he began, his voice too earnest for my liking.

"No, Pablo," I said, flicking his hand off and picking up my pace. "Don't worry about it. I'm a big girl."

He grabbed my hand and held it between both of his, forcing me to stop walking on the corner of Sixty-Fifth and Woodside. A red DON'T WALK sign flashed above us, throwing his face into a pulsing shadow.

"Please," he said, his sincerity alarming me. "I've acted like a real jerk to you in the past. I'm not proud of it. I just want you to know that I'm sorry."

His eyes were wide, and the whites around his dark irises appeared blue against his tan skin, like milk around Cheerios.

"Yeah," I laughed again, self-consciously. "Like I said, don't worry about it."

I shook my hand free of his grasp.

"No big deal."

I cleared my throat and glanced at him. "How's your dad doing?" My voice still had an edge to it that I wished weren't there.

Pablo slowly exhaled.

"Dying," he said, as if surprised to hear himself say it. "He's dying, actually."

Several different emotions scratched at the base of my throat: sadness, anger, empathy, distrust. "Oh, I'm sorry" was all I was able to say.

"Yeah," Pablo continued, "ALS is terrible. He needs help with everything. Can barely raise his hand to his mouth, let alone hold a spoon or a glass."

I focused my attention on the sound of our footsteps on the pavement.

"Who's been taking care of him while you were away?" I asked, wondering if "away" was the polite term for war, like prison, like how we referred to where Kelly's mom was.

"My brother, Ariel," he said. "And Medicaid sends a home attendant."

He shook his head.

"But it's beyond everyone's capabilities at this point." He cleared his throat. "That's why I'm home. I'm trying to help move everybody down to my aunt and uncle's in Florida. There's an assisted-living facility down there that is better"—he searched for the right word—"better equipped."

"Like a hospice?"

Pablo grimaced.

"Yeah," he said. "They have hospice."

We walked a few paces in silence. The autumn night was wet with fog, and I could sense my hair had curled into a crown around my temples. In my head, I heard Mami cursing me for not wearing a hat.

"Damn," I said.

I still didn't want to let him off the hook for his past so easily. Something inside me insisted on holding on to this anger, despite the knowledge that he was watching his second parent die before his very eyes.

"Brian didn't let on that it was this bad," I continued. "I didn't know."

The rubber soles of his sneakers padded along the concrete, slapping like the handballs he used to throw at Broadway Park.

"Brian . . ." He hesitated, as if he were making a calculation. "Brian's no good for you."

I stopped, my boot scraping sharply against the sidewalk.

"What?"

Pablo turned to look at me. We were at the corner of the elementary school where I had gone with Kelly and Brian. We didn't hang out with Pablo until middle school, after he moved here from the Philippines, and joined us in religion class at St. Agnes's.

"I know it's none of my business," Pablo said, shaking his head. "But I've seen you with him, and I've seen you without him, and I can tell you, you're a lot better off when he's not in your life."

I clicked my tongue a couple of times in my open mouth, my hand on my hip, before deciding how to respond.

"He's no good for *me*?" I asked. "Your daddy's dying, and you still making time to hang out with him, why? It's just little old me that can't handle this big, bad Brian?"

Pablo swallowed, the tendons in his neck standing to attention. I inhaled, the cool night air filling my lungs in sharp contrast to the rage that was collecting in my chest.

"Look, Brian's my boy." He frowned. "For better or worse. He was my first friend here in the States, you know. He was there for me when my mom . . ."

He looked past me, toward the large double-door entrance to our old school where parents had gathered to pick us up.

"I know he's fucked up—with women especially, I mean. He's fucked up. You don't even know the half of it. And you deserve better."

I attempted to storm past him, but stopped short, not willing to give up the fight.

"Thanks so much for walking me home, but you're right! This is none of your business."

I walked a few paces, but hearing his footsteps continue behind mine, I turned around again.

"You think just because you apologized, because you are going through this with your dad, that I'm going to listen to what you have to say about Brian now? You think after humiliating me that night at your party in front of all your friends, you can act like now you know what's *best* for me as an adult?"

Pablo looked at his feet, his jaw clenching and unclenching. Quietly, he opened and then closed his mouth. We were talking about what we never talked about.

"I didn't," he finally said. "I didn't force you to—"

"Fuck!" I shoved him, all the shame I'd carried for years burning into an anger that lit my muscles into motion: my chest, shoulders, arms, and fists, all one smooth push into his solid chest, absorbed with frustratingly minimal shock. "Pablo, go fuck yourself."

I was about to turn the corner onto my block, but instead I stepped to him, pointer finger poised at his chest.

"Don't forget that I knew him first. Long before you did. And if it hasn't been clear to you over all these years, I never needed to go halfway round the world for a bullshit war to prove myself, or find myself, or discover a conscience, or whatever it is exactly you did out there for a country that will never give a damn about you."

Pablo winced. I knew he wasn't a citizen, and that that was a huge part in his decision to join the army—to get his citizenship. But I was shooting to kill.

"I have always been able to take care of myself right here in Queens, okay? I certainly don't need you or anybody else looking out for me."

Pablo shook his head and took a breath as if to explain himself further, but I cut him off.

"Thanks again for the walk home, Lancelot!" I shouted over my shoulder, fishing my keys out of my front pocket and sliding them in between each of my fingers to form a jagged metal fist, ready to fight anyone who dared cross the path between me and my front door.

2001

Pablo's father had flown back to Manila for a long-lost uncle's funeral, leaving Pablo's older brother in charge of maintaining the house. Ariel, however, was in his first year at Queensborough Community College and could care less about what Pablo did, as long as he kept out of Ariel's bedroom and didn't touch the porn stash he'd relabeled as Disney movie titles. Naturally, this meant Brian and I convinced Pablo to throw a house party.

It was the old cliché scenario: we invited a set group of close friends, which grew into just a couple of friends of friends, too, which then devolved into the visiting Salvadorian cousin of that one girl in gym class showing up, and before we knew it, five Latin Kings were posing with Olde E and throwing gang signs for pictures on the front stoop.

Pablo lived in Elmhurst, the next zip code over, on the first floor of a one-family house near the park. His father had sliced the second floor up into illegally converted rooms and studio apartments after Pablo's mom died. He rented by the month to day laborers and new immigrants from the Philippines to supplement his income as housekeeping staff at a fancy Manhattan social club called the University Club.

When one of the illegal rooms upstairs was vacant, Pablo, ever the entrepreneur, rented it out to kids who wanted a place to hook up when they cut class. In the backyard, the brothers had erected a shoddily constructed wooden deck, on top of which a girl in a corset was now doing a keg stand.

"That's some white shit right there," I said, nudging my shoulder into Brian's leather jacket. He laughed his high-pitched, delighted guffaw as he popped the cap off a bottle of Corona. I reached for the white bottle of Malibu on the picnic table. "I don't need to do no acrobatics or play no damn games to get drunk."

I lifted the punctured Dole can to mix pineapple juice into my rum and raised the red Solo cup to Brian's eyeline.

"Cheers," he responded, with a dull *thwap* of his beer bottle against my cup.

At that, we heard cheers as the girl finally came up for air, laughing like a hyena louder than all of them.

"Oh no," I heard Brian mutter.

My stomach dropped. "What is she doing here?"

Kelly shook hair from her face and wiped her mouth with the back of her pink-glittered hand, where beer had dribbled down her chin.

Brian sighed. "Pablo's still cool with her, what do you want me to tell you?"

"Nah," I said, setting my drink on the banister. "She should know better than to show her—"

But before I could finish, Brian wrapped his entire hand around my upper arm and pulled me close.

"Why don't we dance?" he asked. He stuck one finger in the air as if to test the winds, when I realized the first strings of Monchy y

Alexandra's "Hoja en Blanco" had come on the playlist. The song had been everywhere that summer, and it was the only song I could ever get him to dance with me. He knew I would agree.

On the concrete patio, stained by barbecue grease and motor oil, I pulled my abs in tight and slowly rolled my pelvis in figure eights from side to side, stepping front to back and around again with Brian's hands on the curve of my hips the entire time.

"It's all about exaggeration," he'd said when he taught me during basement parties with his tías and tíos in Corona. "Everything should be bigger and tighter than you think it should be." It was different from the performative salsa Mami and I danced on Saturday mornings while we cleaned, balancing against the mop or the broom. Bachata was closer, more intimate; bachata belonged to Brian.

Whipping my head around as we traced concentric circles on the pavement, I could sense other people's eyes on us as he spun me out, the skirt of my dress flaring, and twirled me back inside his arms. His hands were hot like fire on my ribs as he worked me back out to arm's length. He didn't lead me so much anymore; rather, he held on for the ride.

I kissed him and tasted the acidity of my pineapple against the brine of his beer. His cheeks were flushed and his eyes, for a moment, felt like they could see only me. It was fleeting though, that moment, and before I knew it, his liquid eyes were back to searching the white lights strung up along the fence for an exit or an empty glass to pour himself into.

"Come on," he said, taking my hand in his plump palm.

I followed him up the stairs to the illegally converted apartments on the second floor and into one of the vacant rooms. It was dark, the only light coming in through the window from the full moon above and the ambient light from the party below. But still, I could just make out the frayed edges of office-gray carpet remnants stapled to the hardwood floors beneath our feet and a dirty pillow slumped in a corner.

"What are we doing here?" I asked.

Brian pushed me up against the wall in response, and again all I could make out was the glint of the moonlight on his teeth from his open-mouthed smile. He pressed his whole hard body against me as he moved to kiss me hungrily on the mouth. I spread my thighs apart slightly, to make room for him to fit closer to my body.

He tilted his head to kiss underneath my chin and down my neck, and scooped my breast out from inside my V-neck. He had always been gentle, always concerned with my pleasure. Still, according to St. Agnes, I was a virgin. He hadn't pushed me for anything more since that failed night after the Nuyorican.

Suddenly, Brian produced a blue Trojan from his back pocket and ripped it open with his teeth.

"Now?" I asked. "Tonight?" I looked down at the torn carpet beneath us. "Here?"

"Why not?" he asked, breathless. I noticed his hair was nubby in spots; I'd already rubbed some of the gel out of his hair with my fingers. It made him look younger, unfinished, like how he looked at the St. Agnes fair when I first kissed him as a child.

"Because I think there are already some rats mating in here, for one thing."

"We'll go to a different room," he said. "You know I've been wanting to try again."

"No." I refused. "Forget it."

I lifted and tucked my breast back inside my bra.

"I'm not trying to have my first time be in some kind of squatter's den, anyway."

I buttoned my dress back up across my chest and made my way back downstairs to where the party out back had gone dark. The lights strung overhead had been turned off since we'd gone upstairs, and now I could only make out shadows and silhouettes around citronella candles and the occasional flicks of Zippo lighters against Newports.

"What's going on?" I asked.

"We're playing truth or dare," a voice I recognized as Pablo's answered.

"Oh good," I mumbled as I reached for a new cup and the bottle of Malibu, "another game."

"Naveen," I heard Pablo start, "it's your turn."

"Kelly," Naveen said, slamming his bottle of beer on the table, "I dare you to go upstairs with me for twenty minutes."

"Twenty?" she slurred. "I thought it was supposed to be seven minutes in heaven."

"Not with me it isn't," he said to a round of hollering.

Kelly stood up, the sparkle of gel in her hair catching what little light was left. I sensed Brian next to me on the deck where I was frozen, watching Kelly.

"Let's go," she said.

The party clapped and whistled as they disappeared through the back door and inside the house. I sucked my teeth and sat down in a metal folding chair outside the circle.

"Brisma," Pablo turned to me. "Truth or dare."

"Oh"—I swallowed a gulp of rum I'd just raised to my lips— "I'm not playing."

"If you're out here, you're playing," he said. I heard Brian scrape the legs of an empty chair up next to me.

"So truth or dare," Pablo repeated.

"Truth, I guess."

Everyone groaned.

"How many times have you and Brian had sex?"

The crowd giggled. I heard some girls mutter under their breath, "puta." Brian tensed up beside me.

"Never," I said, immediately regretting how Brian might feel at my public acknowledgment of our virginity.

"Big surprise," Pablo snickered.

"What does that mean?" I asked, as someone flicked a Bic lighter, rigged so that the flame was tall and slender, to light a cigarette.

"It means you've probably never even touched his dick," Pablo laughed. "You're a prude."

"I've touched it plenty," I said.

"Oh yeah?" I didn't like the tone of Pablo's voice. "Prove it."

The whites of his eyes caught the light of the moon in that moment, and stories about werewolves, and silver bullets, and animal instincts came rushing back to me.

"I dare you to go down on him right here in front of everyone," Pablo said.

The crowd erupted in a Greek chorus of "oh snaps" and stifled, stunned laughter.

"I already chose truth," I said, full of self-satisfaction. "And you already asked me my question."

Pablo groaned. "Yeah, so the answer is"—he waved his hand—"you a prude."

Everyone laughed.

Brian looped his fingers around the arm of my chair and pulled me closer.

"It would be kind of hot," he whispered.

I stared at him, willing the irises of my eyes to burn a hole through the darkness and into his.

"Look at your friend." Pablo nodded up at Kelly in his house. "She's down."

"She's not my friend," I shot back.

Again, the crowd whooped and hollered.

"Come on," Brian whispered. "It's dark, anyway."

My blood ran hot through my veins, from the rum or adrenaline, I was unsure. I didn't just want to make Brian happy, I wanted to let everyone know that he was mine, that I deserved him, and that I could hold a man everyone else wanted. Maybe most of all, I wanted to prove that Kelly was not more desirable than me, not more *down* than I was.

I reached for the zipper of Brian's pants, and it made a sound so loud that everyone knew I'd agreed to the dare. Multiple chairs scraped against wood, rubber soles of sneakers clamoring to get a better look, as best they could in the dark.

He was hard already, the idea of doing this in front of a crowd no doubt a huge turn-on for him. He always liked to invite the existence of other people into our relationship—new girls he'd met, classmates who had a crush on him. He liked to see me jealous. I could tell this was to make everyone else jealous, too. He thrived on it. And this was something I could give him. This moment.

I slipped him inside my mouth and tasted sour sweat and beer. My eyes shut, despite the dark, I kept my lips wet so everyone would hear, the desire to perform silencing all else. It was only for a few moments, maybe seconds—chickenheads, Pablo used to call Kelly and me—before I heard a loud screech of metal against wood, followed by a deep retching sound. One of the girls had started puking, and the others laughed and groaned in response.

I broke apart from Brian and wiped my mouth.

"Brisma's the one to suck a dick," Pablo said, waving a thumb at the girl bent over behind the cooler, "but Yahaira's the one to choke on it."

People laughed and stomped on the deck, and it felt like rolling thunder underneath me, rattling my bones.

Mortified, I stood up to leave. I heard Brian zip up his pants and start to follow me, but I was too quick and sped down the stoop and the sidewalk before he could catch up. Around the corner, I stood in the deserted midnight street, remembering how Kelly and I used to play our own game of chicken by sitting on the double-yellow lines as cars came barreling down the hill of Clement Moore Avenue. I thought about last summer with the Maspeth boys, how guys always wanted her and not me, how she always seemed to be better at playing the game than I was.

I stood there, the rum still warm in my chest, the soggy weight of my body swaying from side to side, until a car turned off Corona Avenue and flashed its high beams at me. I squinted at it, feeling the blood course quicker through my veins, down my arms, and into my cold fists. Chicken, just like when we were kids. Chickenheads. My eyes remained focused on the two headlights as the car barreled toward me, but I was also very aware of my surroundings: the yellow cabs parallel parked in front of the gas station to my right and the glowing white light of the Q58 Bus Station shelter to my left. Above me, a pair of bootleg Jordans hung from a streetlamp and cast a shadow that teased the white ladder crosswalk between corners. Inside my fist, my pinkie nail pinched the flesh of my palm.

I stepped aside just as the Corolla blew past me, horn blaring. I didn't jump, leap, or run. I took a step. I didn't know if that was a measure of my cool so much as evidence of how much liquor had impaired my depth perception. I watched the red brake lights grow small and then disappear as the car turned onto Broadway. The street was quiet again except for the beat of my heart pounding in my ears.

I checked behind me one more time toward Pablo's house to make sure Brian wasn't following and scuttled off to the sidewalk to continue my walk home.

☙

The next morning, I woke to my StarTAC buzzing between my stomach and the bare mattress. The fitted sheet had come undone in the middle of the night, and my sweating skin stuck to the poly-ester casing. I'd spent the early sunlight hours picking at the cuticle on my thumb and replaying the events from the night before over and over in my head. Each time I heard Brian's fly zip open, I felt the vibration in my fingers as each tooth came apart from the oth-ers, the metal cool and denim rough against my skin, and I was slammed with a new wave of guilt and shame and buried my nose deeper inside my pillow.

I fished out the phone from underneath me and flipped open the cover to discover that Brian had called me six times. I'd already missed first period, thanks to Mami working an early shift at the hospital. It was unusual for me to up and disappear on him like I did; just as he thrived on my jealousy, I fed off his need for forgive-ness. I was a wholesaler of his drama.

I wondered, the sheets tangled around my legs, whether I had been too hasty in leaving the party when I did. I wondered if I had overreacted to the whole thing in the first place. After all, Kelly had done more or less the exact same thing, and everybody always wanted to be her friend or her boyfriend. Why couldn't I get away with it, too?

At that moment, I heard a light rasping at my back door. My bedroom had the second exit in the apartment, down a set of stairs into the backyard to a brick-lined square of concrete, where an old wooden doghouse lay rotting for decades, built by the old Mexican man who owned the building for a dog that died before my dad left.

I yanked on a pair of Old Navy shorts and peeled back the blinds to see Kelly standing on the back step. Her eyes were cast low, crumbs of last night's makeup still crusted along her lash line. For a moment, I felt relieved to see her there before quickly pulling up the more familiar cloak of anger I'd been holding on to since last summer.

I opened the door and leaned against the black metal door-frame. The autumn breeze was cool against my flushed face.

"Are you here to gloat?"

Kelly frowned.

"What?" she asked. She looked confused and upset that I was opening our conversation with such aggression.

"No," she said, looking toward the boulevard. "I thought you might want to go take a walk with me. Down to the bodega?"

I stared at her pockmarked skin in the bright sun. Birds were chirping in the large, stubborn elm tree that grew out of the concrete driveway next door. Beneath the wind, it was warmer than it should have been for October.

"Wow," I said out loud, realizing so much of the year was already behind us.

"Never mind," Kelly said, waving. She turned to make her way back to the gate.

"No," I called after her. "Hang on. Let me just put some pants on."

Down on Queens Boulevard, the roads were quieter, less populated than they usually were on a weekday. I loved that time of morning whenever we cut class, when everyone else was making the mad dash to wherever it was their lives required them to be. I felt like I held some secret key on those mornings, that I'd walked through a hidden doorway in the space-time continuum where I could spy on them living their hard, ordinary lives without participating myself. I preferred life there in the in-between; it was a fleeting privilege to which I understood I wouldn't always have access.

Kelly kicked a can of Vanilla Coke in our path off the curb.

"The Yankees lost last night," she said, referring to the most recent postseason game against the Oakland A's. Despite making it to the World Series last year, and despite a flare of hope around their emotional first game post–9/11, the Mets weren't even able to make it to the playoffs.

"Fuck the Yankees," I responded.

"Fuck the Yankees."

We still agreed, then, that the Mets were the only New York team worth rooting for, even if New York had come to stand for much more than hot dogs, and subway tokens, and John Rocker's derogatory comments about the 7 Train these days. From our houses on the hill, we'd watched the Manhattan skyline smolder in the distance for weeks.

"I saw you last night," she said.

"Yeah," I snorted. "I saw *you*, too."

Kelly's head snapped to attention.

"What does that mean?"

I made sure not to shrug, to keep my eyes focused straight ahead.

"Nothing."

"Did you—" She took her keys out of the front pocket of her green hoodie. "Did you see Nicky there, too?"

"Nicky?" I asked. "Gargiullo? From St. Agnes's?"

Kelly nodded her head yes and tucked a strand of hair behind her ear. I noticed she'd gotten a new tragus piercing.

"No," I said, listening to the beat of our sneakers scraping against the concrete. "Why would he have been there?"

Kelly shrugged.

"Maybe he's friends with Pablo? I guess he knows him from CYO? Or religion?"

I inhaled sharply as my mind constructed scenes of Kelly being cheered and applauded by everyone at the party after coming downstairs with Naveen and then flirting with Nicky after all those years and getting his number.

"He was there when I woke up."

I frowned at her.

"Woke up where?"

"At the party," she said. "After Naveen . . . I just kind of passed out."

To our left, a truck jumped the curb to make a right turn into the service lane.

"And Nicky was on top of me."

My skin prickled with awareness; the pins and needles I felt when my foot fell asleep was how my brain felt when she said that. I was enraged. I was afraid.

"That doesn't make any sense," I said.

I looked at Kelly, but she didn't look at me. Her eyes were dull and squinting toward the distance at the traffic headed for the Brooklyn-Queens Expressway. I was losing her again.

"Like," I began, trying to find the right words, "like he was having sex with you?"

Kelly laughed, but it was more in bewilderment, more like shock. She looked at me with a tired smile, her lips almost gray.

"Isn't that some shit?"

"Fuck," I said, surprised at the conviction in my voice, ashamed that I couldn't keep a more calm, disaffected tone.

I didn't want her to feel like I was judging her or that she deserved any pity. It felt like we were eleven again, hiding in the weeds of the dugout, and I was looking to her as my guide to a crazy world of treacherous men and ignorant women. It felt like I had been training for this moment since Timothy.

We walked in strained silence until we arrived at Sandro's on the corner. Sandro himself was at the register, and Kelly acted her normal self, chatting him up about his calico cat, complimenting him on the gold chain he wore around his hairy neck. She was flirting with him, winking beneath the mascara she'd rubbed after waking up underneath Nicky, and I wasn't sure if she even knew she was doing it. I watched him ring her up for only half the items she placed on the counter: milk, bread, Devil Dogs, and pizza-flavored Combos. He blew a quick kiss when we left, charmed by her as ever.

She was smiling as she climbed down the steps, but after a furtive glance at me, she lowered her eyes again to the sidewalk.

"I was thinking last night," I said, "about how we used to play in traffic. Jumping out in front of a car speeding down the hill and back to safety again. Just as quick. Throwing our Hula-Hoops out underneath cars and forcing the younger kids on the block to run and get them."

"Yeah," Kelly said. "We were the worst."

She gave me a crooked smile. "Sitting in the middle of the road cross-legged like a monk, until the oncoming car swerved out of the way."

I tilted my head and thought for a second.

"We used to run out and save each other, didn't we?"

"That's not how I remember it," she said.

We passed by a blue-haired woman in a housecoat sweeping the sidewalk in front of her house. Her husband banged a rug against the fence, and the chain-link echoed and rattled between its posts.

Kelly turned toward me, a clammy finger on my wrist.

"I'm sorry," she said. "For the roof. I was wrong."

I swallowed, my mouth dry, dehydrated from the night before. Every so often, I felt like I could still taste Brian under my tongue.

"Yeah," I replied. It bothered me for some reason that she didn't reference him by name, but the memory of her roof and last summer was already fading like a balloon into the stratosphere. She and Brian both had that effect on me: the ability to confuse me out of being angry at them.

"Yeah," I repeated, the memory of last night much fresher in my mind than our original beef. "Brian ain't shit, anyway."

Kelly slid her thumbnail between her teeth for a second, as if weighing something in her mind. She looked up toward the crest of the hill, the morning sun dappling the blacktop through the brilliant leaves.

"He's not worth it," Kelly said. "No man is."

At the gate to my house, I reached into her bag and ripped open the two-pack of Devil Dogs. I bit into mine and handed her the other one, which she grabbed with a fist.

I looked up at the brick facade of my three-family house, at the shadows cast on the windows by the bristling dead leaves of the elm tree next door. I turned back to Kelly and shrugged.

"School's already shot for the day," I said. "Wanna head to the dugout?"

Kelly smiled and nodded toward the empty lot down the street. We crossed without playing in traffic. We were too old for that now; we knew how reckless people could be. But we spent the rest of the day listening to the radio in the patch of soil where grass still wouldn't grow. We'd salted the earth with our sweat as children— with our fear.

We caught up on each other's life in the months that had passed without a word between us. We ordered Chinese food from the joint down on Broadway that sometimes packed fortune cookies with two slips of paper in them. This time, the paper bag contained no cookies at all, but I wasn't surprised. It made sense that no fortune could reach us there in the in-between, the borrowed time of truancy.

For that day, for those few suspended hours, we were safe.

NOVEMBER 2006

Janet guided me into a room in her family's Pelham Bay house that she called the salon and asked me to wait there while she washed up from her workout. It made me uncomfortable whenever people referred to salons, or dens, or drawing rooms; the luxury of gratuitous rooms made me itchy.

She'd moved back home after the incident, I'd learned, when we spoke briefly over the phone so I could get directions to her parents' house in Westchester.

I figured the house was going to be intimidating, but I didn't expect to be greeted by landscaped cypresses lining the enormous, sprawling lawn leading up to the red-painted door when I stepped out of the cab. Standing at the threshold, peeking in the windows that lined the doorframe, I had taken a moment to gather the resolve to press the doorbell.

In the salon, a fire glowed in the hearth between twin peach-colored armchairs. Delicate-looking designer wallpaper had been pasted above wainscoting that covered the walls. In our apartment at home, Mami hung crucifixes on the cement walls with 3M tape to not upset our landlord.

I picked up a framed picture on the sideboard next to the couch. A younger Janet stood on a podium in a tracksuit holding flowers.

So she was an athlete, too. The photo next to it showed Janet as a kid, maybe twelve or thirteen, wearing frayed denim shorts and a FILA top, crouching on a wooden dock with six other girls, their arms around each other's shoulders, skin red and pink from the sun, cousins, maybe, or camp friends. In the back row were pairs of parents, some men with heavy mustaches, others with aviator sunglasses. Everyone's face was wide and open, smiling as if in midconversation, mid-"cheese." My throat felt sore then, my eyes welling for reasons I couldn't dare explain.

I turned my attention to the bookcases, which appeared to be filled with hundreds of hardcover books, but when I picked one up, three others came off the shelf with it, attached and hollow.

"The hell . . ." I panicked, placing it back down quickly.

"They're ridiculous, I know," Janet said behind me, and I jumped, embarrassed. "Why not just take your time and build an actual library?"

She rolled her eyes before placing a tray holding two glasses of water on an ottoman, ice clinking.

"My dad has no patience," she said, picking up one of the glasses and handing it to me. "Just wants things to look put together right away."

I took the glass from her and nodded.

"Your parents still together?" I asked. *Of course they are*, I thought. *What a stupid question.*

"Yeah," she said, frowning slightly, scooping her own glass up and onto a coaster beside one of the peach armchairs. "Why do you ask?"

"Oh," I said, clearing my throat as I sat down in the chair opposite her, "it's just kind of rare, don't you think? Don't know if I know anyone whose parents aren't split up."

Janet raised her eyebrows.

"Guess I'm lucky."

I stared at the plush, pink carpet beneath my feet and thought about how nice it must feel to sink your bare toes into the soft fibers. I wondered how lucky Janet had felt in her hospital gown, the fluorescent spotlight cutting through the bile of an encroaching hangover. I thought of the open smiles in that photo on the lake, and the lines in Griselda's sour face, and the gravel-scrape of Frances's taunting laugh, and the towel Mami clutched to her chest that cold night with El Cochino, and I wondered where in this house Janet had developed the tools to make the leap from yes, to no, to help. *Security*, the report said she'd yelled. How different that word must feel in her mouth than in mine, in Kelly's.

This anger, though old and constant, would get me nowhere. I looked at Janet nervously looping her hair behind her ear and then in front of it again. We were both just girls, and at that moment, in that house, regardless of the forms and functions of the families and neighborhoods we came from, we needed each other.

OCTOBER 2006

Neither of us had heard from Brian in over a week, but Kelly was the last to have seen him that season-ending night of the Mets' called strike three. We had made vague plans to watch the World Series games together, the four of us, but Pablo bailed—no surprise to me after our showdown on the block—and Brian simply fell off. His phone was going straight to voicemail, he hadn't returned any of our emails or Myspace messages, and Kelly maintained that there was nothing out of the ordinary about how their night had ended, claiming that they drunkenly split apart not long after Pablo and I left.

"I don't know," I said, carving a pattern of half-moons along the wet edge of my cocktail napkin. "You think he's taking this that badly?"

We were back at PJ Moore's for Game 3 of the World Series between St. Louis and Detroit. With the Mets no longer in the pennant race, the pub had dropped its cover charge and we settled back into our usual spots at the bar, only this time there was a lot less orange and blue and quite a few more Yankees and Cardinals hats. Whenever Albert Pujols, the star player for St. Louis, came up to bat, Kelly and I booed.

"Who, Pujols?" she asked, grabbing a handful of nuts from the bowl between us. "He can't hear us booing, girl, what you talking about?"

"No," I said, frowning. "Brian. You think he's MIA because of the Mets?"

Kelly spit a peanut skin off her lip with a *pfft*.

"He plays ball," she said, clearing her throat. She kept her eyes trained on the screen. "He knows sometimes you win, sometimes you lose. It's part of the game."

I rolled the fibers from the wet piece of napkin pinched between my nails to mulch.

"Do you think something could have happened to him?" I asked.

Kelly frowned, her mouth full, and my breath caught in my throat.

"He's grown, Brisma," Kelly said, and swallowed. When she saw I was unmoved, she took a deep breath and ran her fingers through her hair, her scalp blue-white beneath her black mane.

"He was laughing and waving at me from the sidewalk when I left. He busted his ass trying to do a cartwheel. Drunk, definitely, but I'm sure he's been publicly intoxicated before. In fact, I'm sure half the borough were on their asses that night!"

"Yeah," I said. "But not all of them were brown Latino kids outside an Irish pub."

She took a swig of her beer, keeping her eyes on the television screen.

"He's probably fine," she said, quieter this time. "You shouldn't be so caught up on him, anyway."

I was quiet, afraid that I had tipped my hand. That she suspected I still had feelings for him . . . Did I still have feelings for him? It was all so confusing.

"Aren't your sights set on bigger and better things these days?" she asked, as the inning came to an end. "Did you submit that application?"

"Yes," I said, crossing my arms. "A while ago."

"That's great," she said. Kelly had dropped a second course, making her a part-time student and affecting the amount of funding FAFSA was willing to cover. She picked up a second shift at Riviera, in addition to her hours at the bakery, to make up the difference and still have enough to pay her portion of the mortgage and send her mom a few bucks on JPay each month.

Her eyes flitted toward me, a tentative curiosity.

"What's your script about, anyway?"

I couldn't help myself.

"It's about a girl who abandons her friend's drunk ex-boyfriend in the gutter to die a grisly death."

Kelly slammed her pint glass down on the table.

"Oh please," she said, swiveling off of her stool. "That reminds me. I need to change my tampon. Hopefully, you'll have moved on to a new subject to torture me with by the time I get back."

In her absence, I looked around the bar at the other people watching the game. There was a good mix of both men and women, but from what I could tell, most of the women were there as companions—furtive looks between the TV and their men's faces, quick glances at their watches between pitches, as if to ask, how long would this game drag on? Kelly and I followed trade deals, knew statistics. It was this fandom that had informed my pilot script, after all. We weren't just fans who were female; this was an area of our lives where I could join Kelly in finally feeling like one of the cool girls.

It was then, feeling smug, that I felt a buzzing in the back pocket of my jeans. I figured it was Kelly texting me for a tampon. Instead, it was Brian calling me from his cell.

"Hey," I answered, relief audible in my voice. "Where have you been?"

I heard him choke out a distant chuckle away from the receiver.

"You won't believe it," he said, his voice small like a child's.

My ears pitched back involuntarily, the muscles in my neck tightening in fear.

"You'll never guess."

Again, I looked toward the bathroom door and considered what Kelly would say in this situation, how she would react. I grabbed my purse and made my way out the door so I could hear him better on the line.

"You're right," I said. "Because if I were to guess, I'd say you were either arrested or abducted by aliens."

"Ha," he said. "Yes."

The fear dropped from my tight jaw straight through to my gut.

"What do you mean, 'yes'?"

"I mean, yes," he repeated. "I was arrested last week."

A 7 Train rumbled in through the rickety station overhead, providing cover for my momentary speechlessness. I walked a little farther down Sixtieth Street, hoping the noise wouldn't shoo him off the phone. I didn't want to lose him again.

"I just got back," he continued. "I couldn't afford bail, so I had to spend five nights in jail before a judge would see me."

"What were you arrested for?" I asked. "Was it because you were drunk?"

"Can you meet up right now?" he said with a cough. "I'm in Sunnyside."

"Yes," I told him. "Of course."

I walked back toward the bar, but then thought better of it and continued past it to the elevated subway station to take the 7 to Mel's apartment near 46th and Bliss. I didn't bother going in to tell Kelly in person, I just sent her a text saying I needed to leave. She would probably be furious at me, but I didn't care. Brian had called me when he needed help, when he needed someone to confide in. He'd called me, and not Kelly.

❧

Brian had been charged with breaking and entering and sexual assault in the second degree. He told me this as we sat in his uncle's Sebring on the Astoria Park strip underneath the Hell Gate Bridge, listening to Tego Calderón on 105.9 La Kalle. A warrant for his arrest had been out since that weekend he accompanied his St. John's coach to Connecticut. He and a few teammates crashed a party at Sacred Heart University, where Brian hooked up with a freshman in her dorm. The cops caught him last Friday, the day after the Mets lost, when he'd traveled back up to Fairfield County to pick up the team's jersey order for next season.

"I don't understand," I told him. "Did you hook up with her or not? Who is this girl? How did you know her? Was she white?"

"She was just a girl," he said. "A girl that hung around us baseball players, you know. She knew my stats from last season and everything. She and her girlfriends invited us to a party that night, so I went with my buddy."

He placed his hand on my wrist with an urgency that shook me from the questions cycling through my mind.

"She was all over me, Brisma," he said, eyes wide. "I swear. She brought me back to her room."

"Yeah, okay," I said. "But where does the sexual assault come in?"

It was uncomfortable to hear the intimate details of his actions with another woman, but it also upset me that he put himself in that kind of position—that he wasn't smarter about protecting himself.

Brian shifted in his seat, pulling his right knee up onto the stick shift, resting his ankle on his left thigh. His hips were open and facing me. He clapped his hands together in the space between us as he spoke.

"So, we go back to her place, and we're making out. Hooking up—"

"Which is it," I interjected, "making out or hooking up?"

He pursed his lips under heavy, lidded eyes.

"Hooking up. She was drunk though, okay? She had drank a lot at the party. But she was down. *She* was on top of *me*!"

He held his hands to his chest, not blinking. I was reminded of the little boy at the St. Agnes fair in a washed-out T-shirt, worn deep and loose at the neck. What a contrast he was to the man protecting the chest that now filled out his sweater, the broad shoulders that he claimed bore no responsibility.

"Go on," I said. I felt like a St. Agnes nun, like he had come to me for absolution. That's why he'd called me and not Kelly. I inhaled sharply, contracting the muscles around my rib cage, bracing myself.

"So at one point, the girl just falls asleep. Like"—he threw his head back against the headrest, eyes closed, jaw slack—"snoring. Lights out. Of course, I'm not going to stick around like that! I'm not an animal. So, I leave."

I exhaled and tucked a piece of hair behind my ear.

"But then when I'm out on the quad, about to go find my buddy back at the party, I realize I forgot something."

I turned back to face him.

"My watch."

"You went back for a watch?"

"Yeah," he exclaimed, "it was an expensive watch! I got it at last year's sports awards dinner. I wasn't about to leave it at some random chick's dorm room, never to be seen again."

"Why would you have taken off a watch in the first place?"

Brian huffed and pumped the steering wheel with both hands. He looked at me, and I could see a bit of sweat beading on his upper lip.

"It's cold on my wrist," he said. "I don't like it when I'm . . ." He shook his head. "It doesn't matter."

I rolled my eyes and crossed my arms, settling in to hear the rest of his story, relieved that he might just be a stupid prima donna, after all.

"I go back to her building, but I can't get back in this time, right? I don't have the key. So I try throwing rocks at her window. Small ones, pebbles. I'm not trying to break the school's windows or nothing."

I laughed despite myself, and sucked my teeth.

"You are so dumb," I said. "That is some movie shit. It doesn't work in real life."

Brian smiled, and I felt uneasy. It struck me as odd that he was willing to play coy with me, just one week after being arrested for something so serious.

"Yeah, well, I get no response from the rock throwing, and I realize I can reach her window if I pull over a garbage can to stand on and climb up to the ledge."

I narrowed my eyes at him.

"You did all this for a Bolex?"

"I told you," he said, "it was expensive! I love that watch."

I cleared my throat and raised my eyebrows, waiting for him to continue.

"So I climb in through her window, which I could lift because it was already open about two inches, but I was clumsy, and my foot clipped the windowsill, and I fell inside."

Brian raised both hands to grab at his black hair.

"And this girl screams so loud that half the dorm wakes up."

His hands fell heavily back into his lap, meaty fists against fabric, the only sound between us.

"So that was it?" I asked, my face still screwed up into a frown. "You pulled an Alternate 1985 Marty McFly?"

"Yes," he said, squeezing my shoulder. "I knew you'd understand.

"She's screaming bloody murder," he continued, gesturing with both hands toward the side-view mirror before swinging wildly toward the right. "Her RA comes in, half asleep, and calls campus security over, which is when I jet, right? Because all of a sudden, she claims she has no idea who I am and never met me."

"What?" I shook my head.

"Like I told you, she was drunk. She must have blacked out."

"Well," I said, "that's the breaking and entering. But how'd they get sexual assault?"

Brian sighed, pressing his broad shoulders back against the driver's seat.

"Because she wasn't wearing any pants," he said.

I frowned at him again.

"When I fell," he said, "her bed was right beneath the window. And I fell right on top of her."

I let out a thin whine of air like a balloon loosened slightly at the knot.

"Uh-huh," I said. "With your dick out?"

"No," he laughed. "I think she was embarrassed. I think she was trying to cover up for earlier, for inviting me over in the first place."

"Was she white?"

He laughed again.

"Why do you ask?"

I cut my eyes at him sideways.

"Come on," I said. "Was she?"

"Yeah," he responded. "I think. Or no, Spanish maybe."

I sighed and scratched my chin. Not many people were out parked by the water that night, but a cop car still periodically swept through the strip to keep an eye out for drug deals or solicitation. Each time I saw a flash of blue and white pass by, I felt my heart slam louder in my chest, the blood pump harder in my ears.

"What about your teammates?" I asked. "Have they come to your defense at all? What about your coach?"

Brian rubbed the back of his neck and peered through the windshield at the night sky.

"They want me to shut it down." He swallowed.

"Okay," I said. "So what do you do now? Do you have to go to trial?"

"I might," he said, his eyes scared for the first time. "Mel brought me to a lawyer on Roosevelt, but I don't think he really gives a shit."

I slapped my thigh.

"You can't use a 1-800-ABOGADO to fight against a white girl!" I said. "Let me see what I can do. I'll do research at school and see if maybe there are any prelaw or grad students who could recommend someone."

Brian smoothed his palm over the area of my thigh I'd just slapped.

"Thank you, Brisma," he said. "I knew I could count on you."

My heart pounding again, my throat tightening, I looked out onto the shimmering water breaking on the black rocks of the borough's shore.

"Why did you call me?" I asked him.

"What do you mean?" He frowned. When the brown of his irises caught the light of the streetlamps, it reminded me for a moment of the fluttering of cockroach wings.

"Why did you call me?" I repeated.

He turned the dial on the radio down. "You're real. You're my homegirl. Since we were kids. Who else can I depend on?"

With that, he shifted the car into gear and pulled out of our spot. I tried relaxing as he drove me home, I tried to refrain from asking further questions. But as we turned onto the ramp for the eastbound Brooklyn-Queens Expressway, I realized I'd shifted my body all the way to the right of the car away from him, my elbow and my knee against the inside of the door, bones pressing painfully into the armrest and cup holder. Brian was saying things I wanted to hear, but the truth beneath them felt like a pot of water boiling on high. I dimly recalled the saying about frogs not knowing when they were being boiled alive, that the temperature of the water around them would rise and cook them from the inside out before they realized anything was wrong. Something about this situation felt like a demarcation, a point of no return. I had the sense that things would never be the same.

"I'll do whatever I can to help," I told him when he dropped me off.

He grabbed my hand and squeezed it. His palm was sweaty in mine.

"I know you will."

2001

fter the game of truth or dare at Pablo's party, Brian and I
quickly grew apart. The shame I felt over what I'd done was
so thick that no flame I carried for Brian could survive it. In a
weird way, it empowered me to leave him, the clarity I'd reached
not about Brian but about myself: I didn't like what I'd done, and
seeing him every day, kissing him every day, would remind me of it
as long as he remained my boyfriend.

There were calls, and emails, and even a few evenings when
Brian rang our doorbell and Mami told him I wasn't home, but I
could avoid him at school for only so long. A week after Pablo's, he
half-knocked on the back door of my classroom, and I grabbed a
bathroom pass to meet at the top-floor staircase like we always did.

Immediately, he was all hands, and lips, and apologies, but
I placed my hand squarely against his chest and pushed him up
against the caged window.

"It's over, Brian."

Brian snorted and leaned in for my neck.

"No, it's not."

"No." I extended my arm again. "Not like the other times. Let's
just . . ." I sighed and let my hand drop. "Let's just end it. You want
to date other girls anyway, don't you?"

He was silent, lips still parted, sizing me up.

"I don't want to do this anymore," I said. "I don't want to feel like . . ." I watched his jaw tighten. "I don't want to have to prove myself anymore. I'm just done, Brian."

He screwed his lips together and narrowed his eyes at me.

"That sounds mad mature," he said, suspicious.

I shrugged, already feeling lighter.

"Trust me," I said. "Feels far from it."

We never talked about Brian, Kelly and I—and we never spoke about what happened to her that night at Pablo's party. We started hanging out again, slowly; she invited me to a Knicks game her brother got free tickets to, I invited her over for Thanksgiving with Mami. Her parents were living together again, and Kelly liked the opportunity to tell my mom stories about *her parents* as a unit, as a family. I realized, looking at her over a plate of pasteles, that Kelly harbored a peculiar resentment toward Mami that was unique from any of the bad blood between us. Her eagerness to paint a portrait of her finally cohesive family was always trailed by an urgent fear that we knew she didn't really believe it would last, either.

That winter, Kelly indulged me in watching hours-long marathons of *Boy Meets World* on MTV2. The rhythm of the sitcom's laugh track and its tidily solved, one-episode teen problems were soothing to me during this fallow period in both our dating and social lives. While neither of us ever named what it was that we were recovering from, we shared an unspoken understanding that salvation was possible only when we were by each other's side. All winter, we wore sweatpants and ate pounds of cheesy garlic bread toasted in the illegal stove Patrick had installed in the basement as part of a makeshift apartment for himself.

"Do you ever think about our lives as a TV show?" I asked Kelly.

She frowned, straightening the new curtains Frances had hung in their living room in her latest attempt at domesticity. For as long as I could remember, they'd suspended old bedsheets over tension rods.

"No," Kelly clucked.

"Sometimes I do," I said, staring out the window at the overgrown grass of the dugout next door. "Like each school year is a new season of our series."

"That's kind of creepy," she said.

I folded my arms and pulled my knees up. In the year that Kelly and I didn't speak, I had begun writing notes for a TV show I wanted to write about a CYO league baseball team plagued by drama on and off the field, from the perspectives of the kids, coaches, and parents. I had been inspired by all of Brian's games and scrimmages I'd attended. After Kelly's reaction, I wished I hadn't mentioned TV at all. Picking up on that, perhaps, she curled up on the other end of the couch and stretched out one leg so that her foot rested against my thigh.

"Who would play me?" she asked.

"Jessica Alba," I said. "Or maybe Jessica Biel."

I ripped a piece of garlic bread between my hands and pulled the cheese apart. "Someone named Jessica, for sure."

She nodded, pleased with those options.

"And you?"

We both smiled.

"Rosario Dawson," we said in unison.

Harmony in the Morales house never lasted long; eventually, Frances took out a mortgage on the house she inherited from her mother in order to buy Kelly's dad an Escalade in a last-ditch effort to keep him in the States. Frances noticed he'd been withdrawing increasingly larger amounts of money from their bank account, which put her on high alert that he was planning on moving back to Barranquilla again, where we all suspected he maintained a separate family. It didn't work, and he drove that Escalade to the west side of Manhattan where he shipped it back to Colombia so it was waiting for him when his Avianca flight landed just before our senior year. Frances spiraled into a deep depression afterward and became entirely dependent on the income Kelly and Patrick were able to bring in to pay the mortgage. Kelly managed to structure her class schedule to be out of school by two and available to work full-time in the mall at Auntie Anne's, where she slipped me free pretzels until her shift ended at nine. Part of her, I think, liked to be too busy to think—about her parents, about Nicky, about anything.

Brian and I barely spoke in the halls at school, which was easy enough in a school of two thousand kids. But I saw that he was profiled by the Public Schools Athletic League as a rising baseball star to watch, and he started dating the captain of the girls' volleyball team, forming the picture-perfect high school couple. Teachers, priests, even Sandro at the bodega started squinting at me and asking if I still hung out with Brian, if I had heard about the latest college courting him, if I was proud of him. And the thing is, as the sting of our relationship and how it had soured my friendship with Kelly began to wear off under the weight of time, I was. It felt good that it was Brian doing so well, Brian getting the recognition in our community, not dumbass Nicky, or Joey, but the Bolivian kid.

I sought out weekend writing courses through City College (the Harvard of New York, Mami was quick to tell people) because all I was learning in school was how to pass the English Regents with a tight, five-paragraph essay. I craved the opportunity to work on my scripts in a supportive space—or to even just hear my dialogue read aloud. The courses were offered for free to public high school students through the Department of Education's College Now program, and any credits earned transferred to the college of their choice once they enrolled. That's where I first met my mentor, Jackie Acevedo, who taught the Intro to Screenwriting elective I took on Saturday mornings. She wore a head wrap and kept a small diamond stud in her left nostril. She quoted Biggie and grew up in Brooklyn, and it was a revelation to see someone who felt like home at the front of a classroom. We knew so many of our high school teachers drove into Queens from Long Island or Westchester, because they complained about it often.

When it was my turn to workshop my first script, the class was silent and the normally boisterous Professor Acevedo clasped her hands together against her chest and spoke tenderly.

"Have you taken writing classes before?" she asked.

"No," I answered, scratching my cheek, nervous that I was somehow in trouble. "I mean, regular English class. In school."

She placed the script down on her desk.

"You have a good ear," she said. "You're a gifted writer."

No teacher—no adult—had ever acknowledged my writing before. Mami was supportive in that she thought writing was a good exercise that would translate to SAT scores and college acceptance letters, but beyond that, considered it a hobby and nothing more. My high school English teachers consistently scored my essays at a B-, and one even gave me a zero once. But Professor Acevedo saw me. She got me. I couldn't wait to immerse myself in the collegiate world full-time.

I began meeting with Professor Acevedo for one-on-one sessions during office hours and made the decision to apply to Hunter

College because she had accepted a position there in the English Department.

"So, I don't get it," Kelly had said to me one spring morning after she met me at Central Park halfway on my commute home from City College. "Are you like a college student already?"

"No," I said, as we walked through Sheep Meadow, on our way to the 7 Train for a day game at Shea. "I'm just taking, like, an extracurricular class now. For my TV stuff. I guess I might be able to graduate earlier if my credits count. We'll see."

I elbowed her. "Start my real life already, like you."

She plucked Gucci sunglasses out of her purse and slipped them on, without mentioning how much of her Auntie Anne's paycheck they cost her after picking up her portion of the slack on Frances's mortgage and utility bills.

"Damn," she chuckled, unwrapping the plastic on a new pack of Camels. "You're going to be outta here so much quicker than I am."

I frowned.

"Why would I want to leave *New York*?"

I held my arms wide and spun in the meadow, making sure not to step on sunbathing limbs outstretched on beach towels, gesturing to the towers of glass that leered above the trees on all sides.

"This?" I emphasized, looking straight up at the confectionary-blue sky. "Why would I want to leave this?"

She threw the crumpled cellophane at my face, but it floated past me and landed on a man's reddening bare back.

Kelly's eyes grew wide.

"Run!"

She tossed her cigarettes back in her bag and grabbed my hand.

The air, sweet with pollen, burned our lungs as we laughed, laughed up at the sun we'd missed for what felt like an eternity. Running together, hopping over Converse sneakers and wine bottles, breath trapped painfully in our sides, it felt like the two of us were finally back together the way it always should have been, before bills, and boyfriends, and Brian.

OCTOBER 2006

Kelly and I blocked off Friday afternoon to shop for decorations at the Party City on Fourteenth Street. We planned to throw a Halloween fund-raiser to help cover Brian's legal fees. With Frances upstate and Andrés in Colombia, Kelly lived with her older brother alone in that yellow house on Clement Moore Avenue, so we figured we'd host it there, free of any adult presence or intervention, as we still weren't twenty-one ourselves.

I wasn't so concerned about Kelly and Brian anymore. He had, after all, come to me. Brian's assault charge actually brought Kelly and me closer together.

"This rich fucking bitch," Kelly had muttered when I broke the news to her on the 7 Train. "They always go after the wrong ones."

I leaned against her to make room for people to exit, as the doors opened onto the platform at 52nd Street.

"Right," I said. "Right? It's just a misunderstanding."

"To say the least." Kelly looked up at the blinking light at 61st Street Woodside on the subway map.

"He'd never do that," she said, shaking her head. "I mean, he can be a dirtbag, but he doesn't . . ." She met my gaze. "You know he's not like that."

"Of course," I said.

"So how do we help him?"

We would throw a party and charge a cover at the door to help Brian afford to hire someone—anyone—better than a crooked Roosie lawyer. We weren't alone in supporting him, either: the local community showed up, too. Sandro donated heros from his bodega to the party, teachers from our old school banded together to write letters attesting to Brian's character. Brian was a local star athlete they had all watched grow up, had all been charmed by, who was accused of, according to our old history teacher, partying too hard on a college campus. They knew him to keep his nose clean, to be generous with his time, helping out after school and on weekends. So many had hired him to privately coach their own kids when they knew Brian needed the money. I eavesdropped on a phone call Brian took from his former coach Yadiel and heard him tell Brian he *thought* he knew better than to not be careful around white girls. It was almost a joke.

St. Agnes took up a special plate to collect donations for his legal bills, but once the *Queens Gazette* ran his mug shot alongside a small blurb about his arrest, characterizing it as his fall from grace as one of the best catchers in the Public Schools Athletic League— "The pride of Woodside turned predator," they wrote—no one heard from St. Agnes again.

"Can you believe this?" I smacked the paper against Kelly's chest. "The 'pride of Woodside'? How'd they even find out?"

Kelly folded the paper and deposited it in the trash can inside the doors of Party City.

"It's public information, I guess," she said. I was reminded of Frances and how it felt like so much of her battle with the justice system happened in silence, as if on a different AM channel I could never tune in to. Kelly had laughed when she first told me Frances had been sentenced. "She got what was coming to her," she'd said with a shrug—and then never talked ill of her again.

Kelly shook her head and picked up a red shopping basket.

"Who reads the *Gazette* anyway?" she asked. "Early-bird senior citizens at Georgia Diner?"

I picked up my own basket and followed her down the aisle. "This could screw up his scholarship."

"He better hope not," Kelly said over her shoulder. "The kid is dumb as rocks."

I laughed.

"That's not true."

Kelly smiled and pointed toward the back of the store. "C'mon, the adult costumes are over there."

Back in high school, Mami had volunteered me to write alumni updates for the St. Agnes church bulletin twice a year ("¿Qué, qué?" she'd cried. "You like to write, so write!"), and that's how we first learned that Brian had accepted a full baseball scholarship to St. John's University and Pablo had enlisted in the army. Kelly, who didn't want me to include that she was enrolled at LaGuardia, dared me to report that she was working four nights a week at Riviera (which was true, she'd begun bartending there then). That was the last church bulletin I was invited to work on.

"Are you dressing up?" Kelly asked.

"Yeah," I answered. "Maybe a nurse, I was thinking?"

"Like, a sexy nurse, or are you really thinking about showing up in your mom's scrubs to my party?"

I laughed, holding up the round end of a plastic stethoscope to Kelly's face.

"Undecided," I said. "What about you?"

She shrugged, surveying the wall of costumes before us. "I think I might just dress up as a witch again."

"Boring," I said. "Halloween is supposed to be about putting on a costume!" I put the stethoscope back on the rack. "Not showing up as something you *are* every other day of the year."

She smacked me with the hand of a plastic skeleton hanging in front of her.

"Shut up," she said with a smirk. "Not all of us have the imagination of a Hollywood screenwriter, okay?"

She peeked at me out of the corner of her eye. I detected both pride and pain in the tone of her voice. It was a mixture I was intimately familiar with and actively avoided acknowledging; our friendship was a ballet on broken eggshells.

I fingered the thin polyester material of a short, white nurse's outfit, a plastic red cross emblazoned on the chest. The sheen of the white fabric reminded me of the iridescent baby tees we used to wear the summer I got my first period at St. Agnes's. I yearned to go back to that time, to that Fugees record and the way we danced home in defiance, together and alone, against the world. Sometimes I was overwhelmed by the longing to start over, to hit refresh.

"You sure you're cool with this?" I asked. "Raising money for Brian?"

"Of course," she answered, a little too quickly. "He's in a shitty situation."

"Yeah," I said. "But I just mean, there's kind of been some bad blood between you two ever since . . ."

She glanced at me, a nervous blink.

"That's in the past," she said, picking up a glittery pumpkin stress ball. "Right?"

I nodded, reaching to pick up a red latex glove, then thought better of it. "Is it?"

Kelly tossed the stress ball into the pit with the others and turned to face me.

"We were idiot kids, Brisma," she said. "We didn't know no better."

I tugged the strap of my purse tighter across my chest, not sure if I agreed with the blanket lack of responsibility she implied.

"But what I *do* know—" She grabbed the wrist that held on to my purse. "What *we* know is men who really are monsters. And Brian isn't one of them. He's one of us."

I took a deep breath and sighed, looking up at the masks that lined the aisle, gory wounds and rotting flesh.

"It's messed up," was all I could muster.

"Word," she said. "And this bitch had the gall to bring in the cops, too?"

"I know," I said with a tightening in my chest, like I was about to jump off the diving board at Astoria Pool. "Can you imagine running to the cops every time a dude tried to feel up on you?

"Or," I continued as I slammed the nurse's costume back on the hook, "never mind that—bringing home a guy and then acting like you never met him before?"

Kelly laughed.

"You right," she said. "She brought him back there. She took her clothes off!"

"I mean," I said, "no doubt, he should have left that damn watch alone. Forget about, what? Forty-five bucks? He shouldn't have gone back, but for her to feign not even knowing him?"

Kelly pursed her lips at me and turned around the corner to the next aisle.

"She's an entitled bitch!" her disembodied voice called out.

I nodded, yet something nagged at me as we piled onto this girl we'd never met and really knew nothing else about. I felt a rage at the base of my spine heat the blood coursing through my body. I had a difficult time wrapping my mind around how anyone—any woman—could feel they had any right to bring the law into that situation. We all had bad experiences with men. Why was she different? Had she lived such a privileged life free of men's desires and discretions up to that point? Was she too sheltered to know how to handle men? How dare she feel entitled to be treated any other way? Who did she think she was?

In the next aisle, I watched Kelly finger a rack of neon-colored feather boas.

"Have you hooked up with him?" I asked.

Kelly cleared her throat and smoothed a single feather in her hand without looking up at me.

"Brisma, I thought we moved past this," she said.

"Recently, I mean," I said.

Kelly chuckled, her tongue jutting out under her two front teeth, a pitying sound meant to make me feel small for asking.

"Of course not," she emphasized, hooking some Mardi Gras beads delicately around the head of a metal rack. "But, I mean . . . does it even matter? You two aren't together."

I hated that she didn't ask, that she stated it as fact.

"No!" I frowned, embarrassed at how upset I was. "We're not."

She smiled at me, her eyes vacant, locking into a robotic expression light-years from any emotional reality between us.

"Good," she said, fingering the hem of a tulle fairy tutu.

"Brian might not even come tomorrow night, you know." I shook my head. "He might be embarrassed about needing the money."

Kelly held out a She-Devil costume at arm's length, appraising the red, jagged edges of the short dress.

"He'll come," she confidently told the red sequins of the bodice.

"Hey," she said, turning to me, holding the dress against her torso. "What if we do a couple's costume?" she asked, scratching at a strand of hair that had fallen across her eye. "You and me?"

I laughed.

"You want us both to be witches again? Haven't we played that out yet?"

"No," she said, her eyes bright. "We trade the tired old coven in to go as an angel and a devil this time."

"I don't know." I shrugged. "Isn't that kind of tacky?"

"Since when have we ever worried about being tacky?" Kelly spat.

She slung the devil costume over her shoulder and took a few steps down the aisle toward the register.

"You don't have to be an angel, I guess," she said with a shrug. "It was just an idea."

She swung her hips over to the line at the register, leaving me holding the red basket of orange-and-black streamers, Butterfingers, and pipe-cleaner bats. I resented that she expected I'd play the virginal angel, the Goody Two-Shoes, the good conscience. I wanted to be reckless, too. I wanted eyes on me, I wanted men to feel like they needed to have me. It came so easily to Kelly.

I sighed, looking up at the wall of costumes. I needed an outfit that would place me squarely inside my body. Get me out of my head. Like Kelly's devil costume, something dangerous and sexy.

A pair of bright blue shorts caught my eye behind a "Sexy Winnie the Pooh" costume. I peeled the yellow fur away to reveal a Wonder Woman costume: blue bottoms with white stars on them, a red bustier, and a gold belt. High red boots and a crown. This was it. This could work. I remembered those days Brian and I would spend toiling away in his apartment when we should have been in school, turning on TNT in the afternoons, watching old reruns of Lynda Carter as Wonder Woman.

"Now, that is a sexy woman," I remembered him saying, pointing at the TV with the remote in his hand.

"She's beautiful," I agreed. *"You know she's Mexican?"*

Brian had frowned, sitting up in the sheets.

"No way," he'd said. *"She's hot."*

I remember I'd pulled the sheets up and tucked them under my arms, staying still and quiet.

I lifted the costume off the metal hook and checked the price. I imagined walking around the party Saturday night, how Brian would look at me as I bent over to refill drinks in red Solo cups.

A whistle brought me out of my reverie.

"Skee-yu," Kelly sang from where she stood at the register, first in line.

I dropped the Wonder Woman costume in the basket, placed it underneath a bag of cotton spiderwebs, hoping Kelly wouldn't notice it just yet, and made my way up to the front of the store.

2001

Once Kelly and I told Maritza, the owner of Caridad del Cobre, that we weren't interested in a palm reading, she led us behind a door plastered with two solemn silhouettes of the Twin Towers, past rows of bleeding Jesuses and flaming hearts, to the back wall of the botánica. "True Heart or Elemental Storm?" Maritza asked in perfect English, the words hard and round in her mouth without the music of her Spanish.

It was Halloween, only a few weeks after Pablo's terrible party, and Kelly and I weren't totally dressed in costume—she wore a black choker with a plastic spider dangling on her chest, and I wore a black dress with striped orange tights underneath—but it was enough to prompt a few eye rolls from Maritza, who Kelly knew through Frances's short-lived career as a tattoo artist. Kelly thought it was a good idea to use the holiday as an excuse for us to go buy our first deck of tarot cards.

"It's a full moon!" she'd said on the phone. "Do you know what that means?"

"No," I'd said with a frown, still mourning the plans I'd made with Brian to go to a haunted house in Astoria.

"It's very rare," she'd said. "But good for us—good to take back some power. Reclaim our bruja."

I didn't really believe in that stuff anymore, but I was eager to encourage her excitement in anything after her experience with Nicky. I followed Kelly after school up Roosevelt to this botánica sandwiched between Mami's dry cleaner and a check-cashing spot on the corner, where girls posted up after dark. Kelly leaned on the glass countertop and pointed to a deck that pictured a man wielding two large axes over his head.

"Can I see that one?"

Maritza shook her head, her cascading gold earrings bouncing against her cheeks. I didn't blame her for being exasperated by two broke teens, when she could be out on her folding chair on the stoop of the shop, trying to lure in some better customers on what was probably a busy night for her.

"No," she said. "That's Changó. Not for you."

"Oh yeah?" Kelly laughed, glancing at me. She'd recently chopped her hair short into a pixie cut that made her look devastatingly chic in a way I always wished I could pull off. "Which one is for us, then?"

"The two of you?" Maritza asked. "You can't share, you know. Each woman needs her own deck."

I looked at the mechanical waving lucky cat facing the entrance, where the front page of the *Daily News* hung, featuring a photo of Osama bin Laden with the word WANTED printed above it. It was everywhere, in every shop window along Roosevelt, especially the South Asian ones, hoping to be spared from cops and racist vigilantes with any big ideas. I elbowed Kelly.

"Maybe we should forget about this," I said. "Rent a movie instead."

"Nah," Kelly told Maritza. "We're a package deal."

Maritza raised her eyebrows and sucked her teeth.

"Yin and yang." She sighed, digging out a box from behind the counter and placing a black-and-white deck in front of us.

"Light," she said, as she placed an open palm between us before flipping it over, revealing a rosary tattooed across her wrist. "And dark."

She pushed the deck towards us with a tight smile.

"You can't have one without the other."

When I handed Maritza the two tens from my wallet, she reached for them but grabbed my wrist.

"You sure you don't want a reading?" She traced a line running across my palm. "You might be surprised."

I looked at Kelly, who was stuffing the deck into her backpack.

"Don't be weird, Maritza," she said, flicking Maritza's arm. "Let her go."

But Maritza just looked at me. Uncomfortable, I nodded toward her empty hand, resting on the counter.

"Did Frances do that?" I asked.

Maritza looked down and laughed, finally letting me go. She scratched the black ink on her wrist and tugged on the sleeve of her brown sweater.

"Frances wishes," she said to Kelly, who was already walking toward the door. "The janky rose she did for me faded within a year."

Kelly shot up two fingers without turning around and bellowed, "Deuces."

"What do you think she saw in my hand?" I asked inside the dry cleaner's next door, as we waited for the cashier to locate the only skirt suit Mami owned. Mary Kay business had been drying up even before 9/11, and she was planning on attending a seminar that weekend to learn how to adjust to the new economy. A 7 Train roared by on the tracks overhead, drowning out the sound of the television replaying George W. Bush's first pitch at the Yankees' first World Series home game the night before.

Kelly waved her hand.

"The usual," she shouted to be heard. "Big love, big money, big success. The Yankees hopefully about to lose the series."

She unwrapped a pack of Starburst and dropped a pink one into my hand.

"Just kidding. They never give you a bad reading. Never tell you the truth."

I lifted the backpack off her shoulders and let it drop back heavily.

"So why'd we buy a deck from her?"

"If *we* learn the cards," she explained, "then we're in control. We know the truth."

I laid the cellophane-wrapped suit over my arm, and we walked back out onto the gum-stained Roosevelt sidewalk. She hooked her arm through my free one and rested her head on my shoulder. I'd missed her, I realized, like a memory-foam mattress; we fit together. Yin and yang.

"Not gonna trust my fate in anybody else's hands," she said.

OCTOBER 2006

Kelly and I spent Saturday afternoon stringing up the entrance hallway with orange jack-o'-lantern lights and glittering calaveras. Kelly had dated a Mexican coworker at Auntie Anne's, who had taught her how to paint her face into a flowering skull.

"Do I look right?" she asked, smudging charcoal along the line of her widow's peak. "Or is this encroaching, like, blackface territory?"

"Nah," I said, touching up her mascaraed lashes with the edge of a Q-tip. "You look good."

"Come here then!" She grabbed both of my hands in hers and smiled, her excited face ghoulish under the skeletal makeup. "I want to show you something."

She guided me down to the basement, which felt like it had been preserved in amber from our childhood: handed-down strollers still piled in an abandoned heap at the bottom of the stairs, the air still wet with the scent of mildew and watery detergent from the 99 Cents Store.

She plucked something off the floor and held it taut across her chest.

"For me?" I asked.

"Yeah," she said. "It's a lasso. Wonder Woman had one."

I reached for the rope in her hands. It was spray-painted gold, but

I recognized it from our childhood as the rope we used to learn how to double Dutch with the Indian girls down the block.

"Look at you!" I spun the dangling rope in circles two feet off the ground between us. "Getting all crafty."

Kelly beamed.

"I didn't know you had it in you."

"Well," she said, "what can I say? I get it from my momma."

We laughed, but I didn't really know what she meant. Sure, Frances had designed tattoos for a while, but other than that, the house was falling apart around them. I tucked the lasso into my belt.

"I miss playing double Dutch," I said. "Remember you used to be so short you had to stand on a mail crate to turn the rope?"

Kelly grabbed my forearm for balance as she slipped into a pair of black pumps to complete her outfit.

"Ha, ha," she said, towering over me. "Who's laughing now?"

We ribbed each other all the time back then, but Kelly was the best jumper on the block, even if she did have to stand on a box to give my tall self clearance to play. She wouldn't let anyone else take a jab at me as I struggled to keep up though, and she kept a water gun in her back pocket to squirt anyone who dared.

"I didn't know Halloween was a gift-giving type of holiday now. I didn't get you anything," I laughed.

"Don't worry about it," she said. "You'll get me next time."

∽

I set up on a wooden stool just outside Kelly's front door. I was tasked with collecting the suggested ten-dollar donations at the door, while Kelly and I agreed she was more suited to welcoming guests and tending bar inside. It didn't take long sitting still in the cool autumn evening for me to begin shivering underneath my cape, but I warmed up as more people arrived, blood pumping hotter through my veins at every new crunch of leaves. With each new guest, with each new scrape of a boot, high heel, or Roman-esque sandal against the cluttered concrete, my heart leapt at the possibility that it was Brian. It wasn't excitement though, I realized. It was nerves.

I was impressed with the turnout, and I knew Kelly would be, too. She had implemented a mandatory costume rule, one of her big-gest pet peeves being when people refused to participate in a theme because they thought they were too cool or above it somehow. For the most part, everyone showed up in costume, except for one kid who barely got a pass, turning up in an I ♥ NY T-shirt and claiming to be dressed as a tourist.

After a brief lull at the door, a shadow wearing a long black cape stepped gingerly down the stairs. He wore polished black dress shoes that shone in the light of the streetlamps, and which, I could tell from where I sat, must have been at least two sizes too big for him. It was Pablo, but the shoes must have belonged to his older brother. At ground level, he turned back up to the railing and extended a white-gloved hand to help a girl wearing a red mop on her head down the steps.

"And who are you?" I asked, uncurling my lasso to hang like a whip at my side. "The Count from Sesame Street?"

The red mop blinked at me behind large painted-on freckles be-fore laughing.

"Oh, she got jokes," she said. Her teeth were like Chiclets, round and fat in her mouth. She turned to Pablo. "She's funny!"

Pablo lifted a white half-mask that had been hanging off the back of his neck up and over toward me for inspection.

"Phantom of the Opera."

"And who's this?" I asked, nodding at the girl's wig. "The janitor of the opera?"

"Mm-hmm, I'll let that one slide," she said, fingering the rope of her wig, "cuz I know you know I'm dressed as Raggedy Ann."

I looked at Pablo and back at Raggedy Ann, the white petticoat beneath her blue skirt barely covering the tops of her thighs.

"Oh," I exhaled before mumbling under my breath, "*Raggedy Ann does Hunts Point* is more like it."

"How long do we have to be here again?" she asked, as she turned to Pablo, who placed a gloved hand on her shoulder.

"Not too long," he assured her. "I promise."

She sighed and shook her head at me.

"Just point me to the beer," she said.

I opened the door with a loud whine and let it bang against my heel.

"Straight back and into the kitchen," I said, before closing the door behind her.

"And who are you tonight?" Pablo gestured toward my blue briefs. "RuPaul?"

"Close!" I smiled and smacked my lasso across his forearm. "Wonder Woman."

Pablo nodded in acknowledgment and reached for the thin metal handle on the screen door. I stomped it closed with the toe of my red knee-high boot, jerking it from the grasp of his white gloves.

"Forgetting something?"

I extended the extra-large wallet toward him, open, and tapped my long fingernail against the Velcro button on the front.

"Oh, I'm not here for Brian," Pablo said.

I repositioned my foot against the front door of Kelly's house.

"Brian is literally the entire point of this party," I said, shaking the wallet at him.

Pablo rolled his eyes and made a production out of lifting his cape and taking off his gloves to reach inside his pocket from which he produced two crisp ten-dollar bills.

I nudged the door back open with my elbow and nodded him in. A cardboard skeleton with gold-clasped joints rattled against the inside of the window screen.

Pablo took a few steps before pausing to turn back toward me with a serious look on his face. The same look from the night he walked me home.

"Brisma, can we—"

"Hey there!" I waved to a fairy and a bee hopping down the steps. "Welcome to the party!"

I leaned into the hallway inside, and Pablo took a step closer to hear me better.

"Night's young," I said to him. "No need to ruin it so soon."

And with that I slammed the door shut on its hinges, leaving him a silhouette of a cape inside the dark hallway adorned with tiny, glowing jack-o'-lanterns.

Brian turned the corner just then, fashionably late to his own fund-raiser. He was dressed as Frankenstein, his face painted a bright green, his hair patted down with gel over his eyebrows.

"The man of the hour!" I held out my arm to embrace him.

He wrapped himself around me tightly and nudged my hair with his nose. He smelled nice. I wished he didn't. Vanilla and coconut, and fresh laundry. I felt my muscles stiffen against him.

He pulled back to look at me and bit his lip.

"Are there a lot of people in there?"

"Yeah." I patted his arm. "Tons. It's a great turnout."

He stared off to the right of me, his head tilted toward the traffic on the street above. He hadn't let go of my hip. In fact, with the nail of his middle finger, he was lightly tracing the hem of the high-cut brief where it met my stockings.

"What if we bounced?" He gave me a squeeze. "Cut out of here, just you and me?"

"What?" I laughed and stepped back out of his embrace. "That's crazy, everyone's here for you. It's your fund-raiser."

He nodded, shuffling his feet.

"Yeah." He sniffed. "Thank you so much, you know. For doing this for me."

"Of course," I said, hoping my fake eyelashes didn't look as crooked as they felt. "It's the least we can do. We want you to have the best shot in court."

He winced, and I regretted mentioning the word "court." It wasn't a foregone conclusion yet that this would go to trial; getting him a good lawyer was the first step in trying to avoid that very outcome.

The grimace was fleeting, though. His eyes brightened again, and he was back to himself, taking a half step back to appraise my costume. "You look amazing."

I slid his hand off my hip and struck a pose. "Wonder Woman!" I sang out, cupping my right hand at my lips.

Brian laughed and stepped closer again, his lips grazing my cheek as he spoke.

"I was this close to being Superman this year."

I could smell brown liquor on his breath, which meant he'd pre-gamed before showing up to our party. I hardly blamed him. But if he'd pre-gamed, who had he done it with, and why weren't they arriving with him?

"Are your teammates coming?" I asked, taking a seat on the stool.

"No doubt," he said, scratching the tip of his nose and smudging his green makeup. "No doubt," he repeated. "They're on their way."

His distracted eyes locked on mine once again, and I recognized the familiar sparkle in them.

"Why?" he asked with a smirk. "You interested in someone?" He leaned on the brick fence beside me. "I could hook you up maybe with Joel Tejeda—"

"Nah," I said, as I patted his chest beneath the Frankenstein blazer. "I'm good. Just trying to get an estimate of our potential proceeds here." I held up the wallet, its synthetic leather cool and smooth in my hand.

He kissed me on the cheek again, grabbing my chin to do so.

"You're the best," he said. "You always were. No lie. Since we were kids."

I tried to muster an awkward smile and pulled open the screen door for him. I thought it was weird anytime he referenced our past as kids together. Kids not knowing any better. Kids going down on each other. I didn't consider the bulk of our past together juvenile, something embarrassing, and fleeting, and misguided, and I wished he didn't, either.

"Whoa," he said, as he gestured toward the lights, and the skeleton, and the tiny gourds we'd collected from the bodega on Broadway and piled in a basket on a small side table. "You guys went all out!"

I welcomed him inside with an arm pointing toward the back.

"Kelly will be glad to see you at the bar we've set up in the kitchen down the hall."

He smiled at me. That sparkle again.

"Yeah," he said. "I remember."

He snapped his head back quickly toward the direction of the kitchen, and one of the black foam bolts he'd adhered to his neck popped off and bounced against my shield.

What a mess, I thought. *What a metaphor.*

☙

During my time at the door, I welcomed the only two of Brian's teammates who'd come to support him: a mixed kid with blond curls who smelled like milk and baby powder and a Dominican named Rafa, who attempted to dance bachata with every Disney princess in the room. While the majority of the Mets team was Latino that year, St. John's certainly wasn't, and I found it interesting that these couple kids of color were Brian's only teammates to show up. I tapped Rafa on the shoulder to ask when the others would be arriving, and he shrugged.

"You know how they are," he said, as he leaned in. "They can't be bothered with this shit."

He was close enough that I could smell vanilla bourbon underneath his minty aftershave.

"One of their teammates being accused of sexual assault?" I asked.

Rafa lowered his drink and pursed his lips as if to shush me.

"Look," he said, "I know Brian was some big shot over here on your little block. But these folks don't care."

He took a swig of his beer.

"To them, he's just another dirty spic they wish would clean up his own mess."

"Got it," I said, pouring myself a cranberry vodka. Maybe that was why Brian was so dismayed about his future in baseball that night we were on the beach. Maybe he felt he was in over his head in more ways than one, even before the accusation. I hadn't had more than a sip of my drink before I noticed Kelly and Brian dancing together in the strobe-lit living room. His green hands were ultraviolet in the black light against her red fishnets.

I felt a jail-cell slam of anger and nerves hit my gut. I downed the rest of my drink and tossed my plastic cup in the sink. I started over toward them on the dance floor when Pablo cut me off with a white glove to my chest.

"Hey," he said. His mask hung slack on its cheap rubber band around his neck. "Is this a good time to talk?"

I shifted my weight onto my back leg and rested my hands on my hips.

"Does it look like it?"

"Well, it never looks like it," he said. "That's why I'm asking nicely."

I kept my eyes trained on Brian and Kelly on the dance floor while we talked. I sensed Pablo following my line of sight, before he grabbed my wrist gently.

"Let's go outside for a minute."

He tugged on my arm, but I refused to budge, and instead looked at his hand on my wrist as if it were an insect.

"Come on," he said.

I took another glance inside the living room and back toward Pablo at the threshold before following him through the open door.

༄

Pablo brought me out back where people were smoking and making out in dark corners. From our vantage point at the top of the stoop, I could see the tall weeds swaying in the moonlight in the spot where Kelly and I used to hide in the abandoned lot next door.

"Another house party," I said. "Another backyard."

Pablo exhaled loudly as he hopped up to sit on the brick ledge.

"Brisma," he said, his voice pained, "I apologized for that."

The fabric of his gloves gleamed white in the dark evening light, as his hands grasped each of his knees, legs spread wide apart.

"But," he continued, snapping the mask up and off his neck, "do you ever wonder why it is you give Brian a pass for that night?"

I inhaled.

"Do we have to do this again?"

"Yes," he said. "Because we've never actually done it, Brisma." He scratched his collarbone where the string of his cape rested. "It's an honest question. Why do you have such a blind spot for him?"

"I'm not blind," I said, staring past him toward the abandoned lot. "I know who he is. I know he's a dog."

I turned back to look at Pablo.

"But it wasn't his idea," I said, referring to Pablo's backyard dare years before. "It was yours."

"It was my dare," Pablo agreed. "But it was his encouragement. His hand on your neck. It's not like he declined."

"Because what guy would turn down a blow job?" I asked too loudly. A few wigs at the bottom of the steps turned to look up, eyes boring into us from behind deeply parted hair and swooping bangs.

"Besides," I continued, anger curling my fingers into fists. "Wasn't it one of your dares that Nicky made good on that night, too?"

Pablo frowned, putting his drink down on the brick pony wall.

"Nicky?" he asked.

The heavy curtain of shame I'd been carrying about that night crashed down on me once again, and I cringed. I had said too much—more than I'd ever dared to before.

"Never mind," I said, hugging my elbows close.

Pablo leaned back to peer in the kitchen window at the party roaring on inside.

"You have to know," he said quietly. "Brian did it."

"Here we go again," I said, throwing my hands in the air.

"No," he continued. "I mean, Brian's guilty. I don't know for sure about this Sacred Heart girl . . . and that's not really my lane. I can't speak for what went down up there, but I do know he's done shit like that before. With other girls." He cleared his throat. "With you," he added.

"Now I really don't know what you're talking about, Pablo." I twisted the cubic zirconia stud in my earlobe, grateful for the sharp scratch of the post grounding me in the moment.

"He never *attacked* me," I said. "I'm no victim."

"Ashley says she was."

I massaged my temples with my fingers.

"Who the fuck is Ashley?" I exclaimed, shifting the wristlet containing the night's bounty higher up on my forearm.

"Raggedy Ann," he said. "My date."

"Ho-kay," I said as I inhaled. "So you want me to believe this rag doll you dragged in here with you tonight? That's your proof? She's your witness?"

I saw Pablo recoil, his torso tight and shoulders rounded in his seat. "Why are you so angry?"

"Because I don't know why you are so intent on pushing this Latino predator bullshit!" I slapped the wallet down onto the ledge beside him. "I don't know why you ain't defending your boy. We all grew up with him, for Christ's sake. He's one of us. Don't you know how dangerous this is? Are you trying to ruin his life?"

I braced myself against the brick, forcing myself to breathe. I could feel the evening breeze on my skin through my tights, but the emotions and the vodka coursing through my veins were keeping me warm for the moment.

Pablo cleared his throat.

"There are tapes."

I cocked an eyebrow at Pablo beside me.

"What?"

"There are tapes." He cleared his throat again. "He'd film himself with girls and show it to us afterward. Sometimes the girls knew. Sometimes they didn't."

Pablo's eyes flitted toward me briefly, but he looked away just as quickly.

"You didn't, I guess."

I felt the rage inside me turn my body the color of my bustier. The anger boiled my blood to the surface of my skin, burning through melanin, flushing my cheeks. I pressed my hollow plastic shield to Pablo's chest, nearly knocking him off the ledge.

"The fuck you talking about, 'I didn't'?"

Pablo raised his gloved hands in protest, but continued.

"Look, I'm telling you this because I want to make things right with you, Brisma. I know shit was weird—"

"Start talking, Pablo." I slammed the shield on the ledge beside him. "What you mean, 'I didn't know'?"

"He hid a camera in his bookshelf. He showed it to me once. Between his mom's ceramic giraffe and some thick-ass dictionary. He . . ." Pablo lifted his arms to slip the mask back on over his hairline, a nervous tic he'd developed for the evening, a conversational filler for when he didn't want to have to say what came next.

"I think it was the first time you ever had sex."

I laughed.

"You're lying," I said. "We never really had sex. Not full-on."

"No," Pablo said gently. "I know. I mean . . . I saw."

My breath caught inside my throat as a deeply buried memory began to surface through the vodka and the cloying artificial sweetness of the cranberry. The night after the Nuyorican.

"He had put on a condom," Pablo continued. "He tried to put . . ." He watched me, studied my face for a reaction, for recognition. "But—"

I held my hand up to signal him to stop.

"You saw it?"

Pablo nodded, his lips folded in on each other in a neat line.

"Why didn't you tell me?" I asked. "Sooner, I mean. Why didn't you tell me sooner than this?"

Pablo shrugged.

"We were kids," he said. That word again, "kids." "I was an asshole back then. I've copped to that. I wanted . . ." He sighed. "I wanted to be cool? If I'm honest, I was curious, and horned up, and just wanted to be cool."

I gripped the lasso hanging off my belt that Kelly had given me, the fibers of the rope burning the skin of my palm as I twisted it in my hand.

"Plus, after a while, I thought it might have been the kinder thing to do," he said, pinching a fingertip on his left glove. "To not tell you. I thought you'd feel embarrassed if I did."

I wanted to push him straight back again, watch his legs fly up into the air as he tumbled down the stoop. It wasn't high enough to kill him—but it might break a bone.

I imagined Brian showing the videos to his friends. How long did he keep them? Did he have a library? How did his parents not know—his mom? I imagined all those boys looking at my body, pressing pause on a clear shot of my breasts, large and unruly—conspicuous to say the least—that he claimed to have loved despite the porn he showed me, the porn filled with skinny European coeds, nipples pink and proper, translucent as their skin. I had so wanted to please him, to keep him. But I remembered that day, I remembered that it was just too painful to continue and so I made him stop. I wondered if he would have still showed it to his buddies if I had let him continue, if I had successfully passed some kind of test. But of course, I knew the answer.

"I didn't think . . ." Pablo said, looking up at the window. "I thought Brian would eventually grow up, and this would all just fade away and be forgotten. I didn't think he'd still be doing this type of dumb shit with girls."

He shook his head, turning back to me.

"He did it to Ashley, too," Pablo said.

It took me a moment to reorient myself in the current year, to pull my brain out of that evening in 2001 and remember Raggedy Ann, remember I was still talking to Pablo at this Halloween party fund-raiser for Brian to fight charges of sexual assault.

"You're all monsters," I muttered.

"Ashley knew she was being filmed," Pablo said. "Consented to him holding the camcorder while they—"

I could tell he was about to say "fucked" but stopped himself short.

"But," he said as he scratched at his throat, the cape rubbing against his stubble again. "But he was rough with her."

"I don't want to hear this."

"You have to."

"I don't have to do nothing," I yelled and turned to walk back inside.

"Think about it," Pablo called after me. "You know it's true. You know he's not some innocent scapegoat."

I paused at the door.

"So why are you putting this on me?" I cried, my arms flailing at my sides. "Why don't you go to the police with these fucking tapes? Why doesn't"—I hooked my fingers in air quotes—"'Ashley'? Why is she even here?"

"I thought you might believe her, if not me. Besides," he said as he adjusted the mask on his forehead, "we don't have the tapes. And I told you, I'm not trying to get involved like that."

I laughed and felt the bitter acid of citrus and alcohol rise in my throat.

"Yeah, you're really minding your own business here."

"No," he said. "You don't understand. I can't. I'm on Article 15. I need to lay low."

I frowned at him, losing my patience.

"Am I supposed to know what that is?"

"It's kind of like probation," he offered.

"From the army?" I shouted again, too loudly.

Pablo sighed.

"I fought a guy," he said. "My sergeant. He was being inappropriate with a little girl in Fallujah. A civilian."

He wasn't looking at me but at the sparkling brick beneath us.

"She was just a kid," he said, shrugging.

"Just a kid," I repeated.

I bit my lip, until Pablo raised his head to look at me again.

"So was I," I said and stormed back into the kitchen.

It's frightening what we choose to remember and what we choose to forget, I thought, scanning the rows of liquor bottles on the table. The pieces of our lives we cherry-pick to form our identities along the way—different pinches of clay molded together to create a new thing entirely. How quickly we discard whole fragments of ourselves to survive inside these newly formed beings.

I poured myself a shot of vodka at the sink and knocked it back. Someone had lit a blunt and was passing it around the living room. I could still make out Brian and Kelly on the dance floor. His nose was buried in her neck, and she had wrapped her leg up and around his hip. This time I had no one to stop me.

I charged toward them and tapped Kelly on the shoulder, but she didn't seem to feel it.

"Hey," I shouted in her ear. "Can I talk to you?"

She broke apart from Brian to face me and swayed like a sequoia above me. Her eyelids were too heavy to open all the way. She sloppily struck her arm out to push my face away, which only infuriated me more.

"I'm serious," I said, pinching the flesh of her upper arm.

"Ow!"

I grabbed her arm again and yanked her away, not looking at Brian once.

"Let's go."

❦

I pulled her along as far as I could, only halfway up the stairs. She was rabid, twisting her arm out of my grasp. I was afraid she might pop her shoulder out.

"Let me go, bitch!"

It wasn't the way she normally called me bitch. This "bitch" meant psycho.

"We need to talk."

I made my eyes wide, hoping she would see the deeper urgency in them without me having to spell it out there in front of everyone.

"You are such a child," she whined, as she stomped up the stairs past me.

"Look," I said, sliding shut the door to the ramshackle balcony off her mother's bedroom. I exhaled. "Do you think he could have done it?"

Kelly dug a finger in her ear.

"Who?"

"You know I'm talking about Brian," I said. "Do you think he meant to do something more than he did? With the girl in Connecticut?"

"What?" She frowned and flung her arms in the air, exasperated. "What is this you're on about all of a sudden, Brisma?" Her eyes were clear and alive now, bubbling with a long-simmering rage under her calavera makeup.

"Are we not hosting a fucking fund-raiser for him right now? Is he not someone we've known our entire lives?" She gripped the metal railing, still wrapped in multicolored Christmas lights from the year before. "What kind of question is that?"

I shrugged.

"An important one."

I watched Kelly purse her lips together and relax, rearranging the muscles in her face as if seeing me now for the first time. She leaned in and squinted at me, happy, triumphant. "You're jealous."

I shook my head, but she kept on.

"You can't stand to see me with him now."

I leaned back against my corner of the balcony, the cold iron digging into the thin costume material that covered the small of my back.

"So you *are* with him, then?"

"See," she said, jabbing a long, painted fingernail at me. "There," she said, as she sniffed, "I knew it."

"This isn't about me," I said. "I think there's a good chance that Brian really was up to some nefarious shit that night up there."

"Oh." Kelly stepped back toward the door and wound up her arm, as if she were a pitcher about to lob a curveball. "Miss me with that Nefertiti crap, okay?"

Her left hand landed on her hip, gripping it impatiently. "Talk like a real person."

"Brian's a dog," I said.

"Who isn't?"

Close to the glass, she seemed to have caught a glimpse of her own sorry reflection in the window and began trying to tidy up the smeared mascara and faded white paint around her mouth.

"I'm saying," I continued. It felt important to me that she believe me, that she hear me. This would mean something, I thought, to the both of us. "It's more than that. Brian's not a good dude."

"But what? He was good enough for you before tonight?"

She looked at me only through the reflection in the glass, one overplucked eyebrow cocked in my direction.

"Once he starts getting close to me in front of your little friends, that's when you catch feelings? That's when there's a problem?"

"My friends?" I asked. "They're your friends, too."

"I don't care about these people," she said, turning to square her shoulders at me, full-on. "You've always been jealous of my shit."

I laughed. I threw my head back and laughed and felt the spark of danger, of new roads being forged, deep behind my Wonder Woman belt, from my solar plexus. There was no turning back.

"What's there to be jealous of?" I asked. "Your two-timing fucking dad? Your scheming-ass mother who's rightfully rotting away in jail right now because she's a terrible human being who never gave a shit about anybody but herself?"

Kelly remained stone-faced, but I wasn't done. I needed to hurt her. To leave a mark.

"Or am I jealous of all your charming ex-boyfriends?" I asked, spit spraying from my lips on the *f* of "boyfriends." "No wonder you've always been after Brian," I said, the swell of anger cresting inside my chest. "Trade one rapist in for another, right?"

She shoved me then in one animalistic burst I'd dislodged from a place deep inside of her. I had seen glimpses of it before, this beast; I had one, too. I had seen hers on Christmas mornings, when she would invite herself in, and her eyes would glaze over at the gifts stacked for me underneath the tree. I had felt mine in the back room at PJ Moore's, when three guys asked me to dance over the course of the night only so they could chat me up about how to get in with Kelly. We normally kept those sides of ourselves penned in, chained down by our dependence on each other for friendship, for survival. We held each other's secrets without a guidebook, without a manual, without even needing to verbalize the responsibilities of being each other's official keeper, but here I had just spit hers right back into her face. On this night, nearly five years to the day after Pablo's party, after so many tribulations over the same stupid boy who'd been playing us both for so long, we surrendered to our demons. And in a way, it was exhilarating. We had never been more real with each other.

Kelly was strong and her fingernails sharp. When she shoved me, I fell back onto my padded Wonder-bottom, my spine smacking sharply against a single wrought-iron bar in the balcony railing. The knock reverberated through me, and I briefly worried I'd been paralyzed before I caught my breath and wiggled my toes inside my boots. Kelly towered above me, tensed muscles and tight fists. For a moment, I thought I could see steam coming off her cheeks, anger evaporating from her skin like a poison polluting the cool, autumn air.

"Get out," she growled and swiveled on her heels. She slammed the sliding door back on its track so hard that the glass she'd been staring into only moments before shattered on the concrete slab I was laid out on. A violent *bang, crack!* followed by a brilliant crash of crystals, tiny pieces twinkling, tumbling down from the PVC frame in the stunned silence.

I brushed my legs free of debris as I stood up gingerly, my eyes trained on the glittering glass at my feet, shimmering in the moon-light.

Kelly flipped on the light in Frances's old bedroom to reveal piles of clothes on the floor and stacks of magazines on the nightstand. I blinked at her. Her lips were still pursed, but her eyes were half-closed again, as if she were already downstairs, already back on the dance floor, wrapped around Brian's gyrating pelvis.

"You're paying for that," she said.

She flipped off the light switch, leaving me alone in the dark, the detritus of our friendship grinding noisily beneath the heels of my boots.

NOVEMBER 2006

I shredded the seams of the last Sweet'N Low packet between my fingers long after I'd poured it all into my coffee. A glass of ice water perspired on the corner of the peach-lined paper place mat in front of me, sweating from the heat thrown by the windowsill radiators tucked behind the tabletop jukeboxes of Georgia Diner.

Brian had agreed to meet me for lunch the weekend after our fund-raiser. He'd texted me on Tuesday to ask why I had disappeared from the Halloween party without a word. I still held the wallet with the party's cover charge collections, so I knew I would be hearing from him soon enough. Neither Kelly nor I had made any moves to be in touch with each other.

"Are you ready, hon?" the waiter asked, pen poised. He sported a slick black pompadour and a small green-and-white pendant around his neck representing the Pakistani flag. I recognized him from afternoons in the smoking section during high school, when six of us at a time would split one slice of strawberry cheesecake as a pretense for chain-smoking in a warm place during the winter. We ate there so much, we came to refer to him as Elvis, though we never learned his real name.

"Oh, I'm actually waiting to meet someone," I said, stretching my neck to look behind Elvis. I spotted Brian walking in, wearing a black bubble jacket, open to reveal a gray St. John's baseball T-shirt underneath.

"Hey, babe." He smiled and leaned over to kiss me, his cheek cold against the curve of mine. He looked fresh from the crisp weather outside, clean like a Precious Moments figurine of a perfect boyfriend, hot off the assembly line. He'd gotten a tape-up since the party, and the apples of his cheeks were just barely roses from the sudden wintry weather.

"Long night?" I asked, making a show of looking at my watch.

I caught a flash of guilt in his eyes, a brief crease between his eyebrows, which were so thick and defined, they looked as if they'd been threaded like a doll's.

"Not at all," he said, shrugging his shoulders to slip out of his jacket. "It's just that the bus was late."

I straightened the silverware on my right.

"Can't never trust the MTA on a Sunday," I said.

"Hey, chief," Brian called out to our waiter, two fingers in the air, beckoning him back over to us. "Could you bring over a large coffee, please? And a Greek omelet with egg whites?"

He winked at me.

"Spring training's just around the corner."

I blinked back at him.

"So," I said, as I rolled a pink shred of sugar packet between my thumb and forefinger, "everything's still cool with your team, then?"

"Of course," he said, tilting his head, a confused smile on his lips. "Why wouldn't it be?"

I looked at the Red Storm logo on his T-shirt, thinking about the weekend Brian spent in jail, the watch he'd gone back for that night, the pats on the back his coach may have given him when

Brian explained the situation he'd found himself in. I thought about Kelly and me, two pathetic girls raising money for him to hire a lawyer to fight this in court. Brian didn't have to worry about a thing.

Before I could respond, Elvis cut me off.

"And for you, miss?"

I smiled weakly at him.

"I'll just have an order of pancakes. Strawberry jam, no syrup."

Brian leaned over the table once Elvis walked back toward the kitchen with our order.

"How European of you," he said with a smirk.

I screwed up my lips at him.

"What you know about Europe?"

He tapped his fingers on the table between us.

"Napoleon!" he said, raising his voice. He was trying to be cute.

I ripped open another packet of fake sugar and poured it onto the wet saucer my cup sat on, watching the crystals congeal the spilled coffee into a sweet sludge.

"Come on," Brian said, enveloping my fist on the table. "What's wrong?"

I pulled my hand away and looked at the faces of the diners surrounding us.

"Do you remember when we would come here to smoke?" I asked. "After school?"

"*You* came here to smoke." He leaned back, arms wide along the top of the banquette. "You and Kelly."

"You're right," I said as I eyed him. "You came to order whatever was the cheapest thing on the menu."

"Hey," he said, brushing sugar granules off the table. "I happen to like green Jell-O."

I smiled sadly, remembering how we used to pool our coins on the table to count out what we could afford as a group after spending the rest of our money at the local pool hall.

"Can you tell me what happened again?" I asked, looking him in the eyes. "That night?"

"What?" he asked. "Halloween?"

I blinked up at him from under my brow.

"No," I said, "in Connecticut."

"Brisma," he said, his voice approaching something like stern, but belying just a bit of fear around the edges. He licked sugar from his knuckles and balled his napkin into a fist.

"What else is there to say?" he asked.

I rummaged through my large purse, past the spiral notebook in which I'd written the first draft of my spec script, and wrapped my hand around the smooth faux-leather wallet that held the collections from the party. I pulled it out and held it in my lap, my fingers clasped around the Velcro flap. I was acutely aware, suddenly, of my cool, dry skin against the synthetic material.

"Did you go back in there to sleep with her? After she'd passed out?"

"Of course not," he said. "I'm not an animal."

He tapped his fingers on the table and leaned in. "But did I think maybe I had a shot of hooking up with her some more if she woke up?"

He shrugged, but when he saw my eyes go wide at this admission, he laughed self-consciously.

"What is this, anyway?" he asked, looking around at the faces of the diners around us. "An inquisition? You wearing a wire or something?"

He leaned back in and lowered his voice, serious.

"What kind of question is that?"

"No." I shook my head. "I'm not wearing a wire. I wouldn't tape you without your knowledge. That would be wrong."

I placed the wallet on the table between us.

"Wouldn't it?"

He swallowed, and I watched his Adam's apple bob in his throat like a snake digesting its prey. He squinted at me, his high cheekbones a shield.

"Yeah," he said. "That would be wrong."

I brought the ceramic mug to my lips and took a sip of lukewarm coffee. I hoped he wouldn't notice my hand trembling as I set it back down on the table.

"Then why'd *you* do it?" I asked, smacking my lips.

"Hold up," he said, hunching his neck closer over the table. "Now you think I taped this girl?"

His chest against the edge of the table, I could no longer see the red storm on his shirt.

"What's gotten into you?" He frowned. "Kelly said you were acting mad weird at the party, too."

I shot my finger up at him.

"Don't you talk to me about Kelly." I was afraid I'd already given him too much satisfaction, allowed him to think I was jealous of his relationship—or whatever it was—with Kelly.

"This isn't about her," I said. "Not yet, anyway."

"Brisma, you know me," he said, as Elvis came back to set Brian's large coffee down in front of him.

"You've known me since we were kids," he continued, quietly. "You know I'm not a bad guy."

I felt the cotton-like haze of his words begin to distract me again, threaten to sublimate my rage and determination. It would be so easy to simply submit to his suggestion, to dissolve into a more comforting version of events that wouldn't threaten the reality I'd constructed for myself.

"I *have* known you forever," I said. "And I know you think you're hot shit."

Brian clasped his hands and sat back in the booth, as if he were giving up.

"You like to think you're a player and that all these ladies want you," I said, shrugging. "And a lot of them do. But maybe this girl in Connecticut changed her mind and didn't want to finish what you guys started, and you couldn't handle that."

"Brisma," he interjected, "I'm not a fucking rapist."

I looked down, away from his pleading eyes.

"I didn't say you were."

I moved the knife to the edge of the paper place mat. A large halved peach was printed on it, revealing a neon-lined oval pit inside. I inhaled, the burnt coffee from his steaming cup reminding me of old fresh starts, of early mornings in the guidance counselor's office, doing extra credit to make up for cutting class, of Sandro's on hungover Sunday mornings when Kelly and I would split a bacon, egg, and cheese on the corner, watching cars barrel down the boulevard, the Manhattan skyline blocked by the LIRR overpass. I filled my lungs—collecting the nerve to cash in on the psychic energy of all the times I'd given in to Brian in the past, given in to the status quo—and exhaled.

"How many videos do you have?"

"What?" he asked, not missing a beat, not daring to wipe a bit of spittle that had landed on his lip.

"Of women," I clarified, "that you've been with. How many tapes have you made of you hooking up with girls?"

"None," he said, palms pressed against the edge of the table. "I swear."

I looked at him.

"None," he repeated.

"How many people have seen the video you taped of us?"

"Us?" he echoed, incredulous.

"When we tried to have sex that one time," I said. "Was I your first?"

He looked at me, mouth agape, his eyebrows knitting together and back apart, calculating and recalculating his next move.

I let a sad laugh escape through my top teeth.

"Was I the first girl you taped?"

"You sound like a crazy person," Brian said. "I don't know what you're talking about."

"Pablo saw it," I said. "Pablo told me you showed it to a basement full of douchebags in high school."

"Pablo is a hater," he shot back. "The war scrambled his brain. You can't listen to what he says."

I laughed lightly, but it was pressurized air escaping my throat more than anything. I was surprised Brian would be so quick to throw his boy under the bus. To discredit him using the war. I opened the wallet so Brian could see the stack of green inside it, and slid my own twenty-dollar bill out before closing it again and handing it over to him.

"You earned this," I said. "People gave this to you in good faith. It's up to you what you do with it. But I can't."

"You can't what?"

"I can't support this." I gestured to the space between us. "I can't protect you any longer."

I wiped the coffee from the side of my mouth.

"You're messed up, Brian. You need help or something."

"Kelly was right," he said quietly. "Your jealousy is through the roof. It's clouding your judgment."

It was a sore wound to pick at and a poor choice of words. A small part of me wanted to believe he was right; I was being hasty, jumping to conclusions, believing the wrong people. But looking into his cool, lidded eyes as he dismissed me, I felt I was witnessing Brian's true nature once and for all.

"I hope you didn't tape the Connecticut girl," I said, sliding out of the booth. "Or I don't know, maybe I do. For her sake."

I rammed my fist into the sleeve of my peacoat.

"Doesn't sound like those videos would do well for you in court."

"Is that a threat?" he asked, true betrayal in his eyes.

I tugged my collar closed and walked away, buttoning up as I made my way to the exit. I passed Elvis, balancing our orders in his hands near the rotating dessert stand. He opened his mouth to call out to me, but I shook my head. There was too much energy coursing through my veins to turn around. I had set a ball in motion I was not sure I had the guts to follow through on. Was I ready and willing to destroy a man's life? A boy I had known nearly all of my life? Who would believe me? Certainly not Kelly. Was I ready to blow up my friendship with her, too? Had I already done so?

These questions swirled around each other, a vicious circle in my mind. But I pushed the heavy glass doors open and stepped out into the brisk, cold air, which immediately bit at my cheeks and blew back my hair, and I felt like I was entering a different level of the atmosphere. Walking fast, my boots pounding the pavement down Queens Boulevard, I realized I felt clear for the first time in years. I had cut through the cotton haze once and for all. I rubbed the skin of my wrists where I'd worn my Wonder Woman cuff bracelets for the party and ducked my head to skip down into the nearby subway station.

Brian was the bogeyman we'd been warned about our entire lives. And it was my turn to do what I could to protect future girls, future women, from becoming his prey.

2000

Outside of school and Brian, I spent much of my free time in the weeks before Christmas helping Mami pack Mary Kay holiday gift bags for her biggest customers. Some were coworkers at St. Vincent's, some were church ladies, and some were neighbors who lived in the apartment buildings down the block—in all her experience with side hustles, she found anyone who owned property refused to buy from her.

"You know, other kids don't have to do this," I said, tying a red ribbon around candy-cane-printed cellophane.

"Other kids are ungrateful little brats," she said, as she grabbed my chin and smiled. "Lucky for both of us, you're not like them."

I shook her off and lifted up a small velvet box the color of blue fountain ink. I opened it, expecting to find a ring, and instead found a delicate, fine-silver bracelet with a tag that read MAKE ME FEEL IMPORTANT.

I lifted it up.

"What's this?" I asked.

Mami snapped it closed and ripped it from my hands.

"No snooping," she said. "This is a consultant prize."

"So it's yours?"

"No," she said, tucking it into a separate bag, a real Hallmark-type gift bag with a jolly-looking Santa on it.

I grabbed another slip of cellophane to build another bag. "But you're a consultant."

Mami snipped the red ribbon off the spool in her hand and slammed the scissors down on the table.

"Why you asking so many questions?"

I suspected she might have been dating someone at work for a while, but to see that she was planning on regifting a Mary Kay prize to someone she might have feelings for—a prize that said MAKE ME FEEL IMPORTANT, no less!—made me feel all sorts of embarrassed for both of us. It seemed so needy and misguided.

The doorbell rang, and I ran to let Brian into the apartment.

"Feliz Navidad," Brian roared into the kitchen.

"Ay, Brian, Merry Christmas," Mami said, as she got up to hug him. "You want some coquito?"

Brian looked at me, excited.

"Mami, we're fifteen."

"I got *virgin* coquito," she enunciated, walking to the fridge. "Come on, ¿piensas que soy una tonta?"

"I'm only stopping by for a second. I was on my way to my abuela's to help her start preparing for Christmas Eve."

"Ahhh," Mami said, exaggerating her appreciation. "How thoughtful of you. Brisma, you can learn a few things from this one."

"I gotta grab my gift in the bedroom," I said, as I grabbed Brian's hand. "We'll be right back!"

"¡Deja la puerta abierta!" she shouted.

Inside my bedroom, we made out furiously against the wall just inside the open door where Mami couldn't see us. I broke apart from him and reached for my dresser drawer, eager to give him his gift.

"Here," I said, handing him an orange-and-blue binder—Mets colors—bursting with printed computer paper.

"I collected all the letters we've written each other since we started dating, typed them up, and printed them out. I thought it would be cool to have them all in one place, bound up . . . like a book. It's the story of us."

"Aw," he said, as he sat down on the bed to thumb through them. But when he did the springs in my mattress whined in alarm.

"Off the bed!" Mami shouted from the living room.

Brian jumped up, and we walked back into the apartment.

"Don't worry, Mami," I said as Brian held up the binder. "He's leaving now."

Outside, I kept the front door open with one foot while I talked to him.

"Is it too corny, you think?"

"Nah," he said as he kissed my forehead. "It's sweet."

I smiled. Over his shoulder, I saw Kelly walk out of her house and spot us. Before I could react, she turned around and disappeared back into her house. *Good*, I thought. *Let her see us.*

"Oh," he said as he reached into his pocket, "I can't believe I almost forgot."

He took out a skinny rectangle of a gift wrapped in green paper with dogs wearing jingle-bell collars on it. I ripped through it to find a Polaroid i-Zone camera.

"It prints pictures as stickers," he said, pointing to the instructions on the box. "I thought you'd like it."

"I love it."

"Good," he said, as he leaned in. "I thought we could have a

lot of fun with it. Add certain types of"—he raised his eyebrows—
"*pictures* to our letters between class."

"In class?" I laughed. "You're out of your mind. I'm not carrying
around nude photos in school."

"Okay, okay," he said, winking. "Think about it."

I shoved him playfully.

"Boy, you are crazy." I kissed his cheek. "Thank you."

Back inside the apartment, Mami was just about done with her
bags.

"What's that?" she asked, nodding at the box in my hand.

"A camera."

"What?" she exclaimed. "He got money like that?"

"Well," I said, "it's a Polaroid camera. For like, stickers and
stuff."

"Uh-huh," she said, either not understanding or not believing
me. "And what did you give him? Homework?"

"Homework?" I asked.

"Yeah, I saw him carrying out a notebook. Are you doing his
schoolwork or something?"

"Oh my god, no," I cried, rubbing my forehead. "I wrote him
something. You're so paranoid."

"Be careful, that's all I'm saying," she said to the bags, primping
them. "You always writing, writing, writing."

She pointed at me, one of the crinkly bags dangling from her
hand. "Someone might read it someday."

I dropped my arms at my sides. Writing always felt like a fight
with Mami; she was supportive only insofar as it would get me
good grades. Otherwise she taught me to be careful, to be fearful
of real emotions. It's what made the vulnerable MAKE ME FEEL
IMPORTANT plea so ludicrous coming from her.

"Isn't that the point?" I asked. "For other people to read it?"

"The point is," she said, as she dropped the last cellophane gift bag into a large paper Macy's bag, "some things you should keep to yourself. You can't trust everybody."

She slid onto the stool next to the counter and patted her knees. "I just don't want you to get hurt."

NOVEMBER 2006

I could barely sleep the night after giving Brian his cash at the diner. I twisted in my sheets, turning memories over like stones, trying to unearth the objective truth. *Could Brian have really taped me without my knowledge? Did I agree and block it out?* I probably would have agreed if he'd asked me. And the worst question of all: *Does Kelly know? Has Kelly seen the tape, just like Pablo?*

Sirens woke me up at dawn, red-and-blue lights strobing in through my blinds. I jumped out of bed to find Mami standing at the front door, cupping her hand against the glass to cut the glare from her vision to try to make sense of the scene outside.

"Is there a fire?" I sniffed the air for smoke, placing my arm around her shoulder.

"No," she said. "A car crash."

I frowned at the fire trucks and police cars.

"All this for a car crash?"

"Actually," Mami said, shaking her head in disbelief, "it looks like a car crashed into a *house*."

Immediately, I craned my neck out the door to look down the block and make sure Kelly's house was clear.

Mami turned her shoulders to look at me full-on. Her face was pale, in shock. The police lights bounced off the silver pins that kept the net wrapped around her hair in place.

"Julio's house."

I laughed, incredulous.

"What?" I asked. "*Into* his house?"

Mami nodded solemnly.

"I think it's real bad," she said, opening the door and stepping out onto the stoop. She gestured to the street, closed to traffic except for emergency-response vehicles. "Ain't one ambulance," she said. "They left with the driver. Probably drunk."

I sprinted into my bedroom to pull on my hoodie and slippers to join the crowd of neighbors who'd begun milling around the crime scene. Kelly and I hadn't spoken since the fund-raiser, but this was different, this was outside of that fight: I needed to find Kelly.

I weaved through the cop cars, white doors left ajar, black electronics periodically belching to life inside, past a puddle fed by a dribbling, open hydrant, to find Kelly at the front of the crowd, her belly pressed against the yellow tape. Her charcoal-lined eyes were wide and barely blinking as she stared at his house, the red-and-blue lights pulsing across her irises. On her shoulder, she grasped the strap of her backpack; she must have been returning home from Riviera when she arrived at the scene, the wheels of the overturned Honda Civic still rotating in the air.

The crunching sound of glass underfoot as I stepped toward her reminded me of our fight on the balcony, and it alerted her to my presence. She broke from her reverie to glance at me and straightened her spine.

"Did you see what happened?" I asked.

Kelly pursed her lips.

"You don't have eyes?" she asked. "A car crashed into El Cochino's house."

"Is he dead?"

"Killed him on impact," she said. "Eating breakfast." She laughed, looking up at the brightening sky. "Jammed his spoon full of Wheaties right down his throat."

I frowned at her.

"You can't possibly know that."

"Well, it crushed his bones." Kelly shrugged. "It's what the cops said."

From the front door of the house came a deep wail, and I thought for a moment Kelly was wrong, and he'd survived. We watched as two large cops carried El Cochino's elderly grandmother out of what was left of the front entrance, climbing over the front wheels of the car. A new ambulance screeched to the curb, and despite my own experience with her grandson, I felt grief for La Señora, who must have been over ninety. I looked at Kelly as we stepped back to make way for the paramedics. She was smiling.

"Are you happy?" I asked.

"I'm not sad," she said with her chin up. "Good riddance."

I thought about the year he spent watching us, Mami and me, watching Kelly and me, the spell we tried, and the rock I threw at his cheek. We hated him so much, hated that he was allowed to go around violating our space, our privacy, our bodies. Whistling at us, sucking his teeth as we walked by. We hated him together. We were bonded in that anger, so much anger we held, continued to hold—for as unsafe as he made us feel, he was the one safe place we could channel all our rage. And now he was gone.

"Sounds horrible," I said, imagining the cold weight of a metal spoon in my own throat. "A horrible way to die." The white frame of his living room window hung loose, dangling over the undercarriage of the Honda like a pendulum.

Kelly spit on the asphalt over the yellow caution tape.

"People get what they deserve."

"Is that right?" I said, shifting my weight to stand back and appraise her. She wore ripped jeans and platform sandals despite the frosty chill of the early morning. She still carried that anger close, jaw tight, fist clenched around the strap of her bag. She turned to leave, but I called after her.

"How . . . ," I began, my voice unsure. "How can you feel so strongly about Julio, but not—"

"*Julio?*" she asked, disgusted at my use of his government name. It felt, I supposed, like another betrayal. She ran a hand inside the pocket of her backpack to pull out a cigarette.

"Don't try to play me again," Kelly said, continuing down the steps and then stopping. She gestured up toward the flashing lights. "With *Julio*," she mocked, "we were just girls."

She flicked a lighter from inside her fist and sucked on her cigarette. "Brian was with a grown-ass woman."

"He admitted he went back to try and hook up with her after she'd already passed out."

"So?" Kelly stepped back up a stair. "That's happened to me. You know it has. And I've done it, too. I've stuck around after a guy's been so drunk he passed out. Should I go to jail?"

"I don't think Brian—"

"*Brian*," Kelly cut me off, "stopped him. That night."

"What?" I pulled on the drawstring, tightening my hoodie around my neck. "Stopped who?"

The slow glow of Kelly's cigarette burned in the silence between us, a molten eye blinking open, closed. The ambulance door slammed behind us, ready to shuttle La Señora away.

"Brian stopped Nicky. At Pablo's party that one time. When we were . . . Brian came into the room where I was and pulled Nicky off me."

My mind raced, memories jamming together—Nicky, Brian, Pablo, that dirty frayed office carpeting of the rented rooms on Pablo's second floor.

"I thought you were passed out" was all I could say.

"My memories are fuzzy," she said. "But I remember struggling to push Nicky away, telling him to fuck off. Maybe Brian heard me?" She took a deep breath. "Regardless, all I know is Brian pulled him off and told him to leave me alone. Then he personally walked me home all the way to Clement Moore. To my door, Brisma."

I shook my head.

"I don't believe you," I said, searching her face, rewriting every interaction between the three of us over the last five years with that missing piece of the puzzle. "How come you never told me this?"

Kelly sighed and stubbed out her cigarette under her heel.

"He already ruined things for us once." Kelly sighed. "When you agreed to hang out with me that next day, I didn't want to say anything to rock the boat. So . . . I just avoided him—him, and the topic of him, forever. Until he showed up again."

She grabbed my arm and forced me to look at her.

"You understand, he's not that guy, Brisma. To fuck a girl when she's dead to the world. He couldn't have really done this. He was there for me. Don't you understand?"

I tried to understand how this could be the same Brian who supposedly videotaped me without my knowledge, who tried to rouse an unconscious girl and got caught. *How long was Brian in the room before Kelly woke up?* I wondered. *Was there video of Kelly?* I shook my arm loose and rubbed my skin where goose bumps rose up.

"I feel sick," I said, hugging myself. "I've got to go."

"Don't act like you're so innocent, Brisma," she said, defensive again after unloading this secret she'd carried so long. "What are we going to do? Go after every guy who's tried to bust a nut around us?"

She flicked her wrist, turning to finally walk inside.

"Get real," she said. "You start going down this path, no one comes out clean."

2OOI

CaLLiNthaSHoTS7: why u up so late?

SpCLAgEnTxBRiSMA: can't sleep

CaLLiNthaSHoTS7: too many guys hitting you up?

SpCLAgEnTxBRiSMA: ha-ha

CaLLiNthaSHoTS7: these Forest Hills girls won't leave me alone

CaLLiNthaSHoTS7: it's mad annoying

SpCLAgEnTxBRiSMA: wat u talking about

CaLLiNthaSHoTS7: These 2 girls came up to me after the game we
played there last week, wanting to hang out with me.

CaLLiNthaSHoTS7: Alone.

CaLLiNthaSHoTS7: Just the 2 of them . . . and me.;)

SpCLAgEnTxBRiSMA: Gross.

CaLLiNthaSHoTS7: you wanna see their pic?

SpCLAgEnTxBRiSMA: No!

CaLLiNthaSHoTS7: One of them reminds me of you. She's cute.
innocent.

SpCLAgEnTxBRiSMA: ew

SpCLAgEnTxBRiSMA: Since when have I been innocent?

SpCLAgEnTxBRiSMA: u know wat, never mind. I gotta get ready for the
first day of school tomorrow. I start 2nd period
now so I have to wake up by 7am. blech.

CaLLiNthaSHoTS7:	Sent
SpCLAgEnTxBRiSMA:	yo
SpCLAgEnTxBRiSMA:	y u sending this to me??
SpCLAgEnTxBRiSMA:	u think I look like this hamster-faced skank??
CaLLiNthaSHoTS7:	lol
SpCLAgEnTxBRiSMA:	I am much hotter.
CaLLiNthaSHoTS7:	I can't remember.
SpCLAgEnTxBRiSMA:	huh?
CaLLiNthaSHoTS7:	I haven't seen you enough this summer.
SpCLAgEnTxBRiSMA:	I agree.
SpCLAgEnTxBRiSMA:	but . . . things have been weird since that night after the Nuyo.
SpCLAgEnTxBRiSMA:	I thought . . . you were mad at me or something.
CaLLiNthaSHoTS7:	what!! no way.
CaLLiNthaSHoTS7:	that was mad special. <3
CaLLiNthaSHoTS7:	to me, at least.
SpCLAgEnTxBRiSMA:	me too!
SpCLAgEnTxBRiSMA:	never mind. I'm just crazy.
CaLLiNthaSHoTS7:	I've just been busy with summer league.
CaLLiNthaSHoTS7:	Rather be beaned by Taveras on the field than Griselda at home.
SpCLAgEnTxBRiSMA:	:(
SpCLAgEnTxBRiSMA:	is it bad again?
CaLLiNthaSHoTS7:	she's on a rampage. but whatever. nothing I'm not used to.
CaLLiNthaSHoTS7:	Send me a pic?
SpCLAgEnTxBRiSMA:	You know what I look like, son.
CaLLiNthaSHoTS7:	nah, send me a pic of you right now. What you look like right now.
SpCLAgEnTxBRiSMA:	I'm in pajamas! And I don't have a webcam.

CaLLiNthaSHoTS7: Use that polaroid camera I got you and scan it.

CaLLiNthaSHoTS7: cmon

SpCLAgEnTxBRiSMA: uhhh . . . I don't know.

CaLLiNthaSHoTS7: plz? i miss u.

SpCLAgEnTxBRiSMA: gimmie a sex

SpCLAgEnTxBRiSMA: sec* lol

CaLLiNthaSHoTS7: . . . waiting . . .

SpCLAgEnTxBRiSMA: ok, sent.

CaLLiNthaSHoTS7: omg

CaLLiNthaSHoTS7: is that ur bra?

SpCLAgEnTxBRiSMA: ya. Better than Hamster Face?

CaLLiNthaSHoTS7: hahaha yes.

CaLLiNthaSHoTS7: wow.

CaLLiNthaSHoTS7: what a babe.

CaLLiNthaSHoTS7: will I see you mañana?

SpCLAgEnTxBRiSMA: sure, if you're not too busy with your ugly lil FH
girlfriends.

CaLLiNthaSHoTS7: lol stop.

SpCLAgEnTxBRiSMA: meet in the auditorium?

CaLLiNthaSHoTS7: k.

CaLLiNthaSHoTS7: love ya.

SpCLAgEnTxBRiSMA: love you too.

NOVEMBER 2006

Early in my first screen-writing course with Professor Acevedo, she stressed the importance of research.

"Research," she'd said, "is the backbone of your story." She underlined the word on the whiteboard in red marker twice.

"You need research to build a believable story that delivers the truth of your message."

With that in mind, I'd written to a reporter who used to cover the Mets beat for the *Daily News*, and he was surprisingly transparent in his correspondence and generous with his time. He gave me insight into what the mood was like on flights home after a string of away-game losses, how he determined the right player from whom to get a sound bite after a game, and a few instances when the players' off-field drama carried over into the locker room. I couldn't believe all that information was out there, if I could just find the right person and ask the right questions. It was an amazing feeling to discover that access to whole other worlds was only a few keystrokes and a strong-willed nerve away.

I applied this same discipline to Brian's case. If I wanted to know the truth about those sexual assault charges, if I was ever going to convince Kelly of it, I'd need to go to the source—if she'd have me.

I didn't have the Connecticut girl's name, but I had Brian's. I googled his name and found his mug shot pretty quickly—in vivid color this time, not a tiny black-and-white square in the *Queens Gazette*. It was a strange feeling to see his bloated face staring back at me from the news item—like my insides were on the outside. I couldn't bear to look at his tired, red-rimmed eyes, at the familiar crease between his brows, the look he'd give me when he was pulling away, raising up his defenses.

I shook off the unsettling feeling and kept sorting through the search results. A Sacred Heart–branded flyer for a rally scheduled for Election Day to protest sexual assault and harassment on campus. A list of speakers, including deans and RAs, was highlighted on the flyer. At the bottom, scribbled in block letters, was JUSTICE FOR JANET.

Janet? I thought. *Who names their kid Janet anymore?* But it was unique enough that I had a good chance of finding her. I signed up for Facebook with my City University email and searched for Janet at Sacred Heart University. Three came up: Janet Mitchell, a gray-haired professor; Janet Lim, an Asian American freshman; and Janet Wisnewski, a light-skinned girl with a long Dominican blowout—exactly his type, despite the confusing name. I knew it was her. I clicked on her picture and furiously typed a message to her.

"You don't know me, but I know Brian. I don't think he's telling the truth. He's done me dirty before, and I'm sure I'm not the only one. I guess I'm saying . . ."

I hovered over the space bar, my thumb wavering.

"I believe you," I typed. I didn't realize that was true, though, until just then. "I'm here if you want to talk."

I navigated my cursor over the send button, my mind racing wildly with flashes of the past few weeks. I inhaled and clicked send.

Almost immediately, I got a response. One simple question.
"When are you free?"

❧

In the salon, a fire glowed in the hearth between us, both of our
legs crossed against twin peach-colored armchairs.

"You don't look like a Wisnewski," I said, tapping the glass of
water she'd given me, the crystal heavy and substantial in my hands.

Janet coughed and patted down the curling hair at her temples
beneath her blowout.

"What's that?" she asked.

"No," I began. "I just . . . Where are you from?"

She blushed.

"That's your first question?"

"No." I put the glass down on the coffee table. "No, I'm sorry,"
I continued. "It's just—your last name. I was confused. Curious?"

She scratched her collarbone, clearly reconsidering whether she
should have met with me.

"We're Cuban," she said, her hands clasped in her lap, as if that
explained everything.

"Ah," I said, shrugging my bag off my shoulder to hug it in my
lap. "Okay. Cool."

Cool? What was I doing? Why was I asking about her background, and why was it that confirming she was Latina made me
feel at first relieved and then suspicious?

"I really appreciate you talking to me," I said, my eyes narrowing in on the painting that hung behind her: a real, honest-to-god
oil painting hanging beneath a spotlight, the kind where you could
see the chunky, raised acrylic strokes of the artist on the canvas.

Not the printed reproductions Mami bought at church-basement flea markets.

Janet handed me a marble disk from the side table next to her: a coaster. Embarrassed, I grabbed it from her and slid it underneath my glass.

"I'm sorry," I said, wiping sweat from the top of my lip.

"Don't worry about it."

She pursed her full lips at me, and I saw that she had two tiny dark moles on her cheek like poppy seeds.

"I thought about canceling," she said, fingering the ends of her hair at her shoulder.

"Oh?" I said. The truth was, I'd considered it, too.

"Yeah. I've seen you," she said, smoothing the fabric of her sweater on her forearm. It seemed like she didn't quite know what to do with her hands.

"You've seen me?" I asked. "Where?"

"Pictures," she said. "Pictures on his Facebook."

I clicked open the pocket flap of the bag in my lap, nervously.

"I'm barely even on Facebook," I said, trying to remember what kind of photos Brian could have posted with me in them. "I just joined."

I winced, not wanting to sound like I was on the defense.

"I've known him a long time," I added quietly, and it was as if this flipped a switch in her.

"So you're here to try to discredit me, then?" she asked. "To get some dirt on me?"

"No, it's not like that. I told you," I said, waving both of my hands.

She kept her arms folded tight across her chest. I wondered

where her parents were, if they were home, or out playing bridge, or whatever it was people who owned houses like the one we were in did.

"I have my suspicions about him," I said, sucking my teeth. "Enough that I bought a goddamn Metro North ticket to come talk to you in person."

I was glad she wanted to meet on her turf: the train served as a barrier, a palate cleanser between my borough reality and her harsh truth.

"If you're willing," I said, "I'd like to hear your side of the story."

She kept her eyes on me and bit her bottom lip, releasing it only when she placed her glass of water back on the coaster. She told me her story, and I listened intently, wondering all the while how many times she had had to retell those intimate details to detectives, and police officers, and her mother, and her classmates. How many times she'd relived that night out loud and how many more times she must have relived it in her own mind, when it was dark and quiet, when she was lying in bed alone, just like she was that night that Brian crashed down on top of her.

"So," I said, when she appeared to be finished, "he *did* leave his watch there?"

Janet frowned.

"Yeah," she said. "But who cares?"

I didn't know why it was so important to me that that detail was true. It was a toe in the door, a tiny hope that maybe Brian was telling the truth.

"That's when you woke up and screamed?" I asked. "When he crawled back in for the watch?"

"No," she said, her voice trilling louder. "That's when he took off all his clothes and slipped into my bed beside me. I woke up because I couldn't breathe with his cold nose pressed up against mine."

There is a saying that your heart drops when you're scared, when you're sad, when you're disappointed, but I'd never felt the rib-shaking slam of a thud like this before. There was no gray moral area here. What Brian did was horrifying and hard for me to reconcile with what I thought I knew about the boy I once loved. And yet—*and yet!*—there was still a small voice inside my brain that wondered whether Brian did that, stripped off his clothes and slid between the bedsheets of an unconscious girl he'd met only hours before, if he had done that in an attempt at romance.

I gulped down the dread rising in my throat and squared my shoulders at Janet.

"Was he shocked?" I asked.

Janet widened her eyes at me.

"Was *he* shocked?" she asked. "I was! He broke into my room."

"No, I know," I said. "I mean, did he seem surprised that you were upset? How did he react when you screamed?"

Janet considered my question.

"No," she said. "He seemed"—she traced the embroidered vines on the armchair's fabric—"amused."

She shifted her weight from one side to the other in her seat.

"I was drunk that night, yes. But I was so scared in the moment, I was, like, shocked sober."

She swallowed, looking beyond me, squinting at the memory.

"It was dark, but his eyes had a sort of light in them. If I had to describe it, I would say it was excitement."

I was leaning forward, listening to her intently. Feeling nauseated and hot, I squeezed my kneecaps and pushed myself upright in my chair.

"He held a finger up to my mouth," she said. "Told me to shush. I grabbed it, tried to tell him . . ."

Janet laughed.

"I told him I had my period," she said, shrugging. "I didn't. I just thought, for some reason, in the chaos, that it would make him stop. Weird how you never know how you're going to react, what you'll try when . . ."

Her eyes welled up, red blood vessels breaking to the surface under the black, liquid line of her top lid.

"It's just not how you envision your rape to go," she said.

I cleared my throat, feeling the glands under my arms swell and break. I imagined Janet as a young girl, surrounded by stacks of *Seventeen* magazine, reading about rape whistles on campus as if they were something you graduated to, rather than the constant, ever-present threat Kelly and I had felt since we were girls.

"But," I said, "he didn't, uh . . ."

She sucked her teeth and slid a finger under her eye.

"No," she said. "That's when I screamed. I yelled at the top of my lungs for help, and my RA came in a few moments later. Brian had already pulled up his pants and hopped back out the window by then."

It felt dangerous to speak any words into the space between us. I was acutely aware of my sweating skin against the upholstery. My body was painfully present, but my mind was with Kelly on that morning walk we took to Sandro's all those years ago, when we assumed the weight of the night of Pablo's party without question, without protest, when we braided the shame of it into our genomes and kept moving.

"I'm so sorry," I said.

Janet grabbed her phone off the table next to her and flipped it open and closed, a quick glance at the time on the clock.

"Yeah." She cleared her throat. "I actually have to leave. I promised my parents I'd pick up dinner for tonight."

"Oh," I said, as I patted my hair back. "Sure."

I shrugged my bag up onto my shoulder.

"Sure," I repeated.

Janet walked me to her front door in silence, the heaviness of her story hanging in the hallway that led to the foyer, to the long, skinny windows that framed the outside world, where my life hadn't changed yet, where I'd be able to breathe again, if only momentarily. Janet's story deserved oxygen, too.

"Just one thing," I said, turning back to her, my hand on the doorknob. "Do you remember if he . . . taped you at any point? If he had a camera or a camera phone on?"

She frowned and shrugged.

"No," she said. "I doubt it. I don't remember anything like that."

She reached in front of me to open the front door and leaned her weight on the knob.

"Is that what he did to you?"

I was caught off guard by the question. I'd already prepared to leave, thought I'd made it through, without having to share any details about what Pablo said happened to me—how wild to hold out hope, still, that it wasn't true. I took in a sharp breath and intended to laugh, but what came out was more of a cry, my eyes suddenly hot with tears.

"I think so," I said with a nod. "I think so."

She offered a tight-lipped smile and squeezed my hand. I pulled it away quickly, scared at how nice the gesture felt after being in such a dark place with Kelly for so long.

"I'm sorry we didn't get a chance to talk longer," she said, her voice soft. "You have my info. We can chat on the phone, if you want. Email. I don't mind. It would be nice to"—she shrugged—"I don't know, keep in touch. Is that weird?"

She laughed and her smile was warm, her teeth surprisingly not perfect, a slight gap between the top two in front.

"No, it's nice. Thanks. Thank you," I said, as I shook her hand. "You didn't have to share your story with me, but I am so grateful you did."

I crossed the threshold onto the wooden porch and jogged down the two front steps with a lightness that I suspected came from understanding one's purpose, when Janet called out to me one last time.

"You know what?" she said.

I turned around.

"He never even took the damn watch."

⌁

I rode the train back to New York in a daze, as sideways rain pitter-pattered on the dirty, water-stained windows, feeling both more alive than I'd ever felt and more terrified. The rolling thunder of the 7 Train along Queens Boulevard and a rattling LosMets.com ad above my head only seemed to drive me further inside my own thoughts. When I turned the corner onto Clement Moore Avenue to walk up to my apartment, I saw Pablo sitting on my stoop, fists balled inside the pockets of his bomber jacket.

"What are you doing here?" I asked, stomping my boots in place before him.

Pablo cleared his throat.

"My brother and I started going through all the shit in our house before the big move down to Florida. You know, trying to decide what to keep, donate, or toss."

From the pocket of his backpack in front of him, he pulled out a VHS tape with a Post-it note Scotch-taped to the front. I squinted to make out what it read: MAY 2001.

"I found the tape," he said.

Again. For the second time that day, my heart slammed dead in my chest; the blood it pushed to my ears was deafening.

"What?" I asked.

"This whole time we had the tape, Brisma," he repeated, the film shaking inside the plastic cartridge as he handed it to me. "Yours."

2001

Something was wrong with me, I was sure of it.

Lying across from Brian in his twin bed, wrapped in his navy sheet after that evening of poetry at the Nuyorican, I was convinced I was beset with some anatomical anomaly that prevented me from having sex.

His back turned to me, I studied the constellation of beauty marks across Brian's dark shoulders while my heart broke for the times I used to hold on to them with pride, riding his bicycle pegs down Clement Moore, wanting that feeling in the summer sun to last forever. This, too, would be over soon, I understood. And it would be my fault.

The pain was just too great, sparks of red and yellow bursting behind my tightly shut eyes as he tried to enter me. He was far from too big, or too rough—I just couldn't do it. A sad, wounded "Stop," and even more pitiful "I'm sorry," was all I managed to whimper.

I hugged myself, empty and resigned to Brian hating me for the rest of his life. He would find other women, other girls who knew what they were doing, who enjoyed it. *How does Kelly do it?* I found myself wondering.

I pinched the soft flesh of my upper arm, willing myself to

move, to reanimate my body back into my clothing, piece by piece, until I was dressed and ready to leave, to get home before Mami returned from the night shift at St. Vincent's.

I knelt on the bed to kiss Brian on the shoulder, but he barely stirred. I slipped past his dresser, past his bookcase from which a gentle mechanical whirring emanated, a sound I assumed was from a large, glowing alarm clock on the shelf. I slipped out the door, down the back stairs, and into the night, my chest tight with fear and self-loathing as I scurried up Clement Moore Avenue, avoiding catcalls from cars stopped at red lights and skipping past the sound of wet lips smacking inside the shadowed doorway of a halfway house. Mami was always so scared of what could happen to me walking home late at night, as if strangers were ever the only threat.

I turned the key in the lock to our apartment and was relieved to find darkness. Alone, I crawled into bed and pulled the sheets up to my chin, over my clothes, and squeezed my eyes shut, praying for sleep to swallow the night from my memory.

NOVEMBER 2006

The short week of classes before Thanksgiving slogged by. I sat through class after class, carving my thumbnail into the eraser of my pencil, staticky still images of the VHS haunting me anytime I felt my mind wander. Each memory a fresh golpe of shame and regret.

"I don't want you to hate me," I'd said on the tape, out loud, not just in my head.

Pablo had found it in the collection of porn tapes his older brother still kept in his bedroom. It was one of the few that wasn't relabeled *Bambi*, or *Dumbo*, or *Pinocchio*. I wasn't porn. I was "May 2001," like a model in a pinup calendar, except one I didn't know I'd posed for.

Anytime I tried to imagine the scope of this violation, how many people had viewed it, I was assaulted by the image of my body bending over, two-toned like a rhino, tan lines still visible from the summer before. The rip of the condom wrapper and the slap of Brian tossing the latex aside as he told me he'd put it on.

"Brisma?" Professor Acevedo called. "Earth to Brisma?"

I had daydreamed straight through Elements of Screenwriting II, and people around me were already gathering their bags and jackets to leave.

"Can you come up to see me for a moment?"

I closed my blank notebook and made my way to the front of the class.

Professor Acevedo handed me an envelope.

"You did it," she said with a smile.

"What?" I said, frowning.

"The fellowship," she said, tapping the envelope. "You're in!"

I stared at her, my mouth agape.

"I mean, you'll need to complete an interview with the program manager, but that's basically a formality at this point," she said, as she winked. "You'll ace that, no problem—" She stopped short when she realized I wasn't reacting the way she expected me to.

"What's going on?" she asked. "You not sleeping or something?"

"Honestly?" I said. "Something like that."

"Is it serious?"

I looked at her. I knew from taking two previous courses with her that she had grown up in Brooklyn during the '80s, years after Mami. She understood a lot of what I'd written about in her class before: machismo, the heartbreak of perpetually unavailable men, sexism and homophobia in the sports world. I didn't know if I could trust her with this, though. I didn't know if she'd see my side.

I took a chance and spilled everything to her: the watch, the breaking and entering, the Halloween fund-raiser, Kelly and the broken glass door, El Cochino, the train to Pelham, the VHS. When I finished, I felt like I was buzzing in the silence of the empty room, like my body, my mouth, and my fingers were still going, still catching up with my brain. Verbalizing everything for the first time was like releasing a genie from its bottle, and I'd never felt more distant from Kelly; *she* wasn't the one I was spilling my guts to anymore. She had chosen her side. All of our loyalty and fierce protection of each other over the years amounted to what, if not showing up now, showing up for this?

"Have you written about it?" Professor Acevedo asked.

"No," I said, as I tugged on my earlobe. "I mean, yes, of course I have, but only in my journal."

"Well," Professor Acevedo said as she stood up, "maybe you should write about it for real. Sometimes things only become clear after you've written everything down."

She shuffled the sheets from her lesson plan into a neat stack on the desk.

"I do know someone at *Newsday*," she offered. "An old friend who owes me a favor."

"The newspaper?" I asked. "You want me to publish something? I'm not a journalist."

"You don't have to be a journalist to write an op-ed," she said, her eyebrows raised and lips pursed—she knew she was pushing me out of my comfort zone.

"I can't write an op-ed!" I protested.

"Why not?"

"I don't know," I said, though part of me thought maybe she was right. Without Kelly, maybe all I had left was my story. It was tempting.

"Write your story," Professor Acevedo said, flicking her wrist. "And I'll help you share it the best I can."

"Thank you," I said, suddenly slammed with fear. "I might write something for myself. But I can't put people's dirty laundry out there like that."

Professor Acevedo slapped closed a folder from her desk and slid it inside her messenger bag.

"In public, you know. In front of everyone," I continued, quieter. "I don't want to . . ." I looked into Professor Acevedo's eyes. "Destroy his life. For what?"

She took a deep breath and pulled her shoulders back, the threads that held the buttons on her black blazer straining.

"For Janet? You don't owe anything to anyone but yourself, that's true. Maybe you'll write about it, and put it in a drawer, and move on with your life. But what if what you have to say can be used as character testimony against this kid at trial . . ." She tapped her finger on the top of the chair before her. "Are you willing to go to the cops? Or this girl's lawyer?"

"No," I said quickly. "Are you kidding? If I *do* come forward, no one can know it's me."

"Why not?" Professor Acevedo asked.

I squinted at her, and noticed beads of sweat had cropped up at her hairline. What had she been through in her own life, I wondered, that made her so quick to push me to share what I knew?

"It's not how we do things." I shook my head as if she should know better than to ask. "It would have to be anonymous."

She slid the strap of her bag onto her shoulder and sat down on the corner of her desk.

"Brian will know," she said quietly.

I sighed and shook my head. "Thanks for listening," I said, as I zipped up my coat. "It's late, though. I've got to get home and prepare for this interview, yeah?"

Professor Acevedo frowned, and I saw that her brows had already grown in from her last threading session.

"Yes," she said, "of course. Look out for an email from me." She pulled on her hat. "Like I said, I'll put you in touch with my contact."

I folded my lips in on themselves, between my teeth, and fingered the cap of a tube of ChapStick off and on inside my pocket. I wanted to be outside on the train hurtling away from this conversation already.

Professor Acevedo held up her palms. "Just in case," she said. "Think about it."

1996

Kelly snuck out during the final number of the sixth-grade Thanksgiving pageant to come find me. Mr. Hall, our director, had sent me to the teachers' lounge as punishment after Pablo and Brian were taunting Kelly so much backstage that I hip-bumped Pablo hard enough behind the curtain that he fell out onto the stage, all splayed limbs and Vans, at the foot of a life-size horn of plenty.

"Whoa," Kelly chuckled from the doorway. She slapped a palm against the side of the vending machine that sat at the entrance glowing blue. "Brisma in the hot seat!"

She walked over to the coffeemaker and plucked a tiny red straw off the counter to stick between her teeth.

"My mom's gonna kill me," I said, my head in my hands, tiny wisps of white feathers molting around me. Half the class, like me, had been given headbands with feathers hot-glued onto them to represent the Wampanoag tribe at the first Thanksgiving; the other half, like Kelly, received black construction-paper hats as pilgrims.

Kelly plopped down next to me and curled one leg up under her black skirt. "Nah," she said, her choppy new haircut falling into her face. "I'll tell Mr. Hall it was me. What's the worst he could do? Suspend me?"

"Yes," I said, pulling Kelly's pink scrunchie off my wrist and handing it back to her. "That's exactly the move he could pull."

"We're about to go on Thanksgiving vacation, Brisma," she said. "He wants to go home to his family, too."

We sat in silence then, the cheers of the audience in the auditorium a distant roar. I thought of how Kelly's face had crumpled when she looked out at the crowd and saw the empty seat next to Mami and realized her mother wasn't there. Frances had insisted Kelly take chorus because she had such a pretty voice, but Mami told me it was because she refused to cough up the money required to play in the school band. Regardless, it was the only compliment I remember Frances ever giving Kelly. And so it was important to Kelly that she show up. She'd not only been rehearsing her solo, a part in the finale singing "This Land Is Your Land," for weeks now, she asked Patrick's girlfriend to cut layers into her hair, like Rachel from *Friends*. Of course, she cut too much and Kelly ended up looking more like Joey than Rachel. Kelly had pinned it up into a bun as best she could, but pieces of her pin-straight hair kept falling out, and Pablo and Brian, drummers waiting to take the stage with the band, kept pulling even more out until the whole bun collapsed. The boys gasped but couldn't stop their laughter, which was when I decided to shove Pablo hard to shut him up.

"I thought your hair looked really nice," I said quietly.

Kelly allowed herself a brief smile.

"Don't lie," she said. "I look like one of those old-ass Franciscan friar statues at St. Agnes."

"It's not that bad," I laughed.

"You know," she said, as she tucked her other leg up on the seat to hug both knees, "you weren't half bad up there, either. Telling that story."

I smoothed my own hair back up into a ponytail. I was one of only two kids in the whole school who had participated in the citywide storytelling contest that fall; it was sponsored by WFAN and the winners would get to watch Bob Murphy and Gary Cohen call a Mets game from inside the broadcast booth at Shea next year. I was not one of the lucky few. Mr. Hall invited us to recite our stories for the show, anyway, and I told "The Gift of the Magi" by O. Henry during the pageant's intermission.

"You don't think I'm the biggest nerd on the planet?"

"Oh yeah, I do." Kelly tapped her straw against the table. "But it was kind of cool. Other people got to see the Brisma that I know."

"You think?"

She peered beyond me at the door Mr. Hall would walk through any second.

"When you talk," she said, the click of footsteps in the distance growing louder, "people listen."

I turned to see Mr. Hall standing in the doorway.

"Mr. Hall," Kelly said, raising two fingers in the air like she was calling over a waiter, "it was me. I pushed Pablo."

He exhaled then, tired, and walked over to slouch down into the chair opposite us.

"I mean, look at my hair," Kelly said, her body relaxed, her elbows resting on the back of her chair. She spoke to him like they were peers. "It was obviously me they were picking on. If anyone's gonna be punished today, it should be me."

"Kelly's just trying to protect me." I placed a hand on the table in front of her, as if to signal her to stop. "You know she's my best friend."

Mr. Hall stared at us for a few seconds before raising his fingers to his temples.

"I don't have patience for this tonight," he said. "Not for school-yard crushes, and certainly not any of this Spartacus mess."

"No, Mr. Hall, it's not like—" Kelly began, but he shook his head.

"Just go home, okay? And cut these boys some slack. They don't know how else to show they like a girl sometimes."

Kelly grabbed my hand and didn't waste any time pulling me toward the exit.

"Happy Thanksgiving, Mr. Hall!" she shouted over her shoulder as we ran to pick up our coats from a classroom near the auditorium.

"What an idiot," Kelly muttered, and we giggled pulling on our coats.

Outside on the sidewalk, I led Kelly by the hand as we navigated the crowd to find my mother.

"You were great up there," Mami said, hugging us. She plucked off my headband and smoothed back my hair. "No me gusta esto, pero you did a great job. Both of you."

I smiled at Kelly, nervously hoping to keep the teachers' lounge visit from Mami.

"Thank you," I said, still looking at Kelly.

Kelly squeezed my hand and was about to say something, when someone leaned hard on the horn of a car nearby.

"Kelly!" Frances shouted out the passenger side of a beat-up Chrysler. "Get in!"

I squinted in the darkness and made out Frances's boyfriend, Zayid, sitting in the driver's seat. Despite Kelly's allegiance to Andrés, we liked Zayid. He told us jokes, and took us to McDonald's, and asked about our schoolwork—nobody in Kelly's family ever asked about school. But Zayid was Egyptian, and Frances was never going to leave Andrés, no matter how poorly he treated her, for someone born on the African continent.

"Come on," Kelly said to me. "Let's go get McFlurries. Zayid's here."

I turned to Mami, as Kelly climbed into the backseat.

"Can I, please?" I clasped my hands together. "Please? I'll come right home after."

Mami pursed her lips and tightened her scarf around her neck.

"I think you're crazy, but fine." She patted my back. "I'll see you at home."

Kelly and I crowded into the dilapidated backseat, the carpet scratchy against our stockinged legs, cotton peeking through holes in the velvet seat cushion. We were careful to keep the baseball-size hole in the undercarriage between us, so we could watch the road whizzing by as Zayid drove us to the drive-through.

"You're late," Kelly said to her mother.

"You're lucky we got this hunk of junk to take us here at all," Frances spat.

"Kelly, let me see you," Zayid said, at a red light.

She popped up between the front-seat headrests. "You missed my performance."

Frances exhaled smoke from her cigarette out the window.

"I told you," she said, looking at Kelly up close for the first time. "We had car trouble. What the hell did you do to your hair?"

"I cut it," Kelly said, smoothing it down again.

Frances laughed, all gravel and sand, a wheeze.

I watched Zayid quietly appraise her in the rearview mirror.

"Gorgeous," he bellowed with a wink.

"Don't flatter her, Zayid," Frances scolded. "She don't need a bigger head."

"She's your daughter, Fran," he said. "It's not *flattery*."

Kelly plopped down next to me and stuck out her tongue at the back of the front passenger seat where Frances sat. She blew a raspberry at her, and we giggled as Zayid ordered two Oreo McFlurries and paid for them himself.

"Here," Zayid said, as he handed them back to us. "Happy Thanks-for-giving."

Kelly held out her plastic spoon like a trophy, and I tapped mine against hers.

"Happy Thanks Forgiving." We smiled and dug in, watching the road again turn into a blur beneath the rip in the carpet between us.

NOVEMBER 2006

When I stayed in the night before Thanksgiving to write the essay Professor Acevedo had suggested, instead of going out drinking with Kelly like we'd done every year since college started, Mami knew something was up.

"You're not going out tonight?" Mami asked, when I walked into the kitchen to grab a drink. She poked the naked, dimpled skin of the turkey on the table with her butcher knife.

"Good. Grab an onion and start chopping." She wore an open housecoat that used to belong to Abuelita before she passed away, and which Mami now used as an apron. Underneath, she had on thick black tights and a silk camisole that she'd worn that morning to evaluate a foreclosed brownstone in Ridgewood. She bent down, her elbows deep inside the turkey before her.

I wrinkled my nose at her.

"I don't know how you can do that."

"It's just a dumb bird," Mami said. "He doesn't even fly."

I slid onto a stool in front of her and tapped the top of my soda can with my finger.

"I think turkeys can fly," I said.

She lifted the turkey by its wings to expose its round body.

"Look at this gordito," she said. "He ain't going nowhere!"

"Gordita," I corrected her, cracking open the can in my hands.

"¿Ah?" Mami asked, pushing her glasses up on the bridge of her nose with her knuckle.

"The turkey," I said, twisting the tab back and forth. "Statistically, the turkeys we eat on Thanksgiving are usually the hens, not the males."

Mami rolled her eyes and flicked her wrist, still holding the knife, fruit juice running down her forearm. She couldn't stand Kelly, but the two of them used to gang up on me for being a smart-ass whenever I tried to correct them.

"How do you know all of these things?"

I shrugged.

"School?" I said. "The internet."

"Right," Mami began. "And so why is it you are moping around here when your life is about to take off?"

Just that morning, I'd aced my phone interview with the director of the internship program at ABC Studios, just like Professor Acevedo predicted.

"Ay, please," I said to Mami. "It's just a three-month thing. I'll be back before anyone knows it." I picked up a knife on the counter and slid the tip of it into an onion, resting all my weight down on the handle.

Mami kept her lips pursed as she squeezed the remaining orange juice into a bowl to make her signature mojo.

"What did Kelly say when you told her?" she asked.

I sighed. "Things haven't been good."

"Ah," Mami said. "I see."

"No, actually," I said, sliding my diced onions into a bowl, "you don't. Do you remember Brian?"

"Your boyfriend?"

It was quiet then, save for the chopping of steel against wood. How could I communicate what I was feeling? The guilt, the responsibility. The doubt about how I could have been so wrong about someone's character—someone I thought I knew inside and out. I chose my next words carefully.

"Were you ever so sure about who someone was," I began, sliding the blade into a celery stalk, "but then something happened that blew up everything you thought you knew? And the person you thought you knew so well turned out to be someone . . . that frightens you?"

Mami twisted the last orange half with the base of her palm and shifted her weight back onto her stockinged heels.

"Are you in trouble?" Mami asked.

"No," I whined, refusing to look away from the cutting board, permanently scored from years of preparing dinners for two.

"There was a situation," Mami said. "Once. A guy."

I looked up at her, blinking away the onion.

"What happened?"

"I was young," she continued. "Not as young as you are, but old enough to know better. I had just found out he was sleeping with my cousin."

"Who?" I asked. "Which cousin?"

"You never met her," she said, and gestured to the empty space beside her, "obviously."

"How did you find out?"

"He owed her money. He'd been borrowing money from her to pay rent," she said, with a cough. "Our rent."

"You lived together?"

She ignored my question. "She came to me one day with a list of checks she'd written him. She wanted her money back, and he was avoiding her. I thought she was crazy. Jealous." She pursed her lips at me, knowingly.

"But then I looked at our bank statements," she continued, "and I saw they were real. Her checks. He'd deposited every one of them. He was sloppy, really. Never even tried to hide it. I could've looked at our account at any moment, but I never did. I just trusted him, hook, line, and sinker."

"Who was this?" I asked.

"I told you, you don't know her."

"No," I clarified, "I mean, who was the guy?"

She turned to rinse the juguera in the sink, flipping the hot water on full force, steam rising quickly around her.

"You see, he never gave me a goddamn dime for rent," she said, as she scrubbed her nails with the brush she kept by the sink. "He was taking all this money from my cousin, and what was he even doing with it?"

She turned off the faucet and rested her hands on the edge of the sink.

"I confronted him," she continued. "Your grandmother was visiting us, and I was going to wait until she left, but that night he came home and I hadn't cooked anything for dinner I was so upset. He came barreling in, you know? He came in with his"—she balled her hands up in front of her—"his hairy fists banging on the table, pissed that I didn't have food ready for him. Instead, I'd left the copies of my cousin's checks out. I waited for him to notice."

I tried not to move a muscle. I didn't want to spook her from finishing the story.

"I was in the kitchen washing your bottles, and I stayed quiet, I didn't say nothing—"

"Wait—"

"That's when I heard him laugh, mija," Mami said, her top lip curling up. "He laughed. He was never gonna pay her back. Never had any plans to."

The only sound between us was the slow pitter-pattering of water as it dripped from her bare hands onto the cracked linoleum floor.

"I didn't say nothing. Not a word. I thought . . . . I had been a good wife. And Abuelita was trying to stay out of it, she was folding laundry in the next room."

She nodded at the knife in front of me.

"I lunged at him, Brisma. I came at him with a knife."

I watched Mami raise her shoulders in a contrite shrug. She was many things: tough, proud, hardworking, loving. But contrite was not a word I often used to describe her. She reached for the hem of her housecoat, wiping her damp hands on the fabric before looking up at me with red-rimmed eyes.

"I've never felt such an anger before or since," she said. "I could have killed him—I would have killed him. If your grandmother didn't stop me."

"You tried to kill my father."

She sniffed and dabbed the inside of her eye.

"Maybe it would have done us both a favor."

"Don't talk like that," I said, surprising myself.

"You're right," she said, reaching for a hand towel that hung from the oven door. She wiped the ring she wore on her pointer finger, a pearl in a gold setting that had been Abuelita's.

"Our lives could be very different," she said with a sigh. "You asked me if I've ever been shocked to discover someone's true nature. That night I was. I was terrified to realize that I was capable of taking a life, if I was pushed to it.

"That's why I became a nurse." She chuckled. "Not for the money, obviously. To atone for my sin. To help save lives instead."

"How come you never told me this before?" I asked. The turkey glistened between us under the kitchen's fluorescent lights, rivulets of juice dripping slowly down its sloping breast.

"I wanted you to find out your father was an asshole on your own," she said. "Besides"—she adjusted her head wrap down onto her forehead with her thumb and pointer finger—"I wanted to avoid you looking at me like that for as long as possible."

"Like what?"

"Like *you* don't know who I am anymore."

I sat there for a moment, not sure how to respond. I picked up a clove of garlic from a small glass bowl on the table and sliced into its smooth skin with my thumbnail, fishing out the green stem that had sprouted from its head.

"Mami," I started, "you know I won't be able to help you with your real estate plans."

I looked up at her, and she adjusted the glasses on her nose again with pinched fingers.

"When I graduate." I cleared my throat. "If I continue to pursue television. Writing, I mean. I won't be able to—"

"Nah," she snorted, smoothing down the front of her house-coat. "Baby, don't you worry about me."

She pointed her finger at me, Abuelita's pearl shining in the overhead light.

"You do you," she said. "You go after *your* dreams, okay?" She swallowed and straightened up again. "And I'll go after mine," she said, her voice, I thought, wavering a bit.

She ripped off a paper towel from the roll to fold around the knife and wipe it clean. Walking back toward the fridge, she called out over her shoulder, "The only person you can ever really depend on in this life is yourself."

She opened the door and thought for a moment.

"You need to discover your own power."

⌀

I returned to the night of the Nuyorican several times while writing. The shame I'd felt watching Brian's video threatened to annihilate me, if not for Mami's words. I could never again be who I was before viewing it. The weight of protecting other people, and their emotions, and their desires for so long, Brian and Kelly included, had finally broken me in the face of this pixelated evidence.

I had known a part of the real Brian, but looking back, there was so much that he had hidden from me, and that I had refused to see. The glint in his eyes that night at Pablo's party during truth or dare, the free, unrestrained laugh when he admitted that he'd returned to Janet's dorm room to hook up with her. "Of course," he'd said, his white teeth gleaming. How he shrugged me off with those loose, open shoulders, as if anyone would be dumb enough to believe his defense that he'd only wanted his free damn watch back. Maybe he did help Kelly that night with Nicky out of the small, good part of his heart, or perhaps it was something sinister, territorial; whatever his motivation, it didn't erase everything else that he'd done.

I wrote while sitting on the lavender comforter underneath which we'd spent several naked afternoons, pushing and pulling, but ultimately always acquiescing to his desires, the way I'd been taught, the way we all learned to assume responsibility for the impulses of the men in our lives. I watched my fingers fly across the keyboard, angry thoughts about how Kelly and I had willingly played the fool this whole time taking root inside my chest. How enraged we had been when we first heard of Janet's charges against Brian—how upset we were, not that he'd crossed a boundary, but that Janet demanded consequences for it! How entitled we thought she was. We never once stepped back to question the whole paradigm we'd found ourselves in—it wasn't like we'd even thought she was lying. We just hated her for daring to expect something closer to respect. And what about us? Why had we never expected the same for ourselves?

My heart ached for Kelly, and for Janet, and for me. I wanted to run to Kelly, to tell her that we'd been living our lives all wrong this whole time. Janet wasn't a threat—she made a choice, and she rightfully chose herself. I wished I could travel back in time to who we were as young girls sitting in our dugout, listening to games on WFAN through a shower radio we propped on the root of an old elm tree. I wished I could tell those girls not to define themselves by the attention, or lack thereof, from the boys, and the men, and the fathers in their lives. I wanted to forgive them for not having the respect for themselves that maybe they ought to have had . . . but how could we have learned to respect ourselves growing up, when no one ever showed us what that meant?

I folded my arms, rubbing the raised scar on my elbow, a purpled gash where a piece of glass from Kelly's sliding door had cut me, and I knew that too much between us had changed. After all the times I tried to protect Kelly, defend her, she couldn't even meet me halfway on this. "Don't act like you're so innocent," she'd said the night the black body bag was carried out of El Cochino's house. "No one comes out clean."

It would be so easy to hide, keep quiet. Mind my business.

Yet Janet was putting herself out there, seeking justice. I defended him, raised money for him. Denigrated other women for him. I knelt down before him that night at Pablo's in front of everyone. I begged him not to hate me, naked and in pain, and how many people had watched that? I imagined the same laughter he used when he talked about Janet, a girl he never even gave a name to. All of us just nameless girls whose bodies he felt entitled to.

I attached the Word document to an email from an anonymous account I'd set up for this very purpose and double-checked the contact information Professor Acevedo had forwarded me for *Newsday.* I read it and reread it, until I finally clicked send.

If this was going to end my world as I knew it, then I'd have a hand in its destruction with the only weapon left at my disposal: my truth.

DECEMBER 2006

The op-ed was published during finals week, the day before Brian's pretrial conference. The editor chose to run it under the headline "I Believe the Dorm Room Date Rape Victim." I cringed when I saw the words in large italic print. I imagined Janet's parents opening the paper in the perfect peach hues of their living room and blanching at the attention. I cringed, because I never once used that word for Janet, or me: "victim."

Besides a warm nod from Professor Acevedo and Mami buying a few extra copies, life appeared to continue on like normal. No brick through my window, no angry fists pounding on my door. I almost wished for it, though, some violence, because the leaded silence was unbearable.

"What did it even change?" I asked Pablo when he called, tapping the venetian blind cord between my fingers. "What did it do?"

"Brian's left," Pablo said. "Gone down south somewhere to play ball for the winter."

I hesitated. I hated that even then, after everything, a twinge of guilt sprouted in my chest. "You heard from him?"

"His stepdad told me when I called."

"Oh," I said. "Good."

Now Pablo hesitated. "You heard from her?"

"No." I sighed, craning my head at the window to see Kelly's yellow house at the end of the block. "And it kind of kills me. But I guess she's made her choice."

"I think that's all we have in the end," Pablo said. "The opportunity to make better choices. Or our own choices, anyway. And you made a brave-ass one."

I laughed then, a relief.

"I can't believe I'm even talking to *you* about this. After everything that's happened. When have you and I ever talked like this?"

"Things change," Pablo said, as he cleared his throat. "We've changed."

The phone grew hot in my palm. I shut the curtains and relaxed into the chair beside the window. I tried hard not to imagine sixteen-year-old Pablo watching the tape of me.

"You did the right thing," I said, "telling me."

"You were the one with the courage," Pablo said, "to tell everybody else."

I soon began receiving emails from more and more women, girls we went to school with, who reached out to me on Myspace and email with stories of their own about Brian. They'd start their messages with "Did you hear about this?" or "Is this you?" The blue hyperlink to my op-ed glared in each message before they launched into their own experiences with Brian. With each new story someone shared with me, the decision to share mine was reinforced. I wasn't unheard and alone. Each view of that tape had been a new violation. He coerced me that night on Pablo's back deck, too. He'd manipulated me all along. With the truth acknowledged and outside of me now, I felt I could begin to move on. The community of women who showed up for me in my in-box helped.

The op-ed did eventually make small waves on the St. John's campus, too: Brian was quietly removed from any position on the baseball team, including equipment manager, and according to Pablo, when his scholarship was revoked, it was unclear whether he would return to school at all after winter break. A lawyer who Kelly's cousin had used to beat a Xanax charge ended up representing Brian and quietly agreed to a plea deal of community service for the charge of breaking and entering. One short line in the brief article that appeared in the *Stamford Advocate* addressed the rest: "Sexual assault charges were dropped by the prosecution prior to sentencing."

I typed, and deleted, and retyped an email to send to Janet, but decided on a simple heart emoticon: "<3." She responded the next day, writing, "Thanks. I just couldn't do it, you know? A trial. All I want is my life back."

Brian's lawyer, speaking to a reporter for a local news channel, thanked the prosecution for dropping those charges, and for "not ruining a boy's future over a foolish error in judgment that would force him to register as a sex offender for the rest of his life." After two years of good behavior, Brian would have the opportunity to expunge the breaking and entering charge from his record, too. Over the lawyer's shoulder, I saw Brian standing with his hands clasped, looking remorseful—his parents nowhere in sight, but Kelly right beside him. It was a clear line in the sand—cement, really—between us. Kelly had presumably read my essay, learned about the tape, and still chose him. Like the priority Mami gave my father, and El Cochino. Like Frances chose Andrés and Timothy. I remained unconsidered.

But this time, at least, I knew I wasn't alone.

⁂

In the middle of all this, I graduated. No pomp, considering the circumstance. I didn't want to make a big deal out of it, and so Mami and I just roasted a small pernil for Nochebuena and ate cueritos all night while the Yule log cracked on, glowing orange from our television screen.

She gave me a graduation gift: a white-gold tennis bracelet with an engraving on the back.

"A tennis bracelet," she'd said, beaming, as I opened the box. "You've always wanted one, remember?"

I smiled at her. I didn't really know what a bracelet had to do with tennis, but I remembered reading the Babysitter's Club books in third grade and learning that a tennis bracelet was a delicate, elegant thing that a girl was supposed to want. And I remembered that Christmas before Mami's Mary Kay business fizzled out when I found the mysterious MAKE ME FEEL IMPORTANT bracelet among her holiday bags.

"Turn it over," she said.

On the back, she'd had a sentence engraved: AND I KNOW THAT THE HAND OF GOD IS THE PROMISE OF MY OWN.

"Walt Whitman?" I asked, surprised.

Mami nodded, her face alight with satisfaction.

"Yeah, I know a few things, too," she said, shrugging her left shoulder pointedly in my direction. "I read."

"Where'd you learn about Walt Whitman?" I asked, unclasping the chain.

She shrugged.

"School," she said, mocking me, echoing our conversation from Thanksgiving. "The internet."

I wrapped my arms around her shoulders and thanked her, knowing that she hadn't earned anything from her real estate ventures yet, and that it had likely cost many hours of overtime from her last months at the hospital to afford this gift for me. I fingered the engraving that night with the pad of my thumb, as I hovered the cursor of my laptop over a cheap flight to California. The spot in the fellowship was mine for the taking. I just needed to buy the plane ticket.

In one click, my path would depart from JFK to a new life on the opposite coast. I was both excited and terrified; it would be my first time to ever board a plane in my life.

Beneath it all, a current of anxiety rumbled at my core, like a hole in my undercarriage, leaving me exposed to the dangerous, speeding road below. The essay had set me on an entirely different course away from Kelly, and I could feel her coming rage in my bones the way a horse might sense an approaching storm.

1996

That fall after the last St. Agnes fair, after Timothy's VIRGINIA IS FOR LOVERS postcard had long since floated off on a trash barge up the Hudson, a few weeks into the start of sixth grade, Kelly and I spent a Saturday cleaning out the Moraleses' basement—a chore that her older brother had foisted upon us with the dangling carrot of sneaking us in with him to that night's Mets game if we completed the task.

"Ugh," I said, picking up a broom. "We're never going to be done in time. There's so much crap down here."

Kelly jumped down from a mountain of discarded belongings that included a stained high chair, folded playpens, and a random porcelain sink. The soles of her handed-down Keds slapped against the cement floor as she walked over it. In her hand was a white hard-plastic shell that she tossed at my feet.

"Like my brother's old cup?"

Horrified, I kicked it into the trash can.

"Guys are so disgusting."

Kelly dusted off her hands and picked up a stuffed Porky Pig that looked newer than the other items in the pile. Timothy had won it from an arcade game and brought it home for Kelly. It reminded me—I'm sure it reminded both of us—instantly of his Looney Tunes boxers she had buried earlier that summer when he attacked us.

"Sometimes I just want to run away," she said, fingering the pig's snout. "Take my chances"—she turned in the direction of Manhattan—"out there."

"Well," I said, "you're eleven. So I'm guessing you'd die pretty quickly."

Kelly laughed, but it turned sharply into a high-pitched squeal of anger.

"You're right," she said, and shot the pig into a wastebasket. "Let's just throw everything into a garbage bag."

"Why don't you have a sidewalk sale?" I asked. "Make some money off this junk?"

Kelly raised her eyebrows as she snapped a new trash bag open in front of her.

"You would charge people on the block actual cash for your used-up old stuff?" she asked, a smile teasing the corners of her mouth as she turned her back on me. "How embarrassing."

Kelly was recently horrified to learn that Mami turned a (very small) profit on the Mary Kay cosmetics she sold to neighbors. Kelly had looked at me with real betrayal and disdain in her eyes. "You mean she makes money off of us?"

"Us," she had said, as if she or her mother ever cracked open one of the catalogs my mother carefully delivered to them, complete with moisturizer and lipstick samples.

"Here," she said, handing me a corner of a thick blue plastic tarp. "Help me with this."

I grabbed the material and pulled, but only managed to yank it out about a foot or two from behind a tattered old recliner.

"Wait a second," I said, noticing the faded gray dolphins printed on it. "I know what this is!"

Kelly smiled.

"You remember," she said, fingering the silver duct tape that ran along a ripped wave in the painted ocean scenes. "This pool has seen better days."

When we were little, after Ricki Lake and Jenny Jones had aired on Channel 9 and Frances was passed out on her bed upstairs, we would spend the rest of a hot summer afternoon playing *Baywatch* in that inflatable kiddie pool in her backyard. We'd take turns rescuing each other from "drowning," wrapping one of our arms around the other person's torso and lifting them out of the water, sneaking in mouth-to-mouth resuscitation until Frances woke up and yelled at us from the second-floor balcony, "Stop that!" Two words like flat slaps clapping down, sending us sloshing to the sides of the pool in shame.

"I remember," I said quietly. I remembered her birdlike shoulders bouncing against the rim of the pool as I performed fake chest compressions. I remembered the dank suction of her bathing suit against the hollow of my chest as her body lay on top of mine. I remembered pinching her nose closed, and how her cold lips felt as I just barely parted them with my own, gently, and the laughter that followed when I blew a lungful of air into her mouth.

I don't remember how long it was after Timothy arrived that we stopped playing *Baywatch*. I don't remember when the feelings of shame began to lift from my memory, or if they ever did. If they didn't evaporate, but rather enriched the soil from which I continued to grow.

"It's trash now," she said, wrapping the tough plastic under her elbows and yanking hard. She ripped the pool loose from an exposed nail in the wall it was snagged on, but shrieked as she cut her hand on it and tripped backward.

"Look," she said, holding up her hand, blood trickling down her palm.

"Wash it off." I walked to the functioning sink and turned on the faucet full force. "You could get tetanus or something."

Kelly held her bleeding hand as she ran over to the sink and sucked her teeth at me.

"The hell you know about tetanus?"

I shrugged, watching the blood run pink off her hand.

"Do you ever wonder what life would be like without boys?" she asked, still facing the wall. "Without men at all?"

"No," I laughed, grabbing a clean rag. "I mean sure, they're disgusting and terrible. But who else would we obsess over?"

"Imagine if Queens was just filled with girls," she continued. "Wouldn't it be so much more . . . peaceful?"

"A Queens filled with queens?" I smirked.

"Yes!" She splashed water as she turned to me. "Yes, you're right. Fuck that, I don't want to be a girl. Definitely not a princess. I want to be a queen."

"But if we're all queens, doesn't that negate the purpose?"

"Negate the what?" She shook her head. "You're thinking too much. Of course we can all be queens. Each of us rulers of our own world."

Kelly held her wounded palm up close to her face, studying where the nail had ripped a shallow oval crater in her skin.

"Hey, you okay?"

"It's like I'm Jesus," she said with a playful smile, extending both arms out at her sides.

We laughed, but as I watched a drop of blood blot the cement floor red, I had an idea.

"Hold on," I said.

I opened a few drawers of a painted dresser by the stairs, searching for Frances's old tattoo supplies. She had designed tattoos for a few people on the block, but she also got into the idea of doing her own tattoos at home for a while. I grabbed one of the packaged needles I was looking for and held it up to Kelly in triumph.

"I've always wanted to do this." I ripped open the package.

"A tattoo?"

"No," I said, steadying the metal against my finger. "It's just the needle, no ink."

I pierced it under my skin, a shallow puncture, but enough for a single bead of blood to surface on the tip of my finger.

"See?" I grabbed her stigmataed hand and wrapped my finger inside her palm.

Her lips tightened into an *O*, as if in pain, but no sound followed her sharp intake of breath.

"We are blood sisters," I said.

Kelly slowly smiled, her slight underbite teasing me, ready to call me corny, but she didn't. She blinked and repeated back to me, "Blood sisters."

I released her. "You'll never be rid of me now."

I expected her to laugh again, to call me out on some more bruja stuff, but instead her smile wore off.

"I'd never want to be," she said sincerely, before bending down to finish washing the gash in the oversize sink. I saw her glance over at the pile of junk we'd only made a dent in.

"You're the best thing I have," she said, turning off the water and grabbing the clean rag I had thrown over my shoulder.

I didn't know how to respond, beyond the wounded-kitten sound I found myself making and instantly regretting. I felt the weight, not only of the clutter in the basement closing in on us then, but of the soil behind the walls, the storied landfill of Queens Boulevard her family told us about, dumped on that road to make us a thoroughfare. How many generations would it take before the pile of everyone else's shit we'd let grow unabated swallowed us whole? Would we ever be able to dig ourselves out from underneath it all and find ourselves not girls anymore, but queens in our own right?

Kelly sniffed and wrapped her hand once, twice with the cloth, then tucked it in tight.

"All right," she said. "We've got work to do."

NEW YEAR'S EVE 2006

Pablo remained off-base through the holidays as he tried to sell his dad's house in Elmhurst. He'd forwarded me a few links to articles he found on the internet about Brian's case, but there was never any note from him attached to the emails, so I felt no compulsion to respond. I still felt a little raw and exposed after our last phone call. After a few unanswered texts, he emailed me that he had officially cut off contact with Brian and was leaving for Florida after the New Year. They'd received an offer on the house, and he was going to embark on the long drive south to Orlando with his dad and brother in early January.

I decided I couldn't face seeing Pablo in person before he left. I didn't want to feel his eyes on me, the same eyes he'd laid on that VHS tape several times while I remained in the dark. I didn't want to be reminded that I—that we both—had been protecting a predator. I wondered, peeking through my venetian blinds at the curtains drawn closed in the lit window of Kelly's bedroom, if Kelly felt the same way about seeing me. Or if she was still steadfast in her belief in Brian.

Yet Pablo arrived at my door shortly after the sun went down on New Year's Eve.

"Get dressed," he said, his face glowing red and green from the chintzy Christmas decorations Mami had strung up along the iron bars that caged our windows. The shadow of a beard had begun to sprout along his jawline. "We're going to PJ Moore's."

"Like hell we are," I said, pulling the storm door closed. "I'm not going anywhere."

"You can't just hide for the rest of your life," Pablo said, palming the glass pane of the door. "Or until you leave for California."

I looked at him.

"How do you know about that?"

"Your mom told me." He smiled. "I ran into her at Hong Kong Supermarket."

"Goddamn," I muttered. "She can't resist a three-dollar chicken breast."

"She's so proud of you," he continued, ignoring me. He bit his lip. "I am, too."

"Oh," I exhaled. "You're not going to cry, are you?"

"Brisma," he said, his dark eyes trained on me. "Don't do that. You're making moves." He shifted his weight onto the splintered doorframe. "Getting out of here. Don't downplay it."

This new Pablo kept insisting on being genuine instead of playing by the sarcastic ball-busting rules of our block. The army had changed him in some ways better than others.

"Shut up," I said, blushing, but moved aside to make room for him to enter. "Guess you're outta here, too, huh?"

"Yup," he said, his heavy boots stepping into the shared hallway. "We hit the road this Wednesday."

He crossed his fingers.

"I think it's the right thing," he said. "You know?" He swallowed. "I've been struggling with what the right thing to do is, with my dad, with Brian, with you."

His voice cracked a bit, a sheepish vulnerability that felt incongruous with the boy I used to know, with the solid, imposing man who stood in front of me.

"I want you to know," he said, as I pulled the door closed behind him, muting the rattling sound of a truck barreling down the road behind him, "I destroyed all the tapes I could find. Ariel claimed he had no idea how they got mixed up with his stuff."

He squinted at me.

"We don't really get along anymore. I don't know why I ever looked up to him." He took his hat off. "Or Brian."

"Sure you do," I said, sliding the chain into the lock on the doorframe. "We thought they were cool."

We walked up the stairs and into the apartment together.

"Was there . . . ," I started, unsure of how much to reveal. "Did you find any tapes of Kelly?"

Pablo frowned as he unzipped his jacket.

"No," he said. "Was there one?"

I continued on into the kitchen.

"I really hope not."

Pablo shrugged his jacket off before I bent to dig through the bottom shelf of the fridge, my fingers finally grasping the frosty neck of the lone green Heineken bottle rattling around in the back.

"She misses you, you know."

I cracked open the beer with Mami's El Morro bottle opener.

"You've talked to her?"

"No," he said. "She wants nothing to do with me. But I know."

"Don't be so sure," I said, placing the bottle in his hands.

"You guys go so far back," he said. "It would be a shame if you let Brian—"

"It's about more than just Brian now," I interrupted, leading him into the living room.

"Do you really want to leave for California without one last night—at least one last drink—at PJ Moore's?" He lowered himself onto the sofa. "Kelly or no Kelly?"

Pablo remained ramrod straight on the cream chenille cushions, his elbow propped at a ninety-degree angle on the worn-thin couch arm.

"You just want a buddy so you can have *your* last drink at PJ Moore's," I whined.

He smiled and nodded back toward the hallway that led to my bedroom.

"Go ahead, get dressed."

"Sir, yes sir," I joked, bringing my flexed hand to attention at my brow.

"I promise," he laughed, "we'll go just long enough for them to play Journey. First Journey song"—he clapped—"and we're out of there. No harm, no foul."

I smiled and nodded, grateful for the release of tension I realized I'd been holding in my neck and shoulders for the last few weeks. I was so caught up in reevaluating who I'd been in my past, about choosing what to do in my present and how to navigate my next steps forward, that I'd forgotten how it felt to laugh. I'd forgotten that not every man was a monster—and that maybe there was hope even for those who were. If Pablo could change, maybe anyone could, if they were willing to put in the work. Brian wasn't anywhere close to that—that much was clear.

I still had hope for Kelly, though. And so I opened my closet door and searched past the National League Playoff hoodies and Palmer's

Cocoa Butter–branded free Mets T-shirts to grab a scoop-neck T-shirt of shiny black fabric to slip on over my tank top.

"With any luck," I said, "it'll be 'Don't Stop Believin'.'"

Pablo laughed.

"We can only hope."

❧

"This seems a little unceremonious," I said, leaning into the starchy fabric of Pablo's shoulder, silver garland hanging down around us from hooks above the bar. "Don't you think?"

He smelled fresh, like clean laundry and jewelry cleaner.

"What does?" he asked, pulling the drinks he'd ordered close to his chest.

"To be drinking a boring old Smithwick's on New Year's Eve," I answered, taking one from his hands. "On our last New Year's Eve?"

I raised the mug, turning my wrist to examine the caramel-colored beer as best I could in the light thrown from the mini disco balls screwed into the lamps along the wall.

"Here," I added quickly. "Our last New Year's Eve here together. For a while, at least."

"Nah," he said, placing a hand on my elbow. "I think it's perfect."

I smiled as he downed the rest of his whiskey.

"Fuck all that fancy shit, anyway," he said with a cough.

"Pablo!" I laughed. "I thought you were above such language now," I said. "A military man and all."

"You should hear us, Brisma," he said. "Queens ain't got nothing on the Twenty-Sixth Infantry."

I shrugged, laughing and happy to be getting along with him.

That's when I first spotted her. She was dancing by the unlit fireplace in the back, wearing a halter top that matched the decorations hanging in the bar—shiny and silver with straps that tied in a bow at the nape of her neck, like a gift. Her skin sparkled with sweat, or the glittery lotion she'd stocked up on before Bath & Body Works discontinued it, and when I saw her trinity knot tattoo peeking out from beneath the thin fabric as she danced, I could tell she wasn't wearing a bra—a weightless freedom her thin frame could pull off that I never could.

Pablo followed my gaze and cleared his throat.

"I'm gonna go to the bathroom," he said.

"No—" I grabbed his forearm.

"Don't worry," he said. "Order me another beer." He winked. "I'll be right back."

I tried to get the attention of the bartender, but he was deep in conversation with a curly blonde. I pushed off the lip of the bar, keeping one eye trained on Kelly in the back, and crept out the side exit for a cigarette I'd hoped to bum off of someone—an art Kelly and I had perfected before we graduated high school.

"You're not really a smoker," she used to say, "if you never buy your own pack."

There was one lone guy in the smoker's garden area who wasn't part of a larger group. I wasn't in the mood to get roped into a conversation with a whole crew of meatheads and play the part of Flirty Drunk Girl in return for one cigarette's worth of nicotine. He was taller than most of the other smokers, and had longish hair that he wore swept back and over his ears, where I noticed a familiar-looking diamond earring.

"Hey," I said, as I began my old routine, "would you possibly be willing to spare—"

He turned and that's when I realized why he was so familiar: it was Nicky Gargiullo.

I felt the beer in my stomach turn to a solid lead brick. I felt dizzy, the gummy cracks in the sidewalk swinging upward for a moment, disoriented as if I'd time-traveled and arrived at a terrible mistake.

"You okay?" Nicky asked, a heavy brow raised, as he flipped a cigarette out from his soft pack to offer me.

I grabbed the cigarette, squeezing the sponge of thick filter between my fingertips.

"No." I shook my head. "I mean, yes."

I frowned at him, squinting. *Does he not recognize me? How embarrassing*, I thought. *That we shared the same class for years—that he raped my best friend—and he has no idea who I am.*

"I know you, don't I?" I asked, still squinting, as if racking my brain to place him.

Nicky put out his cigarette in a potted plant by the door and blew the last of his smoke out of a crooked mouth.

"Nah," he said, an open palm rubbing the soft T-shirt fabric on his chest. "I don't think so."

He excused himself and walked past me and back in through the side entrance, where at the threshold he bumped into Kelly.

I watched her face go pale, paler than the late-December moon that shone down on us above a billboard that read SMILE: WOODSIDE DENTIST. It looked like a full New Year's moon; I wished I had done the research I remember Kelly had done back when she was on her bruja kick. I wondered how significant the moon was, if its appearance meant something at this time in our lives, that we would ring in *this* new year under the light of a full moon.

Nicky grabbed her by the elbow, and she stiffened as he pulled her into an embrace. Briefly, her eyes met mine over his shoulder, and she blinked her way through what looked like forced pleasant-ries. I felt the lead in my belly slide down and turn my legs into two unmovable pillars, keeping me from walking over there to protect her, as if I could, as if I ever did. It would take a long time, I realized, to be free of those reflexes. Kelly was encoded in my DNA.

It was over as quickly as it began, though, and the flash of vulner-ability on her face was gone as she staggered over to me, teetering on her cheap high heels.

"I knew rats tended to congregate back here," she said, producing a cigarette from the inside of her clenched palm.

"Did you know he'd be here?" I asked. I offered her the lit tip of my cigarette for her to light hers, the smoker's peace offering.

"That asshole?" she said with a frown, towering over me.

Taking my cigarette, she steadied it to the tip of hers, and I felt her body relax next to mine, the muscle memory of a lifelong friend-ship.

"To be honest," she said, as she exhaled a cloud of cold air and Marlboro Red, leaning back on the window ledge behind her, "you're the one I'm surprised to see again."

A group of girls at the other end of the penned-in garden area erupted in excited screams.

"What does that mean?" I asked. "I live down the street from you."

"Not for long though, right?" Her voice rose sweetly at the end of her question, a saccharine affectation of forced excitement, but her eyes locked on mine in a calculating panic.

I broke into a sweat. These were too many reckonings at once.

"Your mom told me," she said, echoing Pablo from earlier in the evening. I knew by the way she said it that it was the ultimate be-trayal, in a season of betrayals, that hurt her.

"Good for you." She dragged loudly on her filter. "Leaving Queens."

"It's a ten-week fellowship," I tried to explain, wincing at the word "fellowship," which I knew would only sound pretentious, a word that meant nothing to her, but me feeling myself.

"It's like an internship," I offered with an eye roll, that familiar urgent need to diminish my own accomplishments to make room for her pain.

"Are you getting paid?" she asked, a brow cocked, her eyes cast downward.

The old bow and arrows of defense rose in my chest.

"Yes," I said, though that wasn't entirely true. I'd receive a stipend and housing but no actual paycheck. So it wasn't entirely false, either. I guess I wasn't ready to lay down my old weapons.

"I'm happy for you," she said, locking her eyes on mine. "I mean it."

Shocked, I looked down at the cigarette burning between my fingers and then back up at her. She had turned to look down the road.

"I'm going to France."

I smiled.

"Oh yeah?"

"Yeah," she said. "One of my professors offered me his house in the South of France over winter break, so I figured, why not?" She brushed a strand of hair off her face, where sweat had caked concealer in the lines around her strained smile.

I knew even if the offer was real, Kelly would never make it onto the plane.

"You hate to travel."

She sucked her teeth.

"No, I don't."

"Are you taking your boyfriend?" I asked, shifting the energy between us immediately. She looked at me, then back in the direction of traffic.

"Brian's at a baseball clinic." She shrugged her left shoulder up to rub an itch on her chin. "All of January. In Arizona."

"Oh," I said. "Pablo told me he was kicked off the team."

"Fuck Pablo," she said, spitting. "You can't listen to anything Major Save-a-Ho has to say."

"Don't call him that," I said, looking at the door, half expecting to see him appear, as if speaking his name would manifest his presence.

"Ah." Kelly smiled. "Who has a boyfriend now?"

"It's not like that," I said, waving my hand. "At all."

"Me neither." She shrugged and bent down to crush the end of her cigarette into a black spot of dried gum on the sidewalk. "For the record. It wasn't like that with Brian."

"Okay." I didn't have the strength to argue with her anymore.

"I swear, I know it probably looked bad," she said, picking up her drink, "and maybe we got somewhat close, but I mainly just didn't want to see him go down like that. After . . ."

She looked toward the door Nicky had disappeared through back into the bar.

"Of all the people out there, I just didn't think he deserved it." She held the glass of half-melted ice up to the light and shook it, appraising how much of her drink she had left. "I thought you'd understood that."

We stood there for a moment studying each other, each of us wondering, perhaps, when it was that we became strangers. I tried to arrange my jaw, and tongue, and teeth to form any kind of response, but I knew on some level that no words could reach Kelly, nothing I said could change the pain and shame that were woven into every fiber of her being, that prevented her from seeing the truth: that we both had deserved better all along. It was then that a redhead bounced out of the open doorway and tugged on Kelly's arm.

"Come on!" she yelped. "Dame más gasolina," she sang along with Daddy Yankee piping in over the outdoor speakers.

Kelly tipped her tumbler of clear alcohol and chewed lime wedge to her mouth and downed what was left of it.

"Who the hell is that?" I asked, an unexpected edge to my voice.

She cut one last look at me, her chin resting on her pockmarked bare shoulder.

"A friend," she said. "You know, someone who's loyal."

She bounded after the redhead as Pablo's voice echoed in my mind, *"Don't do that to yourself."* Kelly's words cut, but then I had expected a certain level of flagellation. I brought the glass of Smithwick's to my mouth. When did I learn that I was responsible for Kelly's pain in addition to my own? When did I take that on?

Inside the bar, I searched for Pablo. He was near the front door, chatting up an Albanian girl I vaguely remembered from high school. I finished my beer and placed it on a high table with a loud clang as I made my way toward him.

"I'm out of here," I said.

Pablo frowned and cocked an ear toward the speakers.

"Uh-uh," he said, pointer finger in the air. "This is reggaetón. I haven't heard Journey yet."

"Yeah, yeah," I said, picking up my jacket from a pile of coats that had slid to the floor beneath a nearby table. "I came, we drank, I talked to Kelly. I'm out."

"How was it?"

I threw my arms open at him, exasperated.

"Not great!"

Pablo's eyes focused on something just beyond my right shoulder. Hours past the new year, the DJ was still amping people up, lots of hip-hop air horns and pig whistles, and he'd just started spinning Fatman Scoop. But under that, I could hear muted *thwap*s of closed fists on soft flesh, like a mallet tenderizing meat, and what sounded like an animal whining in pain.

I turned and saw Kelly being carried out by Wilmer, the bouncer who'd cut his way through the crowd to the dance floor in back. She was kicking and punching wildly, long sweaty hair whipping around her shaking head. As he carried her down the length of the bar, she reached for any and all projectiles she could grab from the tabletops she passed and launched them in the direction of a man's voice shouting back at her, thick with the weight of a Queens accent: Nicky.

"You crazy fuckin' bitch!" I heard. "I don't even know you!"

"I will fucking kill you," she screeched, drunk, her face contorted by a naked rage that I wanted to help her cover, to shield from the public. A naked rage we never directly acknowledged, but which haunted both of us, lurking always at the edges of our vision, in the dark corners of basements and dimly lit apartments. Seeing her rage was seeing my own, and it was in that moment that I understood two things: I would always fight for her because of this shared pain, and until she was willing to do the work she'd never be able to accept the truth about Brian. Acknowledging that he'd done something wrong would mean that she'd need to acknowledge all the times every other man had done her wrong—and that amount of pain was too massive, too overwhelming to consider. So she had to resist it to function. To survive.

Pablo shouldered his way past me, but I grabbed his hand and pulled him back.

"No," I told him, as Wilmer took the shrieking Kelly out the front door. "Not you this time."

I looked back in Nicky's direction to see if he was following, but he was too busy fixing his ripped collar where Kelly had clearly attacked him and shrugging her off as a "crazy bitch" to the friends surrounding him, none of whom I recognized. I watched a white woman with perfectly highlighted extensions wrap her arm around his, and as she brought a glass to her lips, I noticed that she was wearing an engagement ring on her left hand. Nicky was engaged, then. I wondered if she knew the kind of man Nicky was, if she knew what he had done to Kelly, and whether he had done the same to other girls. But the truth, I knew, was a mold that spread quickly through all the rooms in the house of cards we built ourselves to live in.

Wilmer deposited Kelly on the curb next to the red *Village Voice* bins. She stumbled to her feet, her ankles buckling under her. In the cold night air, her anger had been reduced to billowing clouds of condensation from sputtering coughs and whimpers. Her bony shoulders poked out from beneath the black peacoat the bouncer had thrown over her. Before the coat could slide all the way off, I wrapped my arm around her and tugged it on tight.

"For fuck's sake," she cried, laughing when she saw it was me who'd caught her.

"How did I not realize how drunk you are?" I asked.

She chuckled again, licking back a bit of spit that had landed on her lip.

"You weren't looking," she said.

I hailed a black cab, and Wilmer nodded at me as I collected Kelly into the backseat. I checked back over my shoulder to make sure no one—not Nicky or Pablo—followed us.

JANUARY 2007

Kelly's head bobbed listlessly in the corner of the backseat of the Lincoln Town Car as we rolled over the bumps and steel seams of Queens Boulevard; the city had been razing the streets to install parking in two of the three available lanes of the narrow service roads. I reached over to place a hand across her forehead so that it wouldn't bang against the window, which already had grease marks from her sweat and makeup. Behind her through the back window, I could see the faraway lights of Manhattan apartment buildings flickering a cruel farewell in the still darkness of early morning. I wanted to remember that skyline forever. The skyline that had always felt like a birthright, now felt more like a favorite dress I'd outgrown: uncomfortable and unflattering, but full of memories I would always cherish.

Kelly banged her palm against the door handle twice. I thought she was attempting to get out, but she made no other movement until she turned her head in my direction, eyes still closed.

"It's ironic, huh?" she whined through her nose.

The concealer around her mouth that had been caked on thick was now smeared away, revealing red blotches of acne just above her lip. It comforted me to see it, to see the real Kelly as I knew her.

"What is?" I asked, fingering a button on my coat.

"Tonight," she said with a hiccup, raising her eyelids just enough to reveal her pupils. "It took my rapist for us to get past the drama of yours."

She laughed, and it sounded a little bit like Frances's gravel, like a dormant volcano stirring in her lungs. I was uncomfortable so I laughed, too.

"Are we?" I asked. "Past it?"

Kelly rolled her head back to the window, condensation fogging the glass where her breath hit it. She kept her eyes open, but I could tell they weren't focused on any one thing. I gathered the heels she'd kicked off in the backseat and held her feet up on my lap to slip on the extra pair of rolled-up flats I kept in my purse.

The cab pulled over and let us out on the corner where a street that kids on the block called "Cobra Hill" T-boned Clement Moore Avenue. As I handed the cash to the driver through the divider, I noticed the clock on the dash. It was later than I thought—the sun would be up soon.

"Come on, girl," I said, as I wrapped Kelly's arm around my neck and lifted her out of the passenger-side door onto wobbly feet. "We're gonna get you home if it's the last thing I do."

The street was quiet, everyone in bed after the festivities of the night before. The pavement glittered, and the only sound that echoed within the canyon of brick-and-aluminum siding around us was the shuffling of our thin polyester flats across it. The silver sign of a contractor reflected the light of the streetlamps from where it hung on the new chain-link fence that went up around La Señora's house after the car crash in November.

We struggled down the concrete steps, bitten away by salt from last winter's blizzards, and stumbled to her blue front door, which they always left unlocked, daring would-be thieves and criminals to enter.

I tugged Kelly up the carpeted staircase to the second floor, masterfully avoiding the creaky spots on the banister. I managed not to wake up her brother while laying her gently on her bed. I lifted her legs up and placed a wastebasket beside her bed. Her hair was greasy and matted around her pale face, so I gathered it up and tied it in a loose bun. Above her, I noticed pictures of us still taped to her wall: at the St. Agnes carnival, at her brother's birthday party, tailgating with beer and sandwiches at Shea before a Subway Series game. The photos remained there, unchanged, despite everything that had happened. There were no pictures of Brian.

Suddenly, Kelly reached out and grabbed my wrist with a clammy finger bloated by alcohol.

"Don't leave," she whined. It was a whimper on a cloud of vodka. She adjusted herself on the bed, sliding a tangled sheet out from underneath her.

"If you leave," she slurred, "I'll never forgive you."

"Shh," I whispered, not wanting to wake her brother. I leaned my weight against her bed. "Why would you say that?"

She smacked her lips together a few times and turned away from me to nuzzle the left side of her face against her pillow. I watched her chest rise and fall until I suspected she'd finally fallen asleep. I took a step back and grabbed the doorknob to leave.

"You'll never come back," she said, turning onto her other side, the mattress squeaking beneath her.

It was familiar, the feeling of being stabbed in the heart and wanting to apologize for it at the same time. I wanted to tell her she was being stupid, that of course I would come back, that we could go back to how it used to be, that this block was where I came from, that she was my family, that nothing would change that. But I froze and let the feeling turn to anger and then to sadness. She was right.

I closed the door behind me carefully and quickly tiptoed down the stairs, through the front door, and back up the steps to the sidewalk. As I crossed the street, I stopped at the double-yellow lines on the blacktop and looked up toward the crest of the hill. Cars usually came barreling down the hill at all hours, but this morning, in the twilight of a new month, a new year, the road was silent, and I was alone in the brisk January air. I could see the stoplights, a slow, glowing red, then green, just beyond the hill. Behind me, only a few cars accelerated gingerly down Queens Boulevard, drivers nursing hangovers and lingering buzzes from the night before. I closed my eyes and breathed deeply. Far off, I smelled the burn of a firecracker floating on the breeze. The solid cold of the pavement seeped through my thin flats and numbed the arches of my feet.

I felt alive. And alone. It became clear to me then that this was all that mattered. I sat down on the double-yellow lines, like Kelly and I used to do as kids, the cold taking root through my pants, through my flesh, and into the blood flowing through my veins. I sat there, listening to the few remaining birds that hadn't migrated south sing their first sweet notes in the quiet dawn. Like a slugger in a batter's box, I finally understood that life ultimately boils down to you and how you approach the next pitch. Like Mami had told me, even when you're part of a larger team, you can only ever be responsible for yourself.

The question now was, Would I swing? Or would I go down looking?

❦

My flight to Los Angeles was scheduled for January 6. Three Kings Day.

"That's good luck," Mami said, squeezing my hand as we drove down the Van Wyck Expressway. "Little Christmas!"

I had tried to take the AirTrain to JFK, but Mami insisted on not only driving me there, but paying to park her car in the lot and walking me through to security. I would have put up more of a fight if I wasn't feeling jittery about my first solo trip.

"Nobody calls it that," I said, sliding my boarding pass out from a manila folder in my lap for the third time to make sure it was still there.

"The Irish do!" she said, shaking a used tissue out from the pocket of her old coat.

At that, I grabbed my phone to check to see if I'd gotten any text messages. The most recent message was from Pablo, wishing me a safe flight. An email from Hye-Jin with a Yelp link to a Silver Lake restaurant. Nothing from Kelly.

"Well"—I cleared my throat as I tucked my phone back into my jeans pocket—"we're not Irish."

We drove past the color-coded terminals: green, blue, yellow, until finally, we got to orange and Terminal 7.

"Don't let any man buy you a drink," Mami said as she lifted my suitcase out of the trunk. "Or no"—she patted my forearm with her free hand—"they can buy you a drink, but you gotta see them make it."

She stopped rolling the carry-on and poked a finger at my sternum.

"You gotta watch out por lo rufi," she said through gritted teeth.

I laughed, comforted again by her Spanglish. She was always so worried about strangers in the world at large, yet routinely seemed to overlook the threat of men at home.

"I will, Mami," I said, tucking a flyaway hair behind her ear. "Promise."

With my boarding pass in hand again, I hugged her tight before lining up at the security gate.

"I'm going to miss you," she said, her big brown eyes wet, her eyeliner smudged.

"Me too," I said, still uncomfortable about leaving her to run a new business alone. "Thanks"—I gestured toward the suitcase as I grabbed the handle—"for everything."

I meant the long trip to Ozone Park, to this airport on the southern edge of Long Island, but I also hoped she understood that I meant for raising me right, for protecting me as best she could, and for loving me in ways that I knew others weren't lucky enough to be loved. Amid everything I'd gone through, with Kelly and without, I knew that at the end of the day, Mami would always have my back.

"¡Dios te bendiga!" she shouted as I fell in line. I bowed my head in acknowledgement.

At the gate, I handed my boarding pass to the agent and she ripped it, handing back my half ticket with my name and seat assignment: 26C, I repeated to myself, eyeing each row's layout as I passed. 26C. A window seat. As I settled in, my ticket still in hand, I grabbed the new journal Professor Acevedo had gifted me for graduation and opened it to the last page. There, I slid the ticket inside the pocket built into the back cover and closed it quickly, planting it like a time capsule for a future self to rediscover.

Running my hand over the textured leather cover, I imagined how different my life might look after I'd filled all those pages with new words, ideas, dreams, and experiences. I never thought I would leave Queens, and here I was sitting on a plane whose engine had just thrummed to life.

I held my breath the entire climb into the air; some old wives' tale Kelly had taught me rattling around my brain and mixing with another, something about death and warding off the evil eye. Below us, Queens appeared as rows and rows of identical two-story clapboard homes, and then mazelike boxes of brown brick apartment buildings, the roofs of which looked like hieroglyphics from up there, and then finally, the long, fat artery of Queens Boulevard extending far into the darkening distance. So much life flourishing in a borough so often described by its cemeteries and airports. As we continued north, I could just make out the colorful neon pitching and catching figures of Shea Stadium glowing in the twilight, before the plane made a sharp left to head west.

This isn't too bad, I thought, closing my eyes. The loud, constant hum and occasional jostling was like riding the subway, in a way.

We leveled out as we crested the cotton-thin clouds, no Queens below, only heaven, and the planets, and the galaxies above.

I smiled.

This is what it feels like, I thought. *This is what it feels like to swing.*

ACKNOWLEDGMENTS

A huge amount of gratitude to Johanna Castillo for believing in the friendship at the core of this book so strongly that she dedicated her time and expertise to champion Brisma and Kelly's story. Thanks to you, Erin Patterson, Wendolyne Sabrozo, and the support of Writers House.

This book would not be what it is without my amazing editor, Tara Parsons, who *got it* immediately and knew exactly what the story needed. Your enthusiasm was invigorating, and your insights brilliant. Thanks also to Judith Curr, Alexa Frank, Suzanne Quist, Louise Bouzari, Courtney Nobile, Brieana Garcia, Liat Kaplan, Maya Lewis, Terry McGrath, Alicia Tatone for her beautiful cover design, and every other person on the HarperVia team who had a hand in creating and promoting this final product.

Special thanks also to Mallory Soto for editing an early excerpt of this novel that appeared in *Catapult*. I am immensely grateful to all early readers who generously provided invaluable feedback.

Laura Pegram is this book's fairy godmother, in that she encouraged me to pitch it for the first time at the Kweli International Literary Festival in 2018, where I met my agent. I am grateful for Laura's unyielding support of writers of color and the greater Kweli community.

Artist residencies played a huge role in the completion of this novel both before and after I became a mother:

Lemon Tree House in Tuscany showed me that an artistic life was possible. Thank you Erinn Beth Langille and Julie Jolicoeur for creating such a beautiful and safe environment (despite the errant tree limb), where our hearts were opened to new worlds and new dear friends like Ellen Caldwell and .chisaraokwu. (Chisara Asomugha), who also served as some of the earliest readers of this book.

The Jerome Foundation's Emerging Artist Fellowship through the Anderson Center at Tower View allowed me to outline this novel and develop my practice for the creation of the first draft.

Hedgebrook provided peaceful solitude when I needed it as a new(-ish) mother as I revised an early draft. VONA was a jam-packed virtual ride in which Mat Johnson helped me approach my first pages in a new way. I am grateful to every artist and writer I've met on this journey, for each has shown me in their own way that a creative life in service to the communities that made us is possible, including Serena Lin, Dena Simmons, Sahar Delijani, Sharon Van Epps, and many others—I haven't forgotten you.

It's impossible for me to list all the writers whose work has inspired me, but I will say that the work of Julia Alvarez, Toni Morrison, Esmeralda Santiago, Sandra Cisneros, Nicholasa Mohr, Pedro Pietri, and Jamaica Kincaid were some of the first to light me up as a child at the Queens Public Library. Thanks to the Nuyorican Poets Cafe; while I did not step foot inside until I was an adult, I spent many hours poring over *Aloud: Voices from the Nuyorican Poets Cafe* as a teen at home.

The Queens literary community has fortified me in ways known and unknown, and allowed me to give back not just to fellow writ-

ers, but to the next generation of Queens writers—especially the work I've been honored to do through *Newtown Literary* with Tim Fredrick and Jackie Sherbow. My friends in the QCA Artist Peer Circle kept me connected through the length of the pandemic: Micki Spiller, Emily Alta Hockaday, Becky Band Jain, Sherese Francis, and Chris Kibler.

An extra-special thanks to the Queens Council on the Arts, through which I was awarded a 2020 Queens Arts Fund New Work Grant for this novel.

The staff at Espresso 77 and The Queensboro, both in Jackson Heights, kept me in community, coffee, and sweets while I wrote much of this novel. Their hospitality warms my heart, still.

Thank you to the Mets for providing ample opportunity to process heartbreak, but especially to Omar Minaya for spearheading Los Mets, and creating a space for Latinx kids to dream big.

This book is for all the city kids who've had to define for themselves what family is or isn't; who learned how to turn keys into knuckles before learning the Pythagorean theorem; who raised each other, for better or for worse. To Danny, Christina, Pauline, and Nont: thank you for keeping it real with me, always. You *are* family.

Thank you to Lisa Eisenberg and Marla McCormick, who have shown me radical trust, support, and encouragement, and extended grace when I needed it.

As Elisabet Velasquez writes in one of her poems, "some home-girls are not forever." Thank you to any and all homegirls, cousins, aunts who've contributed to the woman and writer I am today, chief among them my late grandma, Laura Torres, who loved to read and taught me how to be tough, how to stand up for myself, but also how to delight in the small joys of life.

To the Northrop family for providing several opportunities for me to escape and work on this book; thank you for opening your doors to me.

To my mother, without whom my work on this novel would literally not be feasible; thank you for your selfless dedication and countless hours spent building cardboard robots and watching *The View* with Charlie.

To Matt, for never wavering in his support. No matter how many anxiety-fueled rabbit holes I lead him down, he lifts me back up each time with love.

And to Charlie, for making me laugh, making me proud, and giving me a million chances to be a better person.

Finally, this book is in part about fictional friends defending a fictional abuser, but I would be remiss to not acknowledge that the real life media's treatment of Brock Turner, Bill Cosby, R. Kelly, and all the other "monsters hiding in plain sight" played a part in my decision to write this book. The defense of Supreme Court Justice Brett Kavanaugh in his confirmation hearings, particularly by high school girl friends who later recanted their support, affirmed and further fueled the rage simmering under some of these pages. My deepest awe and gratitude to Dr. Christine Blasey Ford for her public testimony, and to Chanel Miller for her courage and tenacity in sharing *Know My Name* with the world.

A NOTE FROM THE COVER DESIGNER

Friendship between young girls is a powerful thing: a connection so strong it sometimes feels like a first love. *The Girls in Queens* tells the story of this kind of friendship and its eventual splintering. Brisma and Kelly grew up inseparable throughout their childhood along the train tracks in Queens, and later in life are pulled apart by an accusation made against Brian, Brisma's old boyfriend from the neighborhood.

The cover depicts this fracturing of the friendship as memories resurface and loyalties are tested. I had initially illustrated Brisma and Kelly as overlapping figures, each one's sense of self informed by and intertwined with the other. This didn't feel quite right, though; too clean, too easy. So I cut apart the artwork and put it back together with the characters imperfectly overlapping each other, both together and apart. Train tracks run through the silhouettes as a nod to their home borough—a part of Brisma and Kelly forever, even if they leave.

—Alicia Tatone

Here ends Christine Kandic Torres's
The Girls in Queens.

The first edition of this book was printed and
bound at LSC Communications in
Harrisonburg, Virginia, June 2022.

A NOTE ON THE TYPE

The text of this novel was set in Adobe Garamond Pro, a typeface designed in 1989 by Robert Slimbach. It was based on
two distinctive examples of the French Renaissance style: a
Roman type by Claude Garamond (1499–1561) and an Italic
type by Robert Granjon (1513–1590). The typeface was developed after Slimbach studied the fifteenth-century equipment
at the Plantin-Moretus Museum in Antwerp, Belgium. Adobe
Garamond Pro faithfully captures the original Garamond's
grace and clarity and is used extensively in print for its ele-
gance and readability.

HarperVia

An imprint dedicated to publishing international voices,
offering readers a chance to encounter other lives and
other points of view via the language of the imagination.

BOOK CLUB QUESTIONS

1. Do you identify more with Brisma or Kelly?

2. This is a story about total opposites tied together by a deep, emotional bond. Have you ever had a friend like Brisma or Kelly?

3. *The Girls in Queens* is told from Brisma's perspective. What would Kelly's version of the story sound like?

4. *"Brian had to fight for women to love him his whole life."* What did you make of Brian's role in the story? How does his desire for women's affection shape his character?

5. Did you feel that the Queens setting informed the style or the character arcs? How would the novel change if it was set elsewhere?

6. The novel hops between the late '90s and the early 2000s. How would Brisma's and Kelly's reaction to Brian's scandal change if it happened now?